WINGS
OF
FIRE

WINGS OF FIRE

THE BRIGHTEST NIGHT

by
TUI T. SUTHERLAND

SCHOLASTIC PRESS
NEW YORK

No part of this publication may be reproduced, stored in a retrieval system, or transmitted in any form or by any means, electronic, mechanical, photocopying, recording, or otherwise, without written permission of the publisher. For information regarding permission, write to Scholastic Inc., Attention: Permissions Department, 557 Broadway, New York, NY 10012.

Text copyright © 2014 by Tui T. Sutherland
Map and border design © 2014 by Mike Schley
Dragon illustrations © 2014 by Joy Ang

All rights reserved. Published by Scholastic Press, an imprint of Scholastic Inc., *Publishers since 1920.* SCHOLASTIC, SCHOLASTIC PRESS, and associated logos are trademarks and/or registered trademarks of Scholastic Inc.

Library of Congress Cataloging-in-Publication Data

Sutherland, Tui, 1978– author.
The brightest night / by Tui T. Sutherland.
pages cm. — (Wings of fire ; book 5)
Summary: Sunny has always taken the Dragonet Prophecy very seriously, so Morrowseer's devastating news changes everything — now she must forge a new identity, and find a way to stop the futile and destructive war between the dragon clans.
ISBN 978-0-545-34922-2 (alk. paper)
1. Dragons — Juvenile fiction. 2. Prophecies — Juvenile fiction. 3. Identity (Psychology) — Juvenile fiction. [1. Dragons — Fiction. 2. Prophecies — Fiction. 3. Identity — Fiction. 4. Fantasy.] I. Title. II. Series; Sutherland, Tui, 1978– Wings of fire ; bk. 5.
PZ7.S96694BR 2014
[Fic] — dc23
2013046283

10 9 8 7 6 5 4 3   14 15 16 17 18

Printed in the U.S.A.   23
First printing, April 2014
Book design by Phil Falco

For Adalyn — may you be fierce
and brave and sunny, and may you always
choose your own destiny

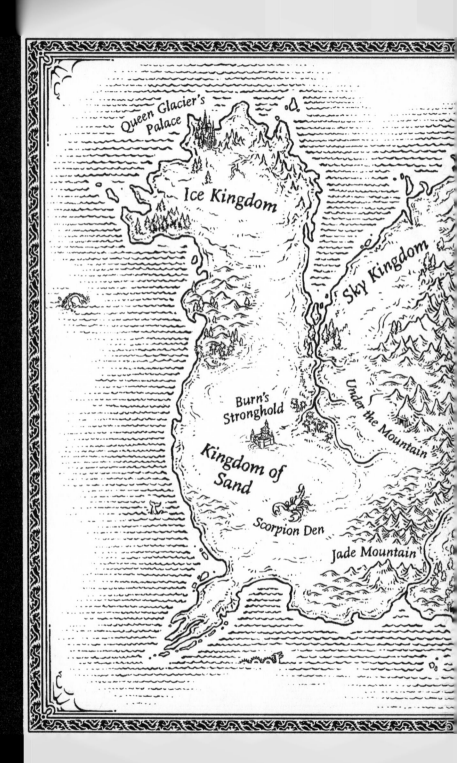

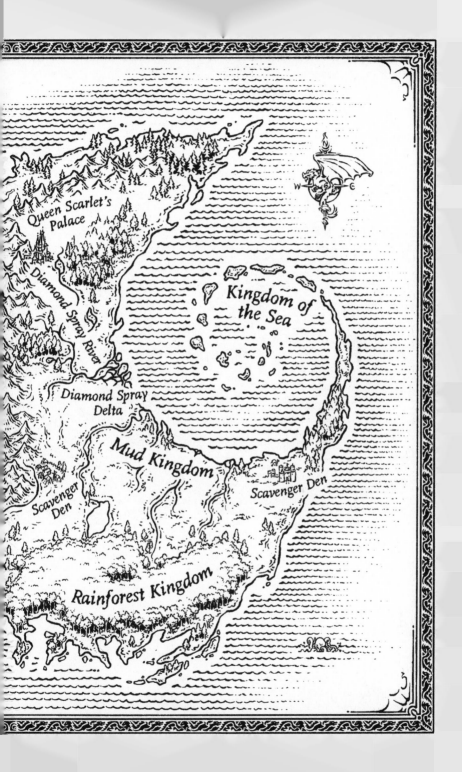

Ice Kingdom

Kingdom

A NIGHTWING GUIDE TO THE
DRAGONS

Sand

Scorpion Den

Jade Mountain

OF PYRRHIA

⌁ SANDWINGS ⌁

Description: pale gold or white scales the color of desert sand; poisonous barbed tail; forked black tongues

Abilities: can survive a long time without water, poison enemies with the tips of their tails like scorpions, bury themselves for camouflage in the desert sand, breathe fire

Queen: Since the death of Queen Oasis, the tribe is split between three rivals for the throne: sisters Burn, Blister, and Blaze.

Alliances: Burn fights alongside SkyWings and MudWings; Blister is allied with the SeaWings; and Blaze has the support of most SandWings as well as an alliance with the IceWings.

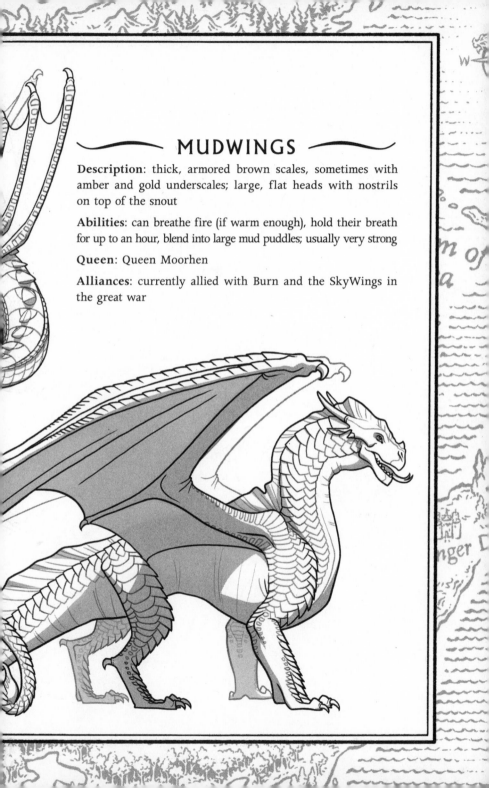

MUDWINGS

Description: thick, armored brown scales, sometimes with amber and gold underscales; large, flat heads with nostrils on top of the snout

Abilities: can breathe fire (if warm enough), hold their breath for up to an hour, blend into large mud puddles; usually very strong

Queen: Queen Moorhen

Alliances: currently allied with Burn and the SkyWings in the great war

SKYWINGS

Description: red-gold or orange scales; enormous wings

Abilities: powerful fighters and fliers, can breathe fire

Queen: Queen Scarlet

Alliances: currently allied with Burn and the MudWings in the great war

SEAWINGS

Description: blue or green or aquamarine scales; webs between their claws; gills on their necks; glow-in-the-dark stripes on their tails/snouts/underbellies

Abilities: can breathe underwater, see in the dark, create huge waves with one splash of their powerful tails; excellent swimmers

Queen: Queen Coral

Alliances: currently allied with Blister in the great war

ICEWINGS

Description: silvery scales like the moon or pale blue like ice; ridged claws to grip the ice; forked blue tongues; tails narrow to a whip-thin end

Abilities: can withstand subzero temperatures and bright light, exhale a deadly freezing breath

Queen: Queen Glacier

Alliances: currently allied with Blaze and most of the SandWings in the great war

RAINWINGS

Description: scales constantly shift colors, usually bright like birds of paradise; prehensile tails

Abilities: can camouflage their scales to blend into their surroundings, use their prehensile tails for climbing; no known natural weapons

Queen: Queen Dazzling

Alliances: not involved in the great war

NIGHTWINGS

Description: purplish-black scales and scattered silver scales on the underside of their wings, like a night sky full of stars; forked black tongues

Abilities: can breathe fire, disappear into dark shadows, read minds, foretell the future

Queen: a closely guarded secret

Alliances: too mysterious and powerful to be part of the war

THE DRAGONET PROPHECY

When the war has lasted twenty years . . .
the dragonets will come.
When the land is soaked in blood and tears . . .
the dragonets will come.

Find the SeaWing egg of deepest blue.
Wings of night shall come to you.
The largest egg in mountain high
will give to you the wings of sky.
For wings of earth, search through the mud
for an egg the color of dragon blood.
And hidden alone from the rival queens,
the SandWing egg awaits unseen.

Of three queens who blister and blaze and burn,
two shall die and one shall learn
if she bows to a fate that is stronger and higher,
she'll have the power of wings of fire.

Five eggs to hatch on brightest night,
five dragons born to end the fight.
Darkness will rise to bring the light.
The dragonets are coming. . . .

PROLOGUE

Twenty years ago . . .

It is nearly impossible to steal from a dragon, particularly a royal one with a palace and guards and very high walls.

At least, that's what Queen Oasis kept telling herself as she hurried along the dark halls, breathing fire to light her way.

Nearly impossible and decidedly stupid.

And yet, she had this terrible feeling. . . .

Something was wrong. There was *something* scrabbling around in her palace. With her exceptionally sharp SandWing hearing, she was sure she could hear squeaking, like faraway mice, and perhaps the clinking of coins.

But mice didn't steal treasure.

So what was it? Was she imagining it? She'd woken from a deep sleep with a start, as if someone had stabbed her in the chest with his venomous tail. It seemed unlikely, but . . . she was going to check on her treasure anyway.

The SandWing queen whirled around a corner and collided with two of her daughters, Blaze and Blister.

"*Ow*," Blaze complained, hopping backward with a grimace. "*Mother*, you stepped on my *foot*."

Blister said nothing, but sidestepped into a corner to get out of the queen's way. Her dark eyes were fixed on every move Oasis made, in that unsettling way she had. Oasis had had a feeling from the moment Blister hatched: this was the daughter who was going to kill her. Her oldest daughter, Burn, was bigger and stronger, but Oasis and Burn actually got along, in a way. They understood each other, apart from Burn's obsession with mutilating animals. And it was easy to distract Burn: give her something creepy-looking and she'd disappear into her rooms for days.

Blister, on the other talon, always seemed to be calculating the moments until her mother's demise, and she'd been like that ever since she was a small dragonet — ever since she'd first realized that killing her mother would make her queen.

Go ahead and challenge me, Oasis thought scornfully, glaring down at Blister. *I'd squash you like a bug and you know it.*

"What's the hurry?" Blister asked smoothly, as if she couldn't sense the malevolence in her mother's gaze. "Is there a royal crisis? Let me guess — Smolder tried to run off with his girlfriend again."

"No, I took care of her," Oasis said. "I'm just going to check the treasury."

"Ooo, sparkly things." Blaze yawned. "Good night, Mother."

Dizzy Blaze, Oasis thought as she hurried on. *She'd be a terrible queen, but she's an acceptable daughter. I don't have to worry about what she'll do to me.*

She heard claws click on the stone behind her and whirled around. Blister held up her talons and flared her wings, filling the narrow passageway.

"Sorry to startle you," she said unconvincingly. "I just wondered if I could come with you."

Oasis hesitated, but she knew if she said no, Blister would find a way to sneak along anyway. It was always better to keep her where you could see her. "Fine. But don't touch anything." *I know what you want to see, you conniving viper. It won't do you any good until I'm dead, though.*

They whisked down the long passage that led to the four treasure rooms.

Everything looked in order — the torches flickered peacefully, the doors were closed and locked.

But there was a strange *smell,* something hairy and woodsy and flowery at the same time. Something had definitely been here.

Oasis crouched to peer under the doors. There was a large gap between the doors and the floor. . . . Not large enough for a dragon, of course, but . . .

"Do you smell scavenger?" she asked Blister.

"I wouldn't know what those smell like," Blister said, wrinkling her nose. "They're too bulky and squishy for my taste."

Queen Oasis selected the right keys from around

her neck and unlocked all the doors, then did a sweep through each room, leaving the doors open.

She came back out glowering with rage.

"That looks ominous," Blister remarked.

"*Scavengers*," spat the queen. "Robbed *me*. How *dare* they?" She lashed her tail, hissing. "They can't have gone far. Wake up Burn and tell her to meet me outside."

"Burn?" Blister echoed, glancing over her mother's shoulder at the treasure rooms.

"Just in case there are a lot of them and we need to fight," Oasis said. "I've seen what their tiny swords can do. I'm not such a fool as to go out there alone."

"Oh, no, of course not," Blister said. "But why Burn, when I'm here?"

Oasis gave her a withering look. "I need a real fighter," she said. "Not someone who thinks she can use her brain to get herself out of anything, and isn't even as smart as she thinks she is."

"I see," Blister said coldly. "I'll wake her at once." She took a step up the corridor, then turned back. "What did they take?"

"Small things, for the most part," Oasis growled. "But they also took the Eye of Onyx."

That actually made Blister's face twitch, as if a hint of a real emotion — worry? surprise? — was trying to come through.

"We'll get it back," Oasis promised. "And we'll have roasted scavenger for breakfast." She pushed past Blister and stormed toward the nearest route to the sky. "I'm going out there. Wake Burn, and hurry."

"Oh, yes. Right away," Blister said.

As Oasis charged into the courtyard, spread her wings, and lifted into the sky, she thought for a moment that she saw Blister turn to look back at the treasure rooms instead. *I forgot to lock them up again,* Oasis thought uneasily. *But this will only take a minute. And if she's stupid enough to take anything, I'll have a good excuse to kill her. She's smarter than that.*

She wheeled toward the outer walls, scanning the sands. A disturbing thought occurred to her: *What if she doesn't wake Burn? What if I'm going to face the thieves alone, with no backup?*

Then she spotted them. Three scavengers — two of them waiting on the sand, the other climbing down from a window. None of them watching the sky. *Scab-infested idiot monkeys.* Oasis growled and folded her wings to drop down silently behind them. Maybe she could scare them to death; prey always tasted better when it died like that.

Only three of them, she thought. *I don't need to wait for Burn, if Blister's even getting her. I can certainly handle three annoying scavengers by myself.*

She narrowed her eyes, advancing up the dunes toward the sound of squeaking.

After all . . . what's the worst that could happen?

Ice Kingdom

Sky Kingdom

Under the Mountain

Burn's
Stronghold

Kingdom of
Sand

Scorpion Den

Jade Mountain

PART ONE

THE SHIFTING SANDS

— CHAPTER 1 —

Sunny had always known that she was the right dragon for a Big Heroic Destiny.

She was going to save the world. She and her friends were going to swoop in on wings of fire, whatever that meant, and bring peace to every dragon in Pyrrhia. It was right there in the prophecy: *five dragons born to end the fight*. That was her fate. That was her *purpose*.

Besides, it explained everything. Why else was she so small and weird-looking? She wasn't a normal SandWing. Her scales and eyes were the wrong color, and she had no venomous barb at the end of her tail. But that didn't matter; in fact, it made sense. Of course a dragon hero with an epic noble quest would be a little different from everyone else. And who would care how strange she looked once she stopped the war?

Then there were her parents, the mysterious dragons who had left her egg buried in the sand in the desert, alone and unguarded. It didn't matter that they obviously didn't want her. It didn't bother Sunny at all, because it was part of the prophecy: *Hidden alone from the rival queens, the SandWing egg awaits unseen*. That was all right; heroes in the scrolls often had no parents. Their heroic destiny was more important than any family.

And her destiny *was* important. There was nothing more important than stopping the war between the dragon tribes. All her life, especially whenever she felt trapped or sad or worried about anything, Sunny had imagined fulfilling the prophecy — how many lives they would save and all the happy, reunited families and all the future dragonets who could grow up in peace, without the constant fear of war.

That was the entire point of her life.

And it was a lie.

Rock walls scraped against her wings as she scrambled away from the NightWing island. She could feel the rumbles of the volcano all the way through her claws. Her friends were behind her, still facing Morrowseer, but she had to get away from them, from him, from everything.

He made up the prophecy. It was all a trick.

No. I don't believe it. He's a vindictive, cruel dragon who's always manipulated us and everyone around him. He would say anything to hurt us.

The prophecy is *real. It has to be.*

She burst out of the tunnel into the rainforest and immediately slammed into the side of a skinny black dragon. The NightWing grunted with surprise and glared at her. Sunny tried to turn and fly the other way, but a floundering wall of black wings and talons and tails drove her back.

In the moonlight, the entire rainforest seemed to be seething with dragons. Roars and hisses and growls drowned out the sound of the raindrops pattering on the leaves all around them. It didn't help that half of the dragons were dark as the shadows and the other half were camouflaged, so claws and corners of wings seemed to suddenly poke out of nowhere. Sunny narrowly avoided a tail in her ear when two NightWings got caught in a dangling vine and whipped around violently as if they were being attacked.

"Everyone calm down!" Glory's voice shouted.

"Listen!" bellowed Grandeur, the old royal RainWing. "Your new queen is speaking!"

Several NightWings muttered under their breath, but none loud enough to be heard, and even they fell silent as others hissed at them.

Sunny ducked and wriggled through the crowd, but she couldn't get any farther than the stream. Several RainWings stood by the water, in shades of blue and purple, holding NightWing spears. Most of them were ruining the effect by peering at the spears with mystified expressions, or holding them upside down.

Still, Sunny decided not to try pushing past them. Those spears would hurt just as much if they poked her by accident as on purpose.

What she really wanted to do was crash away into the rainforest and not come back. She wasn't sure she could face her friends — who acted as if they didn't care about the prophecy at all — and she couldn't even look at the NightWings.

Tsunami wants to believe Morrowseer. She's never wanted to fulfill the prophecy. She doesn't understand how important it is.

Clay would be just as happy if nobody ever noticed how wonderful he is. Then he could sleep and eat and take care of us instead of fighting.

Starflight would love to stop worrying about the prophecy.

And Glory has enough to do here, now that she's queen.

None of them will fight for our destiny. They certainly won't listen to me if I try to explain that Morrowseer must have been lying. They'll give me that look I always get, the one that says: "Oh, silly little Sunny and her crazy dreams, isn't she cute and harmless."

She gazed up at the mass of dark trees overhead, where the moonbeams and raindrops skittered in the wind. Even if she tried to run off, she'd probably get her tail stuck in a tree branch and need to be rescued, and then her friends would get to roll their eyes and pat her on the head again.

It wouldn't be like this in the desert, she thought. She looked across the stream at the other tunnel, the one that led to the Kingdom of Sand. *There I could fly and fly and fly all the way to the horizon without ever stopping to think.*

Not thinking sounded pretty appealing right now.

"You're just as ordinary as any other dragon."

Morrowseer's spiteful words kept going around and around in her head. *"I made up the whole prophecy. . . . Now the war will drag on endlessly, and more dragons will die every day, probably for generations. All of them wondering what happened to the amazing dragonets who were supposed to save them, but obviously failed."*

Sunny clenched her talons and crouched low to the ground.

He was lying, he was lying, *he was lying*. She wouldn't let these NightWings see her cry.

Glory climbed onto a boulder and flapped her wings loudly. Even up there, and even with her queenliest face on, Glory still looked like a dragonet, smaller than almost all the NightWings surrounding her.

If the prophecy is fake, then why was everyone so awful to Glory about not being in it? Sunny thought, feeling another surge of fury at Morrowseer. *Why make her feel so useless — if we're all useless?*

Because it is real. It has to be.

But how can I prove it?

"NightWings," Glory said firmly, speaking up to be heard over the shuffling dragons and the rainstorm. "Your home is gone. Your queen is dead. But this is your chance to start over. If you mess it up, you'll lose this home, too." She pointed to the RainWings. "You will treat these dragons with respect, and in return, because that's the kind of dragons they are, they will be much kinder to you than you deserve."

The RainWing across the stream from Sunny mustered an expression that looked almost fierce.

Rain splattered across Sunny's snout and wings. The storm was picking up strength, ripping through the treetops way over their heads.

"Tonight you'll stay right here," Glory went on. "I don't want any NightWings wandering off until we can count you and write you all down. You will each be assigned two RainWings to keep an eye on you. And yes, if you're feeling like perhaps we don't trust you very much, it's because we don't. None of you are welcome in the RainWing village until you earn that trust. We will find you somewhere else to live."

"We'll get wet out here," one of the burlier NightWings complained.

Glory gave him a steely glare. "Feel free to go back and sleep on your nice dry island instead," she snapped. "I hear it's quite warm there."

Sunny glanced around at the NightWings. Even in the moonlight, she could see that most of them looked badly shaken and subdued. Seeing their home buried by the volcano — even if they knew it would happen eventually, and even though the island had been a terrible place to live — it still must have been an awful shock.

Something like being told your whole life is a lie, I imagine.

A roar suddenly erupted from the crowd behind her. Black dragons surged toward Sunny, flapping their wings in alarm, as two deep-red RainWings dove into their midst and dragged a yowling, petrified NightWing in front of Queen Glory.

"This one!" growled one of the RainWings. "He can't stay here! He's the worst of all of them."

"He's the one who did all the venom experiments on us," said the other. She lashed her tail and hissed at him. Sunny had never seen any RainWings look so angry before, besides Glory. She craned her neck to peer at the NightWing and realized it was Starflight's father, Mastermind, the head scientist of the NightWing tribe. From the look on Glory's face, the queen was probably guessing exactly who it was, too.

The NightWings had been kidnapping RainWings for the last year, imprisoning them and doing experiments to understand their venom-shooting abilities. They'd been planning to invade the rainforest to steal it from the RainWings — either by killing or enslaving all the peaceful rainforest dragons who already lived here.

Sunny had seen the lava-riddled wasteland of an island where the NightWings lived. She knew they were desperate for a new home, and at first, she'd thought Starflight was brilliant for offering to let them come through to the rainforest as long as they pledged their loyalty to Queen Glory — along with a promise to behave peacefully. She liked the idea of dragons from different tribes learning to live together, she felt sorry for the sick and starving black dragons, and she loved the poetic justice of a RainWing becoming the new queen of the NightWings.

But looking at the muttering dragons around her — the NightWings who didn't look as sorry as they should, and the hissing RainWings who were only beginning to realize what their friends had been through — Sunny wondered if this had been a huge mistake. Maybe they should have let the NightWings be swallowed up by the volcano. Maybe it wasn't possible to forgive them. *Maybe we shouldn't even try.*

If they could lie about something as huge and important as the prophecy and stopping the war, what else would they lie about? How could Glory ever trust them?

"I'm sorry," Mastermind croaked weakly. "It was . . . I was just . . . for science . . ." His voice sputtered out, and he cringed away from the RainWings beside him.

Glory flared her wings and several colors rippled quickly through her scales. "Tie him up. We'll figure out what to —"

"Look out!" a dragon by the tunnel roared. "Stand clear!"

Fatespeaker shot out of the hole and a moment later, Tsunami hurtled after her. "Everyone get down!" the SeaWing yelled.

The NightWings by the tunnel all threw themselves to the ground. A blast of scorching heat crackled out of the hole, turning the raindrops around it to hissing steam. Sunny was one of the few still standing, looking at the tunnel, when two more dragons burst out of it.

It was Clay, with his wings shielding Starflight. Starflight's front talons were covering his eyes and long burns were blistering along his scales. As soon as they reached the open air, he collapsed to the ground.

"Stay back!" Tsunami shouted ferociously at the dragons who were flapping around them.

"Starflight!" Sunny cried, feeling a stab of guilt. *He's hurt. I never should have left my friends with Morrowseer.* She jumped forward, trying to squeeze through the crowd of frantic dragons to get to him.

But suddenly talons wrapped around her snout and shoulders, and she was yanked backward into the dark trees.

CHAPTER 2

Sunny thrashed furiously against the huge wings that wrapped around her.

"Quick, while they're all distracted," she heard a voice hiss. A shower of raindrops pattered down on Sunny's head as the dragon holding her ducked through the leaves. It was hard to see much more than black scales, but Sunny realized she was being dragged into the forest, away from the tunnels and the crowd of dragons.

But I have to make sure Starflight is all right! She clawed at the arm that pinned her wings down, but the NightWing only grunted and held her tighter.

Wet leaves squelched and slithered under their talons. From the sounds around her, Sunny guessed there were three NightWings, including her attacker, sneaking away from the scene while everyone was focused on Starflight and Clay.

That's . . . ominous. Maybe she should try to find out what they were up to. She stopped struggling and listened.

The dragons were moving fast and quietly, even without flying; in just a few heartbeats, Sunny couldn't hear what

Glory and Tsunami were shouting anymore. They also moved purposefully, as if they knew the forest well.

A hunting party, Sunny thought with a shiver. *These are probably some of the dragons who came through the tunnel to kidnap RainWings.*

What do they want with me?

"Here," one of the dragons said after a while, and they all stopped. Even with Sunny's sharp hearing, the dragons roaring behind them sounded like distant thunder muttering on the horizon. Rain poured down harder and harder, and the ever-present insect noises of the rainforest had gone into hiding.

Sunny was dumped onto the ground, mud squishing between her claws and splattering her tail. She sprang up and hissed at the dragon who'd been carrying her. He barely glanced down at her before turning to the other two.

"Now what?" he demanded. "The whole plan is ruined. I'm not staying here to kowtow to a RainWing dragonet."

"Me neither," said one of the others, a female who was little more than a dragonet herself. Sunny guessed she was about nine years old. She was bedraggled, wet, bony, and hunched over, and yet when she snorted a burst of flame, Sunny could see her eyes gleaming with stubborn ferocity.

"Plus they'll probably kill me," said the big dragon. "You saw how they were about Mastermind. If they remember that I was his assistant . . . I mean, I was the one who locked them up or stuck them to the walls for him. They'll be after my blood if we stick around here."

"Where are we supposed to go?" hissed the last dragon, another male, much less brawny than the one who'd been carrying Sunny. He had a few missing teeth and his tail was bent at the end, as if it had once been broken and then fixed incorrectly. "We were promised the rainforest. *This* is where I want to live, but not as second-class dragons. Imagine, RainWings telling us what to do!"

"Well, we've got *her*, like you suggested," the big male said to the dragonet, flipping one wing toward Sunny. "So what do we do with her?"

The NightWing dragonet lashed her tail and narrowed her eyes at Sunny. "We use her as a bargaining chip. We can hold her hostage until they take our whole tribe to the RainWing village and make one of us queen."

"Like who?" said the other male. He spat a small flame at the branch that was dripping on his head. "Greatness is weak and won't fight for it. Queen Battlewinner had no brothers or sisters and no other daughters. There's no one else to claim the throne."

"I'll take it," said the dragonet. "That'd be even better than being in the prophecy. If that RainWing can be queen, why not me? I'm bigger than her."

"True," growled the big one behind Sunny.

"Well, I have bad news," Sunny spoke up. "They won't give you anything in exchange for me. I'm nobody. Just a weird-looking SandWing with a useless tail." She snapped her mouth shut before her voice could start wavering. She'd been saying things like that her whole life, but she'd never felt awful about it until today. If there were no prophecy . . . then that meant she really *was* just weird-looking and useless.

No, that's not how it works. I'm weird-looking because I have a destiny. There's a reason I'm like this. There has to be.

The NightWings regarded her with skeptical expressions.

"That would be annoying," said the big one. "I'd be pretty angry if I carried this little thing through the forest and got my scales scratched up for no reason. Fierceteeth, I thought you said she'd be worth something."

Fierceteeth! Sunny remembered what Starflight had told them about the dragonets in the NightWing kingdom. Wasn't Fierceteeth his half sister?

"We can use her if she's who I think she is," said Fierceteeth. She jabbed Sunny painfully in the ribs. "Aren't you Sunny? Starflight yapped on and on about a Sunny whenever he was asleep."

Sunny blinked at her, too startled to answer.

"Yeah, this is her," Fierceteeth said, answering her own question. "My brother's totally in love with her. He'll agree to anything to get her back."

That might actually be true, Sunny thought with alarm. *Does he really talk about me in his sleep?* Only a few hours had passed since she'd stood in the rainforest clearing, in the middle of dragons preparing to invade the NightWing island, and Starflight had told her he loved her — that he'd always loved her.

She still didn't know how she felt about that. She didn't know what this feeling was, the strange ripples of surprise every time she remembered his expression. It was *I don't know what to do* and *somebody loves me* and *don't hurt him* and *really, right now?* and *imagine how happy you could make him* and *why me? really, me?* and *but it's* Starflight. Her sweet, smart, anxious friend. She'd never thought of him like that, not once.

It was still hard for her to believe that he meant it. None of the other dragonets took her seriously. She'd always assumed he was the same way — that he thought she was too little and cheerful to be worth listening to.

Focus. Don't let them use you to hurt your friends.

"Didn't you see Starflight's injuries?" she said. "He's too wounded to have any say in what happens next. And Glory couldn't care less about me. Face it, you can't use me. You should go back and rejoin the other NightWings."

"Nice try," Fierceteeth said.

"What if she's right?" said the NightWing with the missing teeth. "What if they don't want her? What if we expose ourselves and then they just kill us?"

"Strongwings won't let them do that," Fierceteeth said, stepping closer to the burly dragon.

They're a couple, Sunny realized. *A really strange couple.* Strongwings was nearly twice the size of Fierceteeth, but he kept turning toward her and ducking his head as though he was waiting for her to order him around.

"I know how we could find out," said the other male. He drew something flat and shiny and oval-shaped from under his wing. In the moonlight, it shone like polished black glass and fit neatly between his front talons. And it stayed perfectly dry; the raindrops seemed to swerve to avoiding raining on it.

"The Obsidian Mirror," said Strongwings with a hiss of admiration. "Nice work, Preyhunter. I wondered if someone would think to save it." He leaned in and touched the smooth surface with one claw. "No surprise that it wasn't Greatness. She was more worried about saving her own scales."

"She never used it anyway," snorted Preyhunter. "Even when we needed to know what the RainWings were up to. She said she didn't trust anything that was enchanted by an animus. Coward. I don't think the queen knew she wasn't checking it."

"It doesn't work as well as it used to," Strongwings said. "Everyone thinks Stonemover did something to it before he disappeared."

"What is it?" Fierceteeth asked.

"A really old animus-touched piece of treasure," Strongwings explained. "This was one of the most important things we had to save from the treasure room when the volcano erupted and buried that part of the fortress, back when I was a small dragonet. We use it for —" He stopped and glanced at Sunny. "Hmm."

"Don't worry, we'll kill her before she can tell anyone anything important," said Preyhunter.

Go ahead and try, Sunny thought fiercely. *No one else has managed it yet.*

He tilted the mirror so it caught the light of the two moons glowing through the clouds above them. The third moon was just a thin crescent, barely cresting the tops of the trees. The rain had slowed to a misty drizzle.

"Show me how it works," Fierceteeth demanded. She snapped a branch off the nearest tree and set the end on fire, leaves crackling wetly in the flames.

"We just need a name," said Strongwings. "Uh. Someone important."

"That RainWing queen, obviously," Fierceteeth snapped. He looked blank and she hissed at him. "Glory."

"Glory," whispered the dragon holding the Obsidian Mirror. He breathed a plume of smoke across the dark glass. The smoke coiled and twisted, winding like a thin snake around the outer rim of the mirror for a few heartbeats. All at once the smoke vanished as if it had been sucked into the mirror, and a moment later, one tendril curled up from the center of the glass, white tinted with purple, curving like a dragon's neck.

"Mangrove!" the tendril barked abruptly in Glory's voice. "Make sure none of them have any more of those spears. Jambu, you and Grandeur start counting them — the NightWings, just to be clear, not the spears."

Fierceteeth grinned, her teeth gleaming whitely in the moonlight. "This is happening right now?" she whispered, and Strongwings nodded. "Brilliant."

Yes, I can see how that would be a useful trick, Sunny thought bitterly. *Especially for convincing other dragons that you have mystical mind-reading abilities.*

A pinkish wisp of smoke curled up on the mirror next to the first one.

"You bet, no problem, Your Majesty," it said. "Except, uh . . . so, counting. Um. Don't get me wrong, I'm really good at it. Up to, like . . . twenty? That's a pretty big number, right? There probably aren't more NightWings here than that."

"Jambu, there are at least two hundred NightWings here," Glory snapped.

"Hum," he said. "That's like . . . two twenties? Maybe three?"

"I cannot even roll my eyes at you right now," Glory said. "Find me a RainWing who can count."

"I'll do it." A darker coil of smoke appeared, right next to the first. It took Sunny a moment to recognize the voice of Deathbringer, the assassin who had been ordered to kill Glory but instead helped her escape the NightWings.

"Funny," Glory said. "Tell me another. I love jokes about trusting NightWings."

"You exasperating creature," Deathbringer said. "Haven't I *not* killed you multiple times already?"

"I knew it," snarled Preyhunter, curling his claws around the mirror. "I knew Vengeance was right about him. Deathbringer is a traitor."

"We'll take care of him when the rainforest is ours," hissed Strongwings.

"Fine," Glory's voice said. "Go count NightWings. I'll have Starflight check your numbers when he wakes up."

"A ringing vote of confidence," Deathbringer answered, sounding amused. The dark wisp of smoke coiled back into the mirror, as did the pinkish one. Glory's tendril of smoke twisted for a moment, alone on the glass.

"He *will* wake up, right?" she finally said quietly.

"I think so." A new spiral of mud-colored smoke wound its way up from the mirror, and Sunny felt her heart jump hopefully at the sound of Clay's voice. He always made her feel better — even from the other side of the rainforest. "But he was burned pretty badly. We should use the darts to make him keep sleeping until he's healed as much as possible, I think. It'll hurt a lot when he wakes up."

Oh, poor Starflight. Sunny curled her tail around her talons.

"And his eyes?" Glory asked. "Will they be all right?"

"I don't know," Clay said.

"All right, I did a perimeter sweep," Tsunami's voice said bossily as a blue twist of smoke appeared on the mirror. "I made sure any gaps were filled with RainWings holding spears and blowguns, and I added a few more guards on the tunnels. *I* don't think they look very scary, but hopefully the NightWings will." The blue smoke whisked around the other two tendrils as if Tsunami was circling them to land.

"That's why I need you two here," Glory said. "The healers who took Starflight back to the village can look after him until we get there. But for corralling NightWings, you're the most intimidating dragons I have."

"Mwa ha!" Clay said. "That's me! Intimidating! Roar!"

"Well, you are until you do *that*," Tsunami said.

"Hey, at least you're not bright pink," Glory said. "That's extremely helpful right now."

"It's all right," Clay said. "Sunny's probably at the village already. She'll look after Starflight, no matter how upset she is."

Sunny winced and Fierceteeth gave her a sharp look.

"Why is she upset?" Glory asked.

"That slime lizard Morrowseer," Tsunami answered. "He told us that the prophecy is fake. He made it all up as part of the plan for the NightWings to take over the rainforest."

There was a long pause. The three dragons around the mirror all glanced at Sunny. She stared down at her claws.

"WHAT?" Glory exploded. Her curl of smoke shot up to twice its previous size.

"Yeah," Clay said. "Isn't that crazy? I guess that's why Morrowseer wanted us to choose Blister as the next queen — he had this whole —"

"I AM GOING TO BITE THAT DRAGON'S HEAD OFF AND STUFF HIM IN A VOLCANO," Glory roared.

"Too late," Tsunami said. "Since that's kind of already happened. The volcano part, I mean. He's a pile of ashes now."

"Are you serious?" Glory demanded, talking over her. "*The whole thing was made up?* There's no destiny, no wings of fire? No reason for us to be trapped in a cave our whole lives? No amazing mythical SkyWing who's infinitely better than me? *Absolutely no need for any of us after all?*"

"Hey, I'm mad, too," Tsunami said. "But —"

"LET'S GO BACK AND KILL HIM AGAIN."

"At least we don't have to worry about it anymore," Tsunami pointed out. "No destiny means we can do whatever we want. The Talons of Peace can go shove a puffer fish up their noses."

"But Sunny was really upset," Clay said. "She was always kind of excited about the prophecy."

Kind of excited? Sunny lashed her tail. *It wasn't just some fun adventure I was looking forward to, Clay.*

"Oh, Sunny will be fine," said Tsunami. "You know her. She's always happy about everything. By tomorrow she'll be smiling again, and by next week she probably won't even remember the prophecy. She just needs something new to care about, like making Starflight better."

"Well, I can think of lots of ways to keep her busy," Glory said. "For one, she can find me someone to yell at. *I seriously cannot believe this.* If I didn't have to act like a queen right now, rrrrrrrrrrrrrrgh." Her voice trailed off into muffled growling.

Sunny glared at the Obsidian Mirror. This was exactly what she hated most about the way her friends saw her, although hearing them say it so bluntly made it much worse. *As if acting happy means I don't really care about anything. As if I just need to be* distracted *and I'll forget about the whole point of our existence and all the dragons who are counting on us. As if my* brain *were the size of a* blueberry, *three MOONS.*

She caught Fierceteeth looking at her with a wry smirk.

"Not too impressed with your intelligence, are they?" said the NightWing.

Sunny scowled back at her.

"It sounds like they *like* her," said Strongwings dubiously. "But not like they think she's particularly useful or important. I'm not sure they will give us the rainforest in exchange for her."

I'm not either, Sunny thought. *Not that they should. But . . . what* would *they do to get me back? Anything? Or will they figure, "Hey, she'll be fine as a hostage. Remember she's always happy about everything. And that should be pretty distracting for her! Perfect!"?*

Perhaps I'll just rescue myself, then. That'll show them. And then I'll fulfill the prophecy all by myself, too, and then they'll see that it was real all along.

She knew that was exactly the kind of thing her friends would roll their eyes at her for saying. But if no one else cared about their destiny anymore . . . if she was the only dragonet who still believed in it . . . what was she supposed to do?

The NightWing holding the mirror tilted the glass so the smoke tendrils swirled together, and then he shot a small burst of fire across the surface. The smoke vanished, and the black glass went still.

"There's another option," Preyhunter said, regarding the others with a sly expression. "Someone else who definitely does want this stunted SandWing — pretty badly, I'd guess."

Fierceteeth inhaled sharply. "You're right. *Three* someones. We could sell her to the highest bidder — whoever's willing to raise an army and take back the rainforest for us."

Uh-oh. Sunny was not about to be handed over to one of the SandWing queens. She'd spent enough time in cages and prisons already, thanks very much. She snuck a look at the leaning trees and tangled vines around them, searching for the closest gaps in the foliage.

"Start with Blister," Strongwings said, his dark eyes glinting in the moonlight. "She always pays her informants well, and she needs us the most."

What does she pay them with? Sunny wondered. *All the SandWing royal treasure was stolen by the scavenger who killed Queen Oasis, wasn't it? And if there's any left, it would be in the SandWing stronghold, which Burn controls.*

"But Burn would love to have this weirdling in her collection," argued Preyhunter. "From what I hear, a deformed dragonet would fit right in with the two-headed creatures and stuffed scavengers."

"I am not *deformed*," Sunny said hotly, but none of them paid any attention to her.

Queen Scarlet had been planning to hand Sunny over to Burn for this ominous "collection" as well. Sunny was quite sure she never wanted to see what else Burn had collected.

"Who has the strongest army?" Fierceteeth asked. "Burn, right? And it would only take us a few days to get to her, if we fly straight over the mountains and don't stop." She flicked Strongwings in the snout as he opened it to speak. "Don't ask stupid questions. We can't use the tunnel to the Kingdom of Sand. They'll be guarding — YEEEEOOOOW!"

Fierceteeth's howl of pain sent raindrops flying off the leaves around them as Sunny sank her teeth into the vulnerable spot on her tail. Strongwings lunged to grab Sunny, pried her jaws loose, and threw her aside.

"Fierceteeth!" he cried, bending over the NightWing dragonet. "Are you all right?"

Behind him, Sunny hit the ground rolling, sprang up with her wings spread, and shot into the trees.

"Don't let her get away!" Fierceteeth shrieked. "Strongwings! Catch her! Kill her if you have to!"

CHAPTER 3

Dangling wet vines smacked against Sunny's snout as she flew up into the treetops. She remembered what she'd learned from the RainWings about rainforest flying and kept her wings tucked close. She couldn't use her tail to swing from the trees like they did, but she was small enough to maneuver through narrow gaps and swerve quickly.

But the three NightWings were right behind her, roaring angrily.

I should lead them back to the tunnels and the others. Glory needs to know that they're not loyal — she needs to lock them up and keep an eye on them.

For how long? Sunny wondered. *Forever? They'll never be trustworthy; they'll always be plotting to overthrow her. What do you do with dragons like that?*

One of her wings hit a branch as she flew past and a family of monkeys went leaping off into the trees, howling and chattering with alarm. She twisted to glance back and saw a bolt of fire engulf one of the monkeys as the NightWings attacked them, thinking it was her.

They won't be foolish enough to follow me all the way back,

Sunny realized, *even if I can keep ahead of them for that long. They won't let themselves be caught.*

What will they do instead?

She narrowly missed knocking herself out with a giant tree branch, ducking to avoid it at the last second.

The same plan, just without me. They'll go to Burn and tell her we're here in the rainforest — where her army can find us easily.

I need to hide. I need to think.

She curled into a ball and threw herself into one of the dragonfruit trees, where the leaves were huge and over-lapped one another like scales. Her momentum nearly carried her out the other side, but she was able to fling her talons out and hook onto the trunk, slamming her body into it. She froze in place, clinging to the rough bark, hoping the NightWings had lost sight of her in the dark.

"By all the moons, Strongwings!" Fierceteeth swore from somewhere to Sunny's left. "How could you let her escape?"

"Sorry," his voice mumbled.

"She's gone," said Preyhunter. "We'll never find her now — not without running the risk of a RainWing spotting us."

"Let's get out of here," said Strongwings. "Before she brings back reinforcements."

"Talons and tails!" Fierceteeth hissed. "We needed her!"

"We still have useful information for the next SandWing queen," said Preyhunter. "They all want to know where the dragonets are. If we hurry, we'll be the only ones selling that information, and we don't need the SandWing as proof. We're NightWings; everyone believes us."

"Makes sense. Let's go," Strongwings said.

And with a flurry of wingbeats, the dragons headed for the dark open sky above the trees.

Sunny's claws were trembling with the effort to stay still. She took a deep breath.

If I go back and tell the others, we can follow them.

But by the time they listen to me — if they listen to me at all — the NightWings will be long gone.

Sunny was used to the way her friends talked over her all the time. If she really wanted to be heard, she usually had to get Clay's attention and have him make her suggestions for her. Which wasn't fair — she had good ideas! — but her friends never expected her to have anything useful to say. They also didn't trust her to keep secrets; they hadn't even told her about it when they were all planning to escape their guardians. All they wanted was for her to be cheerful and supportive and agree with everything they wanted to do.

Would Glory even listen if Sunny tried to tell her about the rogue NightWings? Wouldn't she be too busy? What if she just rolled her eyes at Sunny, the way she often did?

"I don't want to be 'distracted' from worrying about the prophecy," Sunny muttered. "I want to *do something*."

Like stopping the NightWings. *I could follow them right now. I might be the only dragon who can stop them before they tell Burn where we are.*

Maybe if I do, my friends will see that I can do important things, and then maybe they'll listen to me about the prophecy.

She thought guiltily of Starflight and what he would think when he finally woke up and realized she wasn't there, taking care of him.

Then she thought of what her friends had said about her in the Obsidian Mirror, and she thought about Morrowseer's smug, evil face, and she thought of all the dragons in Pyrrhia waiting for the dragonets of destiny to save them.

I'm doing this. Even if I have to fulfill the prophecy alone, I will.

Sunny clambered up through the branches and lifted off, following the black dragons into the night sky.

It was easier to follow the NightWings than Sunny would have expected. Her sharp eyes could catch the movement of their small, silver underwing scales flashing against the sky, and they weren't making much effort to be quiet, either. Or maybe loud and flappy was how NightWings always flew.

They also were slower than Sunny and got tired more quickly, so she had to be careful not to pass them accidentally, especially during their frequent rest stops.

The sun was rising behind them when they reached the far edge of the rainforest, where the jungle shifted into sparser forest and more marshes, the outskirts of MudWing territory.

The Claws of the Clouds mountains stood out sharply up ahead in the growing light, like a line of jagged, broken teeth. Most of the mountains in the southern part of the range were not as tall as the ones in the north, where the SkyWings lived.

But there was one exception: Jade Mountain.

The tallest mountain on the continent was easy to spot, and not just for its towering size. Sunny remembered the picture on the map of Pyrrhia they'd had underground. In reality, the two crags at the top looked even more like sharp fangs sticking up into the air. One of the scrolls had said that from certain approaches, the tip of the mountain looked exactly like the head of a snake, lunging out of the ground to attack the clouds.

Jade Mountain. Sunny frowned. Someone had said something recently about Jade Mountain. Something she needed to remember. *What was it?*

Nothing came to her as the sun slowly lit up the mountain's fangs.

Sunny had been worrying all night about how she would hide from the NightWings in the daylight. They didn't seem to be watching behind them, but it would be hard to miss her golden scales once the sun was reflecting off them. She wished she had Glory's camouflage scales. Really, any of her friends' skills would be helpful, instead of her own total lack of powers.

But as the sky grew pinker and brighter and then started shading from gray to blue, the three NightWings flew lower, their wings drooping, until finally they landed beside a small river.

Sunny kept her distance, choosing the tallest tree she could find and tucking herself among the branches, close to the trunk. She fixed her eyes on where the NightWings had gone down and pricked her ears. She could hear their distant muttering, with Fierceteeth the most distinct. It sounded as if they were planning to sleep for as much of the day as they could and then fly on at dusk.

They've been breathing volcanic ash and living on dying, rotting scraps, probably for their whole lives, Sunny thought. *No wonder they're not exactly in great shape.*

After a while, the trees stopped rustling and the dragon voices fell silent. A few minutes later, one of them — Sunny guessed Strongwings — started snoring like a herd of congested hippos.

Now what do I do? Sunny wondered. This was a perfect opportunity to wreck their plans, if she could figure out how. *Could I fly to the RainWing village and get back with reinforcements before they wake up?*

No. It would take me all day just to get someone to pay attention to me. I can do this myself. I have to.

What would Tsunami do? Would she go down there and kill them?

I don't think I could do that — even if I could do that.

Sunny sighed. A breeze whispered through the trees, curling under her wings as if inviting her to fly. *Yesterday I wouldn't have worried about what was going to happen next with Fierceteeth and the others. I'd be able to follow them knowing for sure that whatever I did would turn out all right.*

She hated Morrowseer for making her feel this way — this awful *doubting* feeling. He'd planted this worry, which she'd never had before, that maybe things *wouldn't* be all right. That in fact she could die, and the war might go on endlessly, and perhaps there wasn't a happy ending all planned out by the universe.

She had to stop thinking about Morrowseer and the prophecy. It was like stabbing icicle-sharp claws between her scales every time she pictured the haughty black dragon sneering about his great lies.

Stupid NightWings and their deceitful all-knowing high-and-mighty —

Sunny sat up so fast she nearly fell off her tree branch.

All-knowing.

There was one thing she could do to slow the NightWings down.

She could steal the Obsidian Mirror.

— CHAPTER 4 —

This was one of those ideas that Sunny's friends would totally ignore if she suggested it, but would love like crazy if it came from Clay or Tsunami. It was also something they would never, ever let her do herself. Too dangerous! Too risky! Send a dragon with fighting skills or camouflage scales. Not their undersized, cheerful, silly little sister.

Well, I'm the only one here. And I know I can do it.

She waited until the sun was halfway up the sky, and then she carefully worked her way closer, hopping from tree to tree and giving herself as much cover as she could. There were a few spots where she was exposed and her golden scales caught the light, but when she finally came to rest on a branch within sight of the NightWings, all three of them were sleeping soundly.

Starflight said there were never any NightWing guards posted in their fortress. They're used to being so isolated that no one could find them to attack them. It didn't even occur to them to leave someone awake to keep watch.

She snorted. *They probably also figured no one would dare attack a group of amazing all-powerful NightWings.*

Fierceteeth was curled in the curve of Strongwings's underbelly, with her tail draped over his and her head resting on his shoulder. Sunny had no idea how Fierceteeth could sleep through those tree-rattling snores.

Preyhunter lay closer to the river, scrunched into a tight, tense ball, with his wings tucked close to him. In the daylight, Sunny could see how dull his scales were and how ill they all looked. Even Strongwings, who was built large and burly, looked underfed, and his snores rasped heavily as if his lungs and throat and nose were lined with claws.

Sunny studied the ground around Preyhunter until she spotted a corner of black glass sticking out from under one of his wings. He was keeping the Obsidian Mirror very close.

How can I get it without waking him up?

She glanced at the other two again, then quietly slid down her tree until her talons touched the grass. The river bubbled over smooth gray rocks, not much more than a stream. Small purple wildflowers bent under her claws as Sunny tiptoed over to the sleeping NightWing.

He looked miserable, even in his sleep. His jaw was clenched, his talons twitched defensively, and his forked black tongue flickered in and out as he muttered something to himself. When Sunny crouched beside him, she realized he was shivering.

I guess it was pretty hot, living on a volcano. The air didn't feel cold to her, here on the outskirts of the jungle, but perhaps he wasn't used to it. Or perhaps he was sick.

It felt strange to be so close to an unfamiliar NightWing. For the first six years of her life, Sunny had known exactly seven dragons: Clay, Tsunami, Starflight, Glory, and their three guardians, Webs, Dune, and Kestrel.

Two of those seven dragons were dead now. She knew the guardians had never been particularly kind to the dragonets, but they were still the only parents she'd ever had, and she missed them. Her friends had never stopped to grieve for Dune and Kestrel — she wasn't even sure they were sad about their deaths at all. She'd tried not to show how it upset her, but at night, curled up beside Clay, when she was sure he'd sleep through it, sometimes she'd let herself cry for them.

She reached toward the sliver of obsidian, but before she even touched it, Preyhunter whimpered in his sleep, and she snatched her talons back.

None of the dragons moved for a long moment.

Maybe this is a bad idea. I could make things worse if I get myself caught.

But if she could get the mirror away from them, that would be one less weapon in their claws. They'd be flying blind, with no idea what Glory was planning and no way to know if Burn would receive them with open wings. Not to mention Sunny could probably use that mirror herself.

She reached out again and noticed the trembling that shuddered through Preyhunter's scales. Maybe he wasn't cold. Maybe it was a nightmare.

Maybe he's dreaming about the terrible things he's done. Or perhaps he's dreaming about the volcano exploding.

She hesitated, and then unfolded one of her wings, spreading it gently over his back. She was too small to cover him completely, but the warmth that radiated from her scales spread as far over him as she could reach. She held her breath, trying not to touch him.

Preyhunter let out a long, shuddering sigh, and then the shivering stopped. He took another deep breath, and Sunny saw the tension in his snout, jaws, and neck relax. A ripple went through his wings and his claws unclenched. He stopped muttering, and even his closed eyes seemed to smooth over, as if he were shifting into a deeper, calmer sleep.

Sunny waited a long moment, feeling sorry for this dragon even though she really didn't want to. She couldn't help wondering what she herself might have been like if she'd grown up on the NightWing island. Desperate and sad? Mean and hungry?

She reached for the mirror again, and suddenly Preyhunter spoke.

"Please."

Sunny froze. His eyes were still closed. Across the clearing, Fierceteeth shifted her wings and coughed.

"Please don't make me," Preyhunter said, more softly. "Mother, it's awful."

A stab of sympathy shot through Sunny, and she curled her tail in closer. *Remember what he's planning and what he said and what he's done.* But it was hard not to imagine herself in his scales.

Gently she used her front talons to slide the mirror out from under his wing. Her warmth had relaxed his grip on it, so he wasn't clutching it so tightly, and it only took a moment until it was resting coldly between her claws. The obsidian felt thin, like a layer of ice, and the edges were sharp as teeth. Sunny could see her distorted reflection in the dark glass.

She took a careful step back, then another, and folded her wings back in. Preyhunter made a lost, mournful noise, and his claws twitched as if he were trying to pull the warmth back into him.

Will they guess I'm the one who stole it? What if they come looking for me?

She glanced around the clearing. A large, flat gray boulder took up most of the ground between the three dragons, with bright yellow dandelions dotting the edges like topaz gemstones around a pendant.

I'll leave them a message. . . . Something that won't sound like me. Maybe something that'll scare them.

Her own heart was drumming frantically against her ribs like a caged bird. She wanted to get out of there before any of them woke up. But she had a strong feeling that there was something to this idea.

She dipped a claw in the dark red mud that lined the river and wrote on the boulder, in tall, jagged letters:

TURN BACK. YOU FLY TOWARD YOUR DEATH.

Totally spooky, she thought with satisfaction. It even looked like maybe it could have been written in blood. *That should at least creep them out, even if it doesn't send them scurrying back to the rainforest.*

Sunny took a step back, and then suddenly Strongwings let out the loudest snore yet, and Fierceteeth rolled over to swat him with her wing.

"Shut your noisy snout or so help me I will rip it off with my claws!" she hollered.

Sunny bolted into the sky and didn't stop flying until she reached the dense green canopy of the jungle again.

When she finally glanced back, there was no movement from the NightWings' copse of trees. Strongwings had even started snoring again.

I guess she was yelling at him in her sleep. Or she went right back to sleep and didn't notice me there.

Sunny carefully tucked the mirror under one wing and used her talons to clamber up and along the trees until she found a spot where the leaves overlapped so thickly it was like a small green cave around her. She studied the mirror. What had Preyhunter done to activate it?

"Starflight," she said softly to the cold obsidian, and then she breathed a small plume of smoke across the surface.

As it had before, the smoke twined and twisted around the mirror, then vanished. Sunny could feel the mirror thrumming faintly between her claws. It was sort of horrible — a sick, slithering sensation through her blood, as if it were pulling something out of Sunny's heart.

A faint black tendril of smoke curled up from the center of the mirror, barely visible in the green-tinted sunshine. It didn't speak, but when Sunny leaned closer, she could hear the faint sound of breath going in and out.

He's alive.

Two pale blue wisps of smoke drifted by, close to the edge of the mirror.

"I've never seen anything like it," whispered one.

"The queen said this is what 'fire' can do," murmured the other. "It seems almost as bad as venom, if you ask me."

From their voices, Sunny guessed they were two of the healer RainWings she'd befriended while she was helping take care of Webs. RainWing healers were odd, specializing mostly in saying comforting things and offering more fruit to eat. But occasionally they were really specifically knowledgeable, like about jaguar bites, or what to do if you ate too many mangoes, or how to make salves for tails that had been used for swinging from rough branches one too many times.

"I'd rather be Kinkajou than him right now," said the first. "She's healing well."

"Did you see the messenger who was here before?" The second curl of blue smoke moved, looping around the black smoke as if checking on it, and then sliding back to the first. "That big brown dragon sent a message for Sunny. I wasn't sure whether to tell him we haven't seen her. I don't want to worry the queen when she has so many NightWings to deal with."

"I say don't start a panic. She's around somewhere."

This was similar to the RainWings' attitude toward their own missing dragons, some of which had been gone as long as a year by the time Glory rescued them. *Well, that's fine,* Sunny thought. *I don't need or want my friends looking for me. They have enough to do.*

The black smoke stirred, as if the faintest breath of wind had touched it. "Sunny?" Starflight whispered.

But . . . poor Starflight. She curled her tail in around her talons and sighed.

"Shh, we woke him by talking about her," admonished the first healer. "Let's get him another sleeping dart."

Sunny cleared the mirror and held it between her claws for a moment. She disliked it more and more the longer she held it. It had a chilling wrongness to it, like the tunnels, that made her scales feel as if invisible spiders were crawling all over her.

But there were things she needed to know — like what the warring SandWing queens were plotting. The Obsidian Mirror could help her figure out if any of them was an immediate threat to Sunny's friends.

I should at least try one of them. The most dangerous one. She hesitated, and then whispered, "Blister," to the dark glass.

The pale yellow twist of smoke that rose from the center this time had the same chilling stillness that Blister had; it barely even moved in the breeze.

"Be careful!" it hissed suddenly, and Sunny flinched away from the mirror. It was unsettling to hear Blister's voice as if she were on the next branch over. "Close it up. Is he ready to go? All right, give him his gold, and tell him I'll be there in a moment with final instructions." The smoke dipped for a moment, then turned as another small twister touched down. "Anything?"

"No sign of any SeaWings, Your Majesty," said the new arrival. "We waited half the day."

Blister hissed, low and long. "I'll win this war without them, then," she growled. "Burn will be dead within a fortnight, and then I'll kill Blaze with my own talons, and the SeaWings will get *nothing* when they come slithering out of the ocean begging for forgiveness. They'll find my claws and the entire force of the SandWing army waiting instead. Coral has no idea what vengeance can really look like. Don't touch that," she snapped abruptly.

"Sorry, Your Majesty. What —"

"It's my plan to end this war once and for all," Blister said in a dark voice. "Without the SeaWings *or* the NightWings. So stay away from it. Any word from our spies in the Ice Kingdom?"

"No sign of the dragonets yet. Perhaps —"

"I know," Blister snapped. "They could be somewhere else." There was the sound of paper crackling. "I've been considering the possibilities. Hiding in the rainforest, perhaps."

Sunny felt a chill down her spine.

"Or perhaps they're dead," said the soldier. "Especially if they tried going to the rainforest, from what I've heard about that place."

"Hmmm," Blister mused. "Dead. They'd never do anything so convenient for me. Even with a NightWing assassin after them, supposedly, if anything Morrowseer says can be trusted. Speaking of dragons I'm going to dismember as soon as I get my claws on them."

She doesn't know he's dead — how could she? Sunny gripped the branch below her, feeling terror shudder through her scales. *At least she's not searching the rainforest yet.*

"It doesn't matter," said Blister, her voice suddenly brisk. "I'm done with prophecies. I mean, I'll still kill the dragonets when I find them, but first I have a war to win. My new plan will take care of Burn — and then the stronghold will fall, and the throne will be mine." There was a chilling rattling sound, and the twist of smoke seemed to get a little darker.

"How —" began the soldier.

But just then Sunny heard a roar from the NightWings' clearing.

Uh-oh.

She wanted to know what Blister's plan was — but she needed to know how the three NightWings were reacting, and if she was in danger right now. She cleared the mirror quickly, whispered "Fierceteeth" to it, then breathed smoke across it again.

Immediately, three curls of black smoke popped up on the glass, rushing around one another like small tornadoes.

"How could you lose it?" Fierceteeth's voice snarled.

"I didn't *lose* it," Preyhunter snapped. "Someone *stole* it."

"Right out from under your snout?" Fierceteeth growled. "How, exactly?"

"I don't know!" Preyhunter yelled.

"I do," said a trembling voice that barely sounded like Strongwings. "It was the Darkstalker."

Sunny tilted her head toward the mirror. *What's the Darkstalker?*

What could be scary enough to terrify a dragon as big as Strongwings?

The other two NightWings didn't respond for a long moment. Finally, Fierceteeth hissed, "That's just a ghost story for little dragonets. There's no Darkstalker, or if there ever was, we killed him centuries ago."

"No, he's *real*," Strongwings said, edging toward hysteria. "Everyone knows he's still out there somewhere, and now he's found us. Look at this message! We're going to die!"

"It could have been someone who wants us to *think* he's the Darkstalker," Preyhunter said dubiously.

"But who else would know we had the mirror? Who else would know that we're flying to our death?"

"Snap out of it, Strongwings," Fierceteeth barked. "Someone is trying to scare us, that's all. You know the story. The Darkstalker, if he did exist, died a long time ago."

"No. He couldn't die," Strongwings whispered. "They buried him, but they always knew he'd come back one day."

Sunny had never heard of this mythical dragon. *It must be a NightWing legend. Lucky for me.* She hadn't expected to tap into an old superstition.

"Maybe it was that SandWing," Fierceteeth said, then immediately let out a dismissive snort. "No, that stunted salamander wouldn't have the teeth for something like this. She must have gone back and told someone we had the mirror. I bet this was Deathbringer. Seems like something he would do, from what I've heard of him."

Sunny was obscurely flattered and offended at the same time. She flicked her tongue at the dark glass.

"But Deathbringer would just kill us," argued Preyhunter. "Strongwings is right about one thing — this is what the Darkstalker does, according to the stories. He plays with his prey for days, making sure they're nearly paralyzed with terror before he strikes."

"Yes, exactly," Strongwings said. "He'll come back the next time we sleep and kill just one of us, or —"

"So let's *not* be paralyzed with terror," Fierceteeth snarled. "Let's *go*. The Kingdom of Sand is on the other side of those mountains. We can be there in a few days if we stop moaning and clutching our tails. Come *on*." Her smoke tendril was nearly interwoven with Strongwings's, as if she were trying to heave him into the sky with brute force.

"But the message —"

"We can't go back," Fierceteeth said. "Glory will kill us more definitely than any old NightWing animus ghost, and if she doesn't, we'll be the RainWings' prisoners. I'll take my chances in the desert, even without that mirror."

The argument didn't go on much longer. Soon the sound of wingbeats thumped across the smooth obsidian.

Sunny tilted the smoke together and breathed fire across it again until there was nothing but silence and darkness on the face of the mirror. The slithering inside of her faded, but she felt more tired and sick than she had in a while. *I hope I don't have to use this thing too often.*

So I'd better try to keep an eye on them.

She ducked through the leaves and flew straight up until she slipped through the whispering green canopy, straight into blinding sunlight.

On the western horizon, already no bigger than claws, she could see the three black shapes winging away toward the mountains. She followed, feeling better and stronger with each moment of sun on her scales.

The Kingdom of Sand. The desert. Just on the other side of those mountains.

I'm going home.

—— CHAPTER 5 ——

Sunny followed the NightWings for three days as they navigated the foothills and then the snowier heights of the mountain crags. They slept in the shadow of Jade Mountain, listening to the wind howling around the twin peaks. She only had to use the mirror once more, when she lost sight of them, and it helped her catch up to them again.

She would have loved to sneak back into their camp and leave more scary messages, but she knew they'd take turns staying awake to keep watch after losing the mirror. And she resisted the temptation to use the mirror on her friends or on Blister again, although she kept worrying about Blister's new plan. Still, she wanted to avoid that sick, slithery feeling as much as possible.

From the mountaintops, they flew down through densely forested foothills, and off in the distance ahead of them Sunny began to see something that shimmered white and hazy across the horizon.

The desert, she thought with a prickle of anticipation. She'd been there once before, when the dragonets found the tunnel from the rainforest into the Kingdom of Sand. They'd had to chase Mangrove all the way to the borderlands of the

Ice Kingdom. So she'd spent two days flying over the desert, but hardly any time down on the sand, where her talons really wanted to be.

And no time at all looking for my parents. Her thoughts kept circling back to that as she flew, with no one to talk to and nothing else to distract her from worrying about the prophecy.

Her friends had all found some kind of family by now — even if some of it was disappointing family, and no one was quite what they'd expected. Clay's mother was awful, but his brothers and sisters were a lot like him, according to Clay. Tsunami's mother was the queen of the SeaWings, who had tried to imprison them, but Tsunami had two little sisters, too: Anemone and Auklet.

Glory had no way to figure out who her parents were, thanks to the way RainWings kept their eggs all together, but she'd found a brother, Jambu (even if he was a bit silly), and also Grandeur, who was perhaps a great-grandmother or great-aunt or something like that. Poor Starflight had really had it the worst of all, between Mastermind for a dad and Fierceteeth as his sister.

But at least they knew — at least they'd found *someone.* They all had dragons who wanted them in some way.

Why did my parents leave me?

She had almost nothing to go on if she ever wanted to look for her family. All Kestrel had said was, "Dune found Sunny's egg in the desert, hidden near the Scorpion Den."

The Scorpion Den. I don't even know what that is. She'd seen it marked on the map, but she didn't remember reading about it in any scrolls.

Oh! Her wings missed a beat as she finally remembered where she'd heard about Jade Mountain. *It was something Kestrel said the last time we saw her. "When you realize you need me, you can send me a message through the dragon of Jade Mountain."*

She twisted to look back at the fanged mountain. So a dragon lived there — one who dealt with at least some of the Talons of Peace. That could be useful to keep in mind. *Although . . . who would live somewhere so sinister?* She wondered which tribe it was from, and why he or she lived alone.

When she turned back around, she saw the distant shapes of the NightWings diving toward the forest below them. *Resting again? When we're so close? We can't be more than an hour's flight from the desert now.* They had only flown for half the night before stopping to sleep, and then risen with the sunrise to fly again a few hours ago.

Now the sun had cleared the eastern horizon, but the day was barely begun. And they already needed a break? *They seriously have no stamina.* She rolled her eyes and folded her wings to drop down into the forest as well.

Wind-flurried green leaves brushed against her scales and a riot of gray squirrels scattered along the branches as she landed, her talons sinking into the soft grass. In the distance, she could hear the NightWings roaring grumpily, and she guessed they were having another unsuccessful hunt. For a trio of menacing killers, they were actually surprisingly bad at catching anything to eat.

Sunny wasn't the world's best hunter herself, but she didn't need much. She'd always eaten less than her friends —

a lizard a day would be enough for her. Kestrel used to grumble that that was probably why Sunny was so stunted and scrawny, but then Dune would shake his head and insist that it was normal for SandWings to be light eaters.

Kestrel and Dune. Our dead guardians.

If only she'd had more time to ask Dune about where her egg came from. He'd always been evasive when the subject came up, but if she'd known her friends were planning an escape — *if they'd trusted me enough to tell me about it,* she thought with a frown — she could have pressed him harder.

Sunny swiveled her head around, listening.

There was an odd noise in this forest.

Actually there were several odd noises. Like thumps and murmurs and a chattery kind of birdsong, almost as though squirrels were trying to imitate their winged neighbors.

But — it sounded as though it was coming from *under* the ground.

She crouched and pressed one ear to the warm earth.

There's definitely something under here. Groundhogs? Rabbits? She didn't think any normal rodents made noises quite like this. And from what she could tell, it wasn't a small warren underneath her — the sounds seemed to be coming from fairly far away as well.

Softly she paced through the forest, stopping occasionally to listen. She kept an eye out for the three NightWings, but they weren't hard to avoid. First there was the roaring and crashing around, and then after a while, snoring that shook the top branches of the trees.

Sunny worked her way cautiously westward, in the direction of the desert. Small brown and red birds chorused from the trees, occasionally pausing as they saw her approach, and then starting again after a moment, as if they realized she was nothing to worry about. Bumblebees and dragonflies buzzed and hummed and flitted around her talons. In the mild morning breeze, Sunny could smell apples and mint leaves. And something else, too, like old burnt wood.

She couldn't hear the sounds from under the ground anymore, but the burnt smell drew her on. Up ahead she could see a break in the trees.

She stepped out into the bright sunlight and stopped, her eyes momentarily full of light.

There was a hole blasted in the forest.

Something had been here once — something that stretched for more than a mile within the forest, bigger than the dragonets' home under the mountain — but it was gone now, all burned to black ashes.

Where Sunny stood, at the edge of it, the forest was trying to rise again. Ashes drifted like dead leaves over her claws, but she could see small green shoots wriggling through here and there.

She spread her wings and took to the air, hoping for a better look. The burnt area stretched in jagged slashes through the trees and ended at the border with the rocky foothills that led to the desert. From above, she could see that the hole in the forest was many wingspans across and black as a

NightWing's scales. It looked like a dark gap in a piece of jewelry where a gemstone had been violently gouged out.

She circled overhead. Everything inside the hole looked twisted and blasted into dark ashes, but as Sunny studied the wreckage, she realized that it wasn't just trees that had been burned here.

Some of the ghostly shapes that remained looked like . . . buildings.

But these buildings were too small for dragons.

Sunny landed next to one of the ruins and stared at it in confusion for a moment. Even she was too big to fit through the stone doorways that leaned silently out of the ashes.

But why would any dragon build houses so small?

She walked around it, her wings stirring up small tornadoes of ash flakes, and saw that in the center of the burnt area was a kind of open square. She could feel hard, cracked stones meeting her claws under the layers of ash. In the middle of the square she found a collapsed pile of round rocks, and tipped sideways among those was a blackened metal bell about the size of Sunny's head.

Somebody definitely built this. Were they keeping some kind of small animal here?

She turned to look at another of the small stone doorways and found a shape sticking out of the wreckage beside it. When she clawed it out, she realized it was a piece of stone, roughly carved into a shape with two legs, no wings, and holding something pointy over its head.

Oh! Sunny inhaled sharply, getting a noseful of old soot smell. *Scavengers!* The statue, if that's what it was, looked a bit like a drawing from one of the old scrolls about scavengers who attacked dragons for their treasure, waving sharp little toothpick claw things called swords.

Did scavengers build this place? Can they do things like make bells and carve statues?

Sunny knew scavengers lived in dens, but she hadn't thought they could build real buildings like this. She always imagined them clustering in caves or digging out holes to live in, or maybe leaning long sticks together to create shelters, at most. Here there was clearly advanced masonry, deliberate foundation work, and a sort of organized street plan, as far as Sunny could tell.

Plus the statue . . . it was crude, but wasn't it art? What kind of prey made art?

Maybe I'm misunderstanding all of this. Maybe dragons built this place and kept scavengers here for some reason.

And then burned it all down? Why would they do that?

She lifted into the sky, feeling unsettled.

The dragonets had studied scavengers in their scrolls, but Webs and Kestrel had never brought any back to their mountain caves for eating or practice hunting. Sunny had seen a few small scavengers in Queen Scarlet's palace, scurrying around under the dragons' feet at a banquet for the visiting SandWings. But she'd been up in a giant birdcage, on display as a gift for Burn, so she hadn't gotten a very close look.

Scavengers were the ones who'd started the dragon war by killing Queen Oasis and stealing all her treasure, leaving Burn, Blaze, and Blister to fight over the throne and the empty treasury. Sunny didn't know much else about scavengers.

She knew they liked shiny things. She'd always imagined scavengers as sort of fierce magpies or squirrels — bigger than either of those, but not much smarter. They couldn't have very much of a brain if they thought attacking dragons was a good idea, right?

She glanced down at the destroyed village once more, then turned back to find a spot where she could hide and wait for the NightWings.

Maybe there's more to scavengers than we were taught.

But what happened here?

Who burned down this scavenger den . . . and why?

— CHAPTER 6 —

Heat blazed across Sunny's scales. She burrowed into the sand, feeling the tiny particles drift across her talons and tail. The Obsidian Mirror caught the sunshine as if it were trying to suck all the light into itself, and the black wisps of smoke on its surface looked like small sandstorms.

"Why wouldn't we go straight to Burn's stronghold?" Fierceteeth's voice demanded.

"Because she'll have us slaughtered the moment she sees us coming," Preyhunter said impatiently. "Burn is a 'kill first, ask questions later' kind of dragon."

"It makes sense to start at the Scorpion Den," Strongwings agreed. "We can find someone there to take a message to Burn that we want to see her."

Sunny closed her eyes. *The Scorpion Den. That might be where my parents live.*

"I thought the Scorpion Den was full of lowlifes and criminals," said Fierceteeth.

"It is," said Preyhunter.

It is? thought Sunny. *Is that what my parents are?*

"But they're the kind of criminals who know how to get things done, from everything I've heard," said Strongwings.

"That's exactly what we need right now. Besides, the Scorpion Den isn't far — just over those dunes."

Sunny sat up and narrowed her eyes against the bright glare of the sun. The NightWings were far ahead of her, but she thought she could see a dark shape against the sand off in the distance, which might be the Scorpion Den.

"All right, all right," Fierceteeth grumbled. "Waste of time, if you ask me."

Sunny cleared the mirror, feeling excitement prickle through her scales. She knew it was unlikely that she'd find out something about her past in the Scorpion Den, but it was still the closest she'd ever been to her parents. Even if they were criminals, she still wanted to know who they were.

Also, a detour to the Scorpion Den would give her more time to slow down the NightWings. She still hadn't come up with any plans to stop them from telling Burn everything.

In the distance she saw the tiny black shapes lift into the sky. Cautiously she followed them. There was really nowhere to hide in the desert, unless she burrowed under the sand, so she was staying as far back as possible.

But it was hard to stop her wings from beating faster and faster as they drew closer to the Scorpion Den. Sunny could see that it was a walled city full of winding alleyways, ramshackle stone buildings, tattered canopies, and dilapidated tents in colors that had been faded by the sun over a long period of time. And it seethed with dragons: scales glittered from every shadow and venomous tails slithered around corners.

She was so preoccupied staring at the town that she had to stop herself abruptly in midair when she realized that the three

NightWings had not gone inside, but were standing outside the tall gates at the single entrance. It looked as though they were arguing with the muscular SandWing guard, who stood with her wings folded back and her tail raised menacingly.

Sunny dropped quickly to the sand, hoping she hadn't been seen. She flattened herself against the dune, even though she knew her scales were not quite the right color for camouflage.

Now that she was still, she could hear the dragons' voices shouting.

"You have no right to stop us!" Fierceteeth roared. "Can't you see that we're NightWings?"

"Yeah," answered the guard. "So read my mind. The part that says go eat your tails."

"We have business in the Scorpion Den," Preyhunter insisted.

"No one gets inside without a contribution to the Outclaws," the guard said firmly.

"The *Outclaws*?" said Preyhunter. "That's what you call yourselves? You must be joking."

"Are you asking for treasure?" Fierceteeth demanded. "Of course we don't have treasure! Our home was just —"

"Surely you can make an exception for us," Strongwings interjected, cutting her off. "I mean, we're *NightWings*."

"And?" said the guard.

There was a pause. Sunny grinned, imagining the apoplectic fit Fierceteeth was probably having.

"We could give you a prophecy," Preyhunter suggested after a moment.

"Hah," the guard said, sounding moderately more interested. "That would be funny. Qibli! Tell Thorn we have three NightWings offering their pathetic services."

"I think you mean *prophetic* services," Fierceteeth said.

"Uh-huh," said the guard skeptically.

There was a long silence as everyone waited. Sunny wriggled higher up on her dune, hoping for a view of the city gates, but a long slope of sand dotted with prickly spheres of cacti blocked her way.

What can I offer the guard to get inside the Scorpion Den? she wondered. She glanced down at the Obsidian Mirror. It was the only thing she had — was it worth giving up her one advantage over the NightWings? On the other talon, she knew she'd be happy to have its sinister weight out of her claws. But on the third talon, she didn't know who would end up with their claws on this potentially dangerous weapon. What might the Outclaws do with it?

Hmmm. Moreover, even if she didn't offer it to them, what was to stop a band of outlaws from just taking it? Sunny thought for a moment, then quickly dug a hole in the sand next to one of the cactus balls and buried the mirror. Of course there wasn't anything here to help her distinguish one brownish rolling sand dune from the next. She'd have to cross all her claws and hope she'd be able to find it again. But a dangerous mirror nobody could find was better than a dangerous mirror floating around the Scorpion Den, surely.

She lifted her head as the guard below spoke. "All right," he said. "Thorn wants to see you, don't ask me why. Follow Qibli — and no funny business."

Sunny waited as long as she could bear it, then scrambled up and started over the dune.

A SandWing was standing there, no more than three steps away, staring straight at her as if he'd been waiting for her. His side was pocked and dented with old scars, and he had six claws on each foreleg, instead of five. She had no idea where he'd come from, or how he'd snuck up on her so quickly and quietly.

"Oh!" she yelped.

"That means you, too," he said calmly.

"M-m-me too what?" Sunny stammered.

He tilted his head and studied her curiously, registering the odd color of her scales and eyes, and no doubt noticing her venomless tail as well.

"You're to come before the Outclaws as well. Thorn wants to know why you're following those scumdwellers." He jerked his head in the direction of the den and the NightWings. Sunny had never heard anyone refer to NightWings with that much disrespect before, except perhaps Tsunami or Glory.

"I'm — I'm not following anybody," Sunny said, folding her wings back. She could hear how unconvincing she sounded.

He shrugged. "Lie to me all you want, but I wouldn't recommend trying it with Thorn." He flicked his tail and she flinched away. "Come."

It was not a request. At least he wasn't threatening to chain her up — and at least going with him would mean getting into the Scorpion Den without the problem of payment.

"Fine," she said, lifting her chin. "Take me to Thorn."

They flew down to the city gates and the guard nodded impassively as they went past her, straight into a crooked stone alleyway with steps leading up and down. Sharp, spicy cooking smells filled the air, along with the scents of smoke and crowds of overheated dragons. The streets around them were lined with rickety stalls and tents, and voices began pressing in on Sunny.

"Crocodile stew? Roasted scorpion? Bag of crickets?"

"Bet you'd like some gold for them golden scales!"

"Stock up on brightsting cactus — you never know when you might need it!"

"Need anyone killed, little lady? Here, take my card."

A small, flat piece of metal, inscribed with a name, was pressed into Sunny's talons, and the SandWing who'd given it to her vanished almost immediately. Sunny blinked and glanced up at the dragon escorting her.

"Whose is it?" he asked, plucking it out of her claws. "Nah, you don't want him. Too expensive, barely competent." He tossed the card into another stall as they went by, and a snout poked out of a pile of carpets to growl at them.

"Ouch!" Sunny yelped as someone rushed past and stepped on her tail. She tried to sidestep a pair of quarreling dragons and got smacked in the face by a sandy wing.

These streets are so narrow . . . and there are so many of them. . . . They must accidentally scratch each other with their tails all the time. She looked more closely at the stalls around her and realized that many of them sold the cactus that was the antidote to SandWing venom. As far as she could see, it was nearly as popular as the giant camel-hide pouches of water being sold by every other merchant, or the tiny blue dragons and shiny black spheres that also seemed to share all the tables with other merchandise.

A wooden signboard caught her eye: three dragons' faces carved under the words WANTED. Sunny twisted to try and stare at the faces as her guard hurried her past. She could have sworn one of them was Dune . . . and one of the others was . . . but surely it couldn't be . . .

Her guard steered her through the tangles of dragons, keeping one wing firmly settled against her back. Other dragons jumped out of his way when they spotted him, or ducked their heads as he went by, or slipped into shadowy corners, hissing. Soon Sunny realized that the same wooden WANTED sign was posted everywhere, hung from walls, pinned to tent flaps, and nailed to the stallboards. She got a chance to peer at one more closely when they paused to let a cart of gold-painted boxes clatter by.

It really does look like Morrowseer. Morrowseer, Dune, and a NightWing I've never seen before. But why? And who's looking for them?

There was small print below the pictures, but Sunny didn't get to read it before her guard hurried her on.

Nearly all the dragons she saw were SandWings, although she also spotted a couple of scarlet SkyWings and even, once, the pale blue scales of an IceWing, who must have been miserable in this heat. She also noticed a lot of war wounds: dragons with missing talons, mangled wings, clawed-up snouts, or ripped ears, many of them huddling in the spaces between the stalls, skinny and wretched.

Although she was sure the Scorpion Den was a dangerous place to live, she guessed that a lot of dragons came here to hide from the war — either before they could be pressed into service, or after they'd been so badly injured that they couldn't bear to fight anymore.

One SandWing limped up to them and did an odd half salute to Sunny's guard. "Going off-duty, sir." He paused and squinted at Sunny, and she realized that he had a long scratch across one of his eyes that had also torn up part of his nose. There was something vaguely familiar about him, but she was sure she would have remembered that scratch.

"Addax, quit reporting to me all the time," the guard said. "That's not how the Outclaws work. Also, I told you to stop calling me 'sir.'"

"Yes. Right. Right." The dragon coughed, clearly swallowing another "sir." "Uh, who's your guest?"

Sunny sidled closer to her escort, wishing Addax would stop staring at her. Her guard seemed to sense this; he casually spread his big wings to shield her from view.

"Just a visitor for Thorn," he said. "Carry on."

Addax bobbed his head and shuffled off into the crowd.

"Some of these former soldiers have a hard time breaking their military habits," the big SandWing said to her. "But Addax is harmless, don't worry."

Sunny twisted to look back and saw that the limping SandWing had stopped in the shade of a stall that seemed to be selling poisons. His black eyes stared through her, and even when she ducked behind her guard's wings again and after they'd crossed several more alleys, she still felt a prickling, creeping feeling along her spine, as if his gaze were following her.

They wound their way toward the center of the city, stooping under torn canopies and tripping over uneven cobblestones. Sunny could smell something new up ahead, like exploded fruit, and she caught a glimpse of dark green through the gaps ahead of her, incongruous against the sand-colored buildings, faded orange tents, and red or black brick walls.

A dragonet suddenly stumbled in front of Sunny, holding out its front claws.

"Hungry!" he bleated.

His pale yellow scales were slathered with dirt, and he was tiny, with bony ribs sticking out along his chest. His black eyes caught Sunny, and she stared down at him helplessly.

"I'm sorry," she said. "I don't have anything."

The dragon beside her leaned forward and caught the dragonet before he could run off again, casually pinning the little one's tail to the ground with one talon.

"Don't hurt him!" Sunny cried, but the guard didn't even look at her.

"Where's your guardian, squirt?" he asked the dragonet.

"Sorry, sorry, sorry," cried a female SandWing, hurrying out of a nearby alley. "I would never have let him bother you, sir. Please forgive us." She grabbed the dragonet and clutched him to her. He drooped, no energy left to wriggle away.

"You must be new here," said the six-clawed dragon, squinting at her. "He shouldn't be starving like that.

Dragonets up to eight years old get a free meal every morning after sunrise at the pool. Start sending him, and he'll be the size of a real dragon soon."

The SandWing shivered and ducked her head. "But, sir," she whispered. "I heard that was a trick."

He sighed impatiently. "Let me guess — we feed them and then grab them to turn them into Outclaws, am I right?" She flinched, and her wings folded closer around the dragonet. "Listen, we're not out to abduct a bunch of scrawny youngsters who'd be more trouble than they're worth. Thorn just wants to make sure no more dragonets die of hunger in the Scorpion Den. It's not complicated."

"Yes, sir," the SandWing whispered.

"Look, send him tomorrow morning, or I'll come after you myself," he said.

She nodded and scuttled away, keeping the dragonet under her wing.

"Some dragons," muttered Sunny's guard.

"Is that true?" Sunny asked. "The . . . um, Outclaws feed all the dragonets in the Scorpion Den?"

He shifted his wings up and down and scowled. "We try to. Dragons don't change easily, though, especially in a place like this. And especially when someone's trying to help them. Brainless worms," he muttered, turning to stalk away again.

Sunny wasn't sure that she would trust a gift from this dragon either.

"What's your name?" she asked as she caught up to walk beside him.

He looked down at her, his black tongue flicking in and out. "Six-Claws."

"Oh," Sunny said, glancing at his odd talons, and then, before she could stop herself, "Your parents were feeling pretty creative."

He barked a laugh that made several dragons around them leap into the nearest hiding place in terror. Sunlight glinted off his light yellowish-brown scales as he held up one of his front legs and examined the six wickedly sharp claws there. "I guess so. Yours?"

"I'm Sunny," she said. "I never met my parents." She chanced a sideways look at his face, but there was no reaction there. He was old enough to be her father, and from the way he walked and talked, she guessed he'd been in the Scorpion Den for a while. Plus he had those six claws — maybe peculiar defects ran in the family. Maybe he hadn't commented on her tail yet because he'd seen other dragons with the same flaw . . . dragons related to him.

Or maybe I'm totally desperate.

They stepped down a set of five stone stairs and their talons sank into sand. Sunny tore her gaze away from Six-Claws and saw that the shadows of tents and canopies had been replaced by the sweeping shade of large palm fronds.

There was an oasis in the middle of the Scorpion Den.

Well, that makes sense, Sunny realized. Why else would dragons build a city here?

She could see a rippling pool of greenish-blue water in the middle of the sand and the palms. She could also see multiple well-armed, dangerous-looking dragons patrolling around the outskirts of it.

"Are those all Outclaws?" she asked. "You guard the water in the Scorpion Den?"

"In the desert, she who controls the water, controls everything," Six-Claws said.

"And here that 'she' is Thorn," Sunny guessed.

Six-Claws nodded toward a large white tent set up beside the water. The walls billowed like swans' wings, and venomous tail points stuck out under the edges here and there. Two particularly mean-looking SandWings guarded the entrance, where a flap had been rolled up to allow dragons to pass through.

As they approached, Sunny spotted a flash of black scales through the doorway and ducked behind Six-Claws.

He peered over his shoulder at her. "Yes?"

"I don't want them to see me," she whispered.

"The NightWings?" he asked. "The ones you were . . . *not* following?"

She nodded.

"Why?"

Sunny had a pretty strong feeling that it wouldn't be wise to reveal her connection to the prophecy. Even if the Outclaws didn't immediately sell her to Burn, someone else in the Scorpion Den was sure to pounce on that opportunity.

"They tried to kill me," she said. That was basically true.

Six-Claws looked amused. "Here's some free advice. When a dragon tries to kill you, fly the *opposite* way."

"I'm keeping an eye on them," she said, bristling. "I need to know what they're planning."

"That's up to Thorn now," he said. "Come along, and stay behind me."

Sunny's heart thumped as they approached the tent. Should she try to run? Wasn't it possible — even likely — that Thorn and the NightWings would team up to sell her to Burn? Thorn was the leader of a gang of criminals, after all.

Sunny wouldn't get far in this city, though, not with the Outclaws after her. Even in a place full of SandWings, she'd stick out like a fire on a dark night. She tried to keep the memory of the hungry dragonet in her head as she ducked under the soft white flap of the tent. A leader of criminals who fed small dragons didn't sound so bad. Maybe Thorn could be reasoned with.

The three NightWings were seated in a row on a bright orange carpet woven with alternating purple and white claw shapes. A skylight in the tent ceiling was positioned to shine a ray of sunlight down on them, beaming bright and hot straight into their faces. Sunny had a feeling that was deliberate. They were surrounded on all sides by SandWings, many of them rippling with scars or missing teeth, as if they'd fought hard for a place in this tent and weren't planning to move anytime soon.

The only clear spot was at the far end of the tent, where a pile of woven sky-blue rugs was arranged on a dais. After a few moments, the sound of laughter came from outside, and five more SandWings pushed their way into the tent.

Sunny could tell which one was Thorn immediately, although she was smaller than the others, and she wasn't wearing more treasure than anybody else. A solitary gold bracelet circled one of her upper forearms: a chain of flying dragons made from twisted wires. Around her neck hung a simple copper chain with a moonstone pendant — an odd jewel to find in the desert, Sunny thought.

Her scales were sandy yellow and dappled with a pattern of small brown speckles down her back and along her wings. She looked young — probably barely twenty years old, if Sunny had to guess. Most dragons grew quickly for the first seven years of their lives, and then a little bit each year after that, so the oldest dragons were usually the largest, like Morrowseer and Burn and Grandeur. But Thorn was wiry and compact and looked as if she might stay that way no matter how long she lived.

What was it that made her seem so clearly the leader of this group? She was laughing with the others as they came in, but she walked a step ahead of them, her wings half open and tilted forward as if she had somewhere to be, and her eyes scanning the room as if she were searching for something. She radiated an intense energy; even Sunny caught herself wanting to follow her wherever she went next.

The laughter dropped from Thorn's eyes when she spotted the three NightWings. She curled her tail up threateningly before stalking around them and climbing onto the dais. Sunny was glad not to be the one under that glare.

"NightWings," Thorn said darkly. "Well, well, well. We haven't had any of you visit our fine city in about seven years."

"Why would we?" Fierceteeth challenged. "We're only here now because we want to make a deal with Burn."

"We need someone to take her a message," Strongwings added.

Thorn leaned forward. "That's irrelevant to me. Where is Morrowseer?"

All three NightWings looked startled.

"You know Morrowseer?" Preyhunter stammered.

"Unfortunately," Thorn growled. "Tell me where he is, and I'll seriously consider not killing you."

Preyhunter flared his wings and several Outclaws took a menacing step toward him. "You can't kill us!" he protested. "We're NightWings!"

"I assure you NightWings die just as easily as any other dragon," Thorn said. "Would you like a demonstration?"

"No, no, no," Strongwings said hurriedly. "We'll tell you what we know."

"In exchange for a messenger to Burn," Fierceteeth interjected.

"In exchange for your lives," Thorn countered calmly. "I'm not sending any of my Outclaws into that deathpit. Most of them are here expressly because they're trying to avoid her."

"But —" Fierceteeth started.

"Morrowseer's dead," Preyhunter blurted out. "He died just a few days ago."

There was a terrible silence. One of the dragons who'd come in last took a step toward Thorn, reaching out tentatively, her expression a surprising mix of horror and sympathy.

Thorn's face contorted into a fury like nothing Sunny had ever seen before. With a cry of rage, she leaped off the dais, seized Preyhunter by the throat, and flung him to the ground, where she pinned him with her claws and swung her tail over his heart.

Fierceteeth and Strongwings didn't have time to react before Outclaws were there, holding them back. It wasn't necessary, though; Sunny could see that they were too terrified to do anything to help Preyhunter.

"Ssssay that again," Thorn hissed in Preyhunter's face.

"H-he's dead!" Preyhunter stammered. "Isn't that good news? It sounded like you hated him — aren't you glad he's dead?"

"He *can't* be dead," Thorn said. "Tell me the truth, you lying bag of bones. Tell me how to get to your secret home and where Morrowseer is and *what he did to* —" She cut herself off abruptly.

"I can't tell you any of that," Preyhunter whined. "We're not allowed to! But I promise you Morrowseer is dead — really, really, really dead."

"No!" Thorn shouted. A burst of flame shot out of her mouth, scorching a spot beside Preyhunter's neck. He screamed with fear, and two Outclaws jumped forward to beat out the flames on the carpet before the fire reached the tent. At the same moment, Preyhunter convulsed and lashed out, slicing at Thorn's underbelly with his sharp talons.

"Moons-blasted crocodile spawn!" Six-Claws roared, knocking dragons aside as he leaped at Preyhunter. Another

SandWing, a male dragonet around Sunny's age, also darted forward from the other side.

But they weren't fast enough.

Thorn's tail stabbed down into the NightWing's heart, and with a shriek of pain, Preyhunter collapsed underneath her, dead.

CHAPTER 7

Sunny stared at the NightWing's body, his wings lying crookedly on either side of him, his snout contorted into a final twist of despair.

He was a bad dragon, she told herself. *The world is better off this way. My friends are safer now that he's dead.*

But he had a horrible life, the other half of her argued. *Maybe he could have changed. Maybe there was a better dragon inside him somewhere, if someone had bothered to try and bring it out.*

Thorn stepped away from the body, taking a deep breath. Six-Claws put one talon on her shoulder, and she gave him a rueful look, as if she hadn't wanted to kill Preyhunter after all.

She might not have, if he hadn't lashed out at her. Or maybe she had to, either way, to make sure the other NightWings know how serious — and dangerous — she is.

"It's all right, Qibli, thank you," Thorn said to the dragonet who'd run forward to help her. He stood on the other side of the body, looking as though he'd very much like to stab it again, just to be sure.

"Let's try this again," Thorn said, turning to Fierceteeth and Strongwings. The two black dragons had their heads down and their wings pressed in close to their bodies. Thorn stopped, eye to eye with Fierceteeth. "Tell me how to find Morrowseer."

Fierceteeth hesitated, only for a moment, then said, "It's an island."

"Fierceteeth!" Strongwings hissed.

"What?" she snapped at him. "What does it matter anymore? It's all destroyed anyway." She returned her scowling gaze to Thorn. "We lived on an island, north of the continent, but the whole place was just wiped out by a volcano. Morrowseer was killed by it. That's the truth, so, sorry if you don't like it." She lifted her chin defiantly.

Thorn's claws twitched and her eyes narrowed.

I can't let Starflight's sister die, Sunny thought. *No matter how terrible she is. Not if I can stop it.* She knew it was foolish to expose herself here, but it felt like clearly the *right* thing to do. That was what being in the prophecy was all about — and if she wanted to keep believing in it, she had to keep acting worthy of it.

"It's true!" she called. She pushed her way through the SandWings, who blinked at her in confusion. "It's true, don't hurt her." She stumbled onto the sand in front of Thorn, half a wingspan from the NightWings who'd tried to kill her.

"You!" Fierceteeth cried.

"I was there, on the NightWing island," Sunny said, ignoring her. Thorn's black eyes were pinning her to the sand like an exotic insect, studying every bizarrely golden scale. "There was a volcano, and it wiped out the NightWings' home and killed Morrowseer. I'm sorry," she added, and she was, although she wasn't quite sure why.

"Who in the blazes are you?" Thorn asked.

"This is the one who was following them," Six-Claws said, nodding at the black dragons. Fierceteeth scowled; Strongwings just looked shocked.

"Ah," said Thorn, tilting her head. "Really. So . . . you're not here to see me about the reward?"

What reward? Sunny shook her head. "I'm just trying to stop them before they hurt my friends," she said, and then added, with a rush of hope, "Please don't let them send a messenger to Burn. It'll put a lot of dragons in danger."

"Really," Thorn said. She twisted to look at the NightWings. "What do you have to say about that?"

"We have information we know Burn will pay handsomely for," Strongwings said, glaring at Sunny. "Not only us — I'm sure she'll reward anyone who helps us get to her. And she'll pay even more if you throw in this puny dragonet."

Thorn regarded Sunny skeptically. "Why?"

Sunny shook her head, but of course that wasn't going to stop him.

"She's one of the dragonets in the prophecy," he said triumphantly.

Every dragon in the tent seemed to sit up at once. A few leaped to their feet and slipped out the front entrance, Sunny noticed uneasily. Most of the others started whispering to each other. She caught snippets like, "why so small?" and "that's why that soldier —" and "but her tail" and "no wonder Burn —" One dragon with a missing eye shifted closer to peer at her and Sunny tucked her tail closer around her talons, shivering.

"And we know where the others are," Strongwings went on.

Fierceteeth smacked him in the snout with her tail. "Shut up!" she snarled.

All of Thorn's burning energy was now fixed on Sunny. She took a step closer, then circled Sunny, inspecting her. Sunny tried to look brave and calm, even as Thorn picked up her harmless tail and flipped it curiously between her claws.

"Hmm," said the leader of the Outclaws. "You're a little unusual."

"I know," Sunny said. "It's all right, though; I don't mind. It's just the way I hatched."

"On the brightest night," Thorn said. "Six years ago." It was not exactly a question, but Sunny answered it anyway.

"Yes."

Thorn walked around Sunny one more time, her talons sending up small clouds of sand between the gaps in the carpets, and then stopped beside her, frowning at the NightWings. "One more question for you cowardly lizards. Can you tell me anything about a NightWing named Stonemover?"

Strongwings snorted. "He took off six or seven years ago and no one's heard from him since. The queen was furious."

This answer didn't seem to make Thorn any happier than anything else they'd said. She hissed quietly, then turned to Six-Claws.

"Put them somewhere unpleasant," she ordered. "I'll decide what to do with them later. You," she said to Sunny, "come with me."

They left on a tide of murmuring dragons. Sunny felt the same way she had when she was in that cage in the Sky Palace, hung up for everyone to stare at. She stayed close to Thorn's tail.

The back wall turned out to divide the tent in two, and when they ducked through a flap, Sunny found herself in a smaller area with fewer rugs, where there were a couple of low black tables, a trunk packed with scrolls, and two startling pictures pinned to the walls.

Sunny gasped when she saw them.

One was Morrowseer, drawn in dark ink, glowering the way he always did. The paper was large and pockmarked with tiny holes. *Like someone's been throwing rather sharp things at it,* Sunny thought.

The other picture was slightly smaller but had received the same treatment.

Staring out at her, looking much younger than she remembered him, was Dune.

Sunny touched the paper lightly with one claw. "Wow," she said. *He still has the scars, but he looks much healthier. This must be back when he was still getting the sun and heat a SandWing needs, before he went into hiding under the mountain to take care of us.*

"You know him?" Thorn asked from behind one of the low tables. She sounded casual, but there was something ferociously intense in her eyes.

Sunny wondered how much to admit, but before she had to answer, the flaps rustled and the same dragonet from before shoved his way in. He was bigger than Sunny, but now that she could see him more clearly, she guessed he was perhaps a year younger. A dark amber earring glowed in one ear and a small, rakish scar zigzagged across his nose.

"Qibli," Thorn warned. "This is a private discussion."

"I'm not leaving you alone with no stranger," Qibli said, shooting a look full of daggers at Sunny. "All prophecy-like or not."

Thorn looked amused. "Your loyalty is charming, but I think I can handle this dragonet as well as you can."

"It's better to have backup," he insisted. He twitched his tail forward to rest on the sand in front of him. "I promise I'll be quiet."

"Well, that I do have to see," she said, rolling her eyes. "All right. You — what was your name?"

"Sunny."

Thorn crossed to the trunk of scrolls, which sat on another sky-blue rug. Wiping her front talons on the fabric to shake off the sand, Thorn leaned in and picked up a sheaf of loose pages.

"Sunny," she echoed. "Before you say anything else — you're really not here for the reward?"

"I don't know anything about a reward," Sunny promised.

Qibli made a scornful noise. Without commenting, Thorn

handed her one of the pages. The thick, yellowish paper crinkled stiffly between her claws.

REWARD REWARD REWARD

For any information leading to the whereabouts of two NightWings once seen around the Scorpion Den, known as Morrowseer and Stonemover.

For any information regarding the present location of a scarred SandWing named Dune, last seen frequenting the night market seven years ago.

For any dragonet hatched in the last six years with unusual features.

Come before Thorn at the Outclaw Pool with anything. Your safety guaranteed.

REWARD REWARD REWARD

Smaller drawings of Morrowseer and Dune accompanied the words, along with another drawing of a subdued-looking NightWing she guessed was Stonemover. She glanced at the other papers that Thorn was holding and saw similar pronouncements with slightly different words —"five years ago" or "in the last three years," for instance. This wasn't a new search, or a new reward. This was the latest update of an ongoing hunt.

Sunny put the paper down slowly. Pieces were starting to come together in her mind, bubbling in a funny, hopeful, confused way.

"You didn't know about this?" Thorn asked.

Sunny shook her head. "I haven't been in the Kingdom of Sand in the last six years." She took a deep breath, then let it all spill out of her. "My egg was found out in the desert, alone, by a dragon named Dune. That dragon." She pointed to the picture on the wall as Thorn inhaled sharply. "He took me to be raised by the Talons of Peace, along with the other dragonets of destiny. After all, I fit the prophecy. . . ." She hesitated, then added, "And my parents clearly didn't want me."

She raised her head and met Thorn's eyes. The leader of the Outclaws dropped the rest of the papers, stepped forward, and seized Sunny's front talons in hers.

"He didn't *find* you," she growled. "He *stole* you. He knew where I'd hidden you for your own safety, and he betrayed me."

Sunny felt as though she couldn't breathe. The claws wrapped around hers, the dark eyes fixed on her. These were the only real things in the tent; everything else was blurring and sliding away.

This is it, she thought wonderingly. *This is the moment we all dreamed about, all those years under the mountain.*

"I wanted you," Thorn said fiercely. "You were the only thing I wanted. I've done everything I could to find you."

Not fulfilling the prophecy . . . but finding our parents.

Thorn gripped her claws tighter. "Sunny. You're my daughter."

CHAPTER 8

Sunny's scales felt as if they were fizzing and humming and trying to leap right off her. She flung herself into Thorn's wings, which folded around her like sunbeams.

"Hey!" Qibli barked, jumping up.

"It's all right, sit down," Thorn said. She rested her head on top of Sunny's and pulled her in more tightly.

"I knew you didn't really abandon me," Sunny said, although she wasn't sure how much she'd ever really known that.

"*I* knew I'd find you one day," said Thorn. "I didn't take over this city for nothing. Never thought you'd just come strolling into my tent, though. Chasing a trio of NightWings, no less." She leaned back and smiled. "Funny brave little dragon."

It was warm, warm, warm, here in her mother's wings, as warm as Sunny had always wanted to be.

"Hang on," Qibli interjected. "Thorn, begging your pardon, but how do you know? She could be anybody. She could be playing you. She could be a con artist!"

"I've met enough con artists in the last six years," Thorn

said calmly, "swaggering in here, hoping to cheat me out of the reward. This is my daughter."

"Where's my father?" Sunny asked. "It's — it's not Dune, is it?"

"Bright smashing suns, no," Thorn said. "What a horrifying thought. No." She shot a glance at Qibli. "He's . . . not around anymore. We can talk about that later. But speaking of Dune, if you can point me at him, he's on this Needs To Be Violently Dismembered list I have."

"He's already dead," Sunny said. "But he wasn't so bad, really. He died trying to protect us."

"Successfully?" Thorn asked.

"Well . . . not very successfully," Sunny admitted. "We kind of all got captured by the SkyWing queen. But we're all right now."

Thorn growled. "Teeth of the viper, I cannot believe my enemies have all died before I could rip their heads off myself. Qibli, give me those drawings."

The dragonet unpinned the drawings of Morrowseer and Dune from the wall, and Thorn kept one wing around Sunny as she tore them into tiny shreds.

"Feel better?" Sunny asked.

"Yes," Thorn said, hugging her close again. "Would you like me to have those NightWings killed for you?"

"No, no," Sunny said quickly. "One of them is the sister of a friend of mine." She hesitated. "I kind of wish you hadn't killed the other one."

"I know," Thorn said. She lifted her talons, checking

them for blood. "It's not my favorite part of the role, but if you want to lead dragons, you have to show them your claws sometimes, beetle."

"Beetle?" Sunny echoed.

Thorn gave her an affectionate grin. "That was my pet name for you when you were still in your egg," she said. "That's what I've been calling you in my head all these years. But I like Sunny. Dune must have been paying attention when I talked about possible names for you." Her face darkened.

"So you were friends," Sunny prompted.

"I thought so." Her mother looked up at the tent ceiling for a moment, her eyes glittering.

"I have so many questions," Sunny said softly. *How did you know I would look weird? Why did you have to hide my egg for safety? What do the NightWings have to do with anything?*

"So do I!" said Thorn. "I want to know everything about everything you've done for the last six years. And we should celebrate! Let me send all my brigands about their duties, and I'll tell Armadillo to plan a party. Free roasted lizards and camel milk for the whole Scorpion Den tonight!" She grinned.

"Wait," Sunny said. "I don't need a party —"

"Perhaps not, but it'll accomplish three things," Thorn said briskly. "First, it'll relieve the tension out there — all those dragons wondering what'll happen with a prophecy dragonet in our midst. Second, it'll let everyone know you're my daughter, so they'll treat you with respect and not just curiosity. And third, it'll make it very clear that you're under Outclaw protection, which you're going to need in this city."

"Oh," Sunny said. For a moment she'd worried that her mother was like Blaze, just looking for any excuse for a party. It was reassuring to realize she had smart reasons for what she was doing.

A commotion erupted in the main tent: dragons yelling, something being knocked over. Thorn whirled around with her tail high, alert for any danger.

But when a SandWing burst through the flaps and threw himself at her feet, she relaxed and waved Qibli back.

"What is it?" Thorn asked.

"Reports of a dragonbite viper," he gasped, "seen near the orphanage."

"Are we sure?" Thorn demanded, grabbing a long spear made of three strands of metal twisted together and split into several sharp points at the end. "Have any Outclaws confirmed that it's really there?"

"No," he said, panting, "but someone panicked and set the nearest stalls on fire. The orphanage will go up in flames if we don't put it out fast."

"And so will the rest of the city," Thorn said. "Sunny, I'm sorry, I have to take care of this."

"Of course," Sunny said, jumping up. "Can I help? What can I do?"

"You can stay here safely so I don't have to worry about you," Thorn said. "Please. Dragonbite vipers are not to be trifled with. I'll be back as soon as I can." She snatched up a bag by the outer flap and ducked out of the tent, gone before the messenger could scramble to his feet and follow her.

Sunny and Qibli stared at each other for a few long moments. Sunny wondered if she should be upset that her mother had brushed aside her offer of help, but honestly, she wasn't sure she'd have been much use. As the excitement of meeting her mother wore off, her wings began to feel like heavy boulders leaning against her sides. Her head was woozy from the strange smells and noises of the Scorpion Den.

"What's a dragonbite viper?" Sunny finally asked.

"Really?" Qibli said. "It's the most dangerous thing in the desert. Probably in all of Pyrrhia, but we get them more than most tribes. It's the only snake in the world that can kill a dragon."

"There's a snake that can do that?" Sunny said. She shuddered from her horns to her wingtips. "Creepy."

He nodded, and she tilted her head at him.

"Is Thorn your mother, too?" she asked.

"Ha!" he said, startled. He touched his snout self-consciously, where a few brown speckles stood out against his light yellow scales, much like the ones all over Thorn. "Moons, no. She *saved* me from my mother. Besides, the way I understand it, there's only ever been one egg for Thorn, and that's you — if you are who you say you are."

"Nobody else?" Sunny asked. "I don't have any brothers or sisters?"

He shook his head. "You're better off. Mine are a pair of dung-snorting hippo-heads who'd rather stab me with their tails than share so much as a fig with me. Joke's on them, now that I'm an Outclaw." Qibli puffed his spines up and made a ferocious face. "And you better not be messing with Thorn either. There's plenty of Outclaws lined up behind me who'll make you sorry if you are."

"I wouldn't know how to mess with her," Sunny said. "I promise, I'm really very nice."

"Hmm," Qibli said skeptically.

There was a tan camel-hair pillow next to one of the black tables that looked softer than anything Sunny had slept on in the last several days — and she hadn't slept much, waking up frequently to make sure the NightWings hadn't flown onward without her. She curled up on the cool sand and rested her head and front talons on the pillow. Qibli kept his dark eyes on her, his brow furrowed as if he hadn't quite decided whether to trust her yet.

"So, what do the Outclaws do?" Sunny asked.

He fluffed his wings, scattering sand in all directions. "Everything. We keep the Scorpion Den from becoming a mess of blood and teeth, which it used to be, with everyone fighting all the time, till we sorted 'em all out. And we make sure those what has too much are convinced to pass some along to them with nothing."

"And what do you do with the pool?" Sunny was genuinely curious, but for some reason, Qibli's answers seemed to be fading in and out.

"We're the boss of it," he explained proudly. "That way we can get water to all the little dragons and the sick dragons and the wounded from the war. When they're not too scared to come around and ask for it anyways. We can be very intimidating," he added with a satisfied nod.

"Mm-hmm," Sunny said, her eyelids drooping.

"Are you falling asleep in the middle of my fascinating explanation?" Qibli demanded, sounding outraged.

"No," Sunny mumbled, inaccurately, and if he said anything else, she didn't hear it.

She woke up in darkness to the sounds of dragons roaring and carousing outside the tent. A small oil lamp, gleaming bronze, was set beside her, and Six-Claws sat beside it, chewing on something that had been skewered on a stick and burned to a crisp.

He dipped his head to her as she sat up and yawned. "Your mother said not to wake you."

The shiver *that* sent down Sunny's spine was both lovely and unsettling. *My mother.*

"You could have. I always feel like I'm missing something when I'm sleeping," Sunny said, stretching. "Where is she?"

"Still trying to put out all the fires and restore order." He flipped one wing at the noises beyond the white, billowing walls. There was something solid about his presence, as though of course he would be there, waiting patiently, whenever she woke up and needed him. Sunny could imagine that her mother would be able to rely on him.

She wondered again if there was any chance he might be her father. Thorn had said "not around," but maybe that just meant "not attached" anymore. Or maybe there was a reason she was keeping it a secret from the other Outclaws.

Most significantly, knowing he had hatched with his unusual sixth claws might be enough to make Thorn think Sunny would have something odd about her, too.

"What happened with the viper?" Sunny asked. "Is everyone all right?"

Six-Claws stopped chewing and looked at her. "We didn't find the viper yet, but we've contained the fire, for the most part. And nobody was bitten, so far. So we're either very lucky or quite unlucky, if there's really a viper out there." He considered her for a moment, then added, "Thanks for asking."

"Oh," Sunny said, flustered. She'd been worried; of course she'd asked. "Of course."

Six-Claws tossed away his stick and rubbed sand over his talons. "Ready to be presented to the Outclaws?" he asked her.

"Not even remotely," Sunny confessed. He chuckled in a rumbling way and lifted the flap so she could step through the tent and out onto the shifting sands, pale in the light of the three moons overhead.

The bright orange-and-yellow flames of torches flickered all around the oasis, reflecting in a dance across the pool. There were too many dragons for Sunny to count, especially in the wavering shadows, and most of them were moving — chasing one another across the sand, calling out insults or threats or jokes, laughing and tossing drinks at each other. As she blinked around, looking for Thorn, one of the

SandWings toppled into the pool with a splash and three others jumped to haul her out.

"Idiots," Six-Claws said with affection, and started forward.

"That's far enough," said a voice in the darkness behind the tent. "Six-Claws. Stop where you are."

Six-Claws swung around with a hiss. "I take orders from Thorn and no one else."

"Oh, it's not an order," said the other dragon. He stepped forward so the torchlight could catch on his yellow scales, and Sunny recognized the SandWing they'd run into on the streets earlier — Addax, the one with the scratch who'd looked familiar. "It's a suggestion I think you'll really want to listen to."

Six-Claws took a menacing step toward him and Addax flicked his tail. Two more beefy dragons appeared behind him. They had a small dragonet pinned between them, perhaps two years old, with nearly white scales and a tail barb that still wasn't fully developed. She squeaked nervously as they dragged her forward.

"The question really," said Addax, "is which daughter do you care about more — the alleged long-lost egg that Thorn has been searching for . . . or yours?"

Sunny glanced up at Six-Claws and saw the fury and fear contorting his face. He sank his talons into the sand, raising his tail. Beyond him, in the shadows, she saw four more SandWings slide out from behind the tent to stand menacingly between them and the pool.

"Ostrich," Six-Claws growled, his eyes fixed on his daughter. "Don't be scared. I won't let them hurt you."

"Don't make a mistake here," Addax warned him. "My friends' tails are much closer to your dragonet than you are to me. If you attack, or even shout for help, she'll be dead in an instant. But this doesn't have to get all violent, Six-Claws. We want the dragonet of destiny. It's a simple, fair trade."

"There was no dragonbite viper, was there?" Six-Claws said. "You set that fire to draw Thorn away. Do you know how many dragonets you could have killed?"

"Yes," said Addax. "Don't make it one more."

Six-Claws growled again, and Sunny saw his eyes dart from her to his daughter. *He loves her so much,* she thought. *That's what I always wanted. That's what I might have, now, with Thorn. Family, and answers, and a place to belong.*

But only if I deserve it. I can't take it at the expense of another family.

"It's all right," she said to Six-Claws. "Make the trade. You have to. I'll be fine." She glanced up at the palm leaves that blocked the view of the stars. Addax had smartly cornered them in a pocket of shadow where they couldn't be spotted from across the pool.

"What do you want her for?" Six-Claws asked.

"Burn wants the dragonets pretty badly," Addax said. "She'll take me back if I show up with one of them."

"Back into her army?" Six-Claws demanded. "Why would you want that? You could be safe here. The war never comes to the Scorpion Den."

Addax shifted, firelight gleaming in his dark eyes. "I was thrown out of her army, but my family wasn't. There are dragons there I need to get back to."

Aw, sad, Sunny thought, and then her brain added, in a voice much like Tsunami's: *Sunny, by all the moons, quit feeling sorry for dragons who want to abduct you and sell you off.*

She glanced down at the six wickedly curved claws that were carving gouges in the sand beside her. She had a bad feeling that Six-Claws was planning to fight, which couldn't possibly go well for either him or Ostrich.

"Six-Claws," she said firmly. "I said *make the trade.* My mother will understand." She wanted to jump forward herself and wrench the little dragonet out of their claws. Ostrich was trembling so badly that Sunny could hear her teeth clicking together.

"But Thorn —" Six-Claws said, twisting around to glance back at the flickering lights by the pool.

"Doesn't have to know," Addax said. "Tell her this one ran off. Woke up, decided she didn't want a criminal thug for a mother, and flew for the hills."

"Don't tell her that!" Sunny protested indignantly. She smacked her tail against the sand. "That's so mean! I wouldn't do that!"

"If he tells her the truth, Thorn is likely to get herself killed trying to rescue you," Addax said. "Would you prefer that?"

"No, but at least come up with something believable," Sunny said spiritedly. She looked up at Six-Claws. "You can tell her I had to go back to my friends, to let them know they're safe from the NightWings. Tell her I'll be back." Six-Claws stared at her, his face unreadable.

Addax flicked his tongue. "You won't be."

"You don't know that," Sunny said. "Now release Ostrich and I'll go with you." She was starting to worry that the little dragonet would have a heart attack and collapse right there.

"No," Addax said. "She flies with us until we have an hour's head start, and then I'll send her back."

That made practical sense, although Sunny didn't want to drag Ostrich any further into danger. But if they left Ostrich behind, Six-Claws and the others would chase them down before they could reach Burn's stronghold.

"All right, then let's go," she said. Even more than Ostrich, she was worried about what Six-Claws might do. She didn't think he'd stand a chance against seven big dragons.

And what if he is my father? And Ostrich is my half sister?

I don't want them to die before I get to know them.

It wasn't until they were aloft, winging north through the cold desert night toward the stronghold of one of the most dangerous dragons in Pyrrhia, that the thought occurred to Sunny that *she* might be the one who was about to die.

Ice Kingdom
Sky Kingdom
Under the Mountain
Burn's Stronghold
Kingdom of Sand
Scorpion Den
Jade Mountain

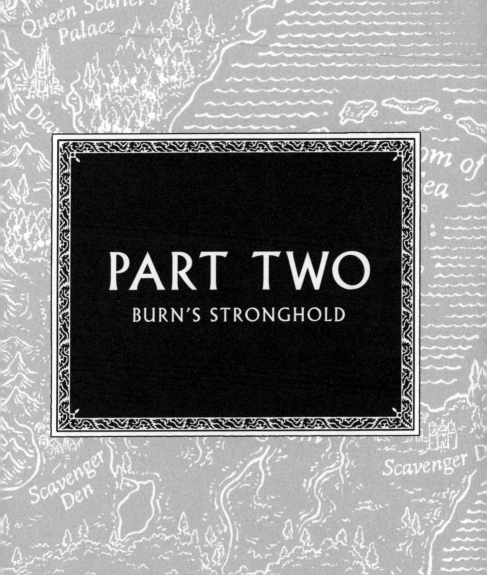

PART TWO

BURN'S STRONGHOLD

CHAPTER 9

The outer walls of the palace were dripping with blood.

Sunny had read the scrolls about the SandWing stronghold, and she'd seen it from afar, but nothing could have prepared her for the smell of the decapitated dragon heads that studded the top of the walls, or the gruesome stains on the stone below them.

They were still more than a mile away when the horrible rotting smell first reached her, making her choke and nearly driving her out of the sky. Addax caught her as she faltered toward the sand.

"Shallow breaths," he advised. "You get used to it."

"*Do* you? Really?" Sunny asked.

He shrugged, which as far as she could tell meant "no."

Ostrich had been released during the night, shooting one last terrified look at Sunny before bolting back toward the distant fires of the Scorpion Den. Sunny thought that Addax had deliberately freed the dragonet while the Den was still visible behind them. Optimistically she thought perhaps he was concerned for Ostrich's safety; it seemed kind not to make her find her way in total darkness.

She could almost hear her friends laughing at her in her

head. *"That's right, Sunny, your kidnapper is a real sweetheart. He's handing you over to Burn out of the goodness of his heart, too."*

But if he was doing this for his family . . . for someone he cared about . . . Sunny glanced over at the scarred dragon and thought, *There's more to his story. There's always more to everyone's story, if you bother to find out what it is.*

The sun had cleared the mountains when they came to the sentries: a pair of SandWings carrying long spears. Relentless heat beat down from the cloudless sky, making the smell much worse. Sunny's wings ached from flying so long without stopping. She could see the brownish-yellow walls of the stronghold up ahead, stained and crusted with the dark red and black gore that dripped from the grisly decorations.

It was a vast palace, far larger than she had realized when she'd seen it from a distance. The ramparts seemed to stretch across the horizon, and Sunny guessed that two or three Scorpion Dens could fit inside, or about a thousand of the caves she'd grown up in.

"Hold it," said one of the sentries, swinging the spear toward them. He squinted. "Addax?"

"Ho there," said Addax. He waved a claw, and the dragons behind him all paused, beating the air and craning to see past his wings.

"Picked up some friends somewhere, I see," said the sentry, half jokingly. "Are you invading, or what's all this?"

"Brought a present for the queen," said Addax. He flicked his tail at Sunny, and she hissed at him. "Recognize this one?"

Both sentries drew in a quick breath. "From the party in the Sky Kingdom," said one of them. "Scarlet was going to give her to Queen Burn."

That's where I've seen Addax before, Sunny realized. *Bowing and scraping behind Burn as she examined me like a deformed gemstone. Before he got his scar.*

"And now I've found her and *I'm* giving her to the queen," said Addax smugly.

The sentry looked skeptically at their entourage. "And you need seven dragons to transport this midget creature safely?"

"I'm terrifying when you get to know me," Sunny volunteered. She heard a couple of the dragons behind her chuckle, but Addax shot them a stern look and they subsided.

"Wait," said the other sentry. "Doesn't that mean she's — I mean, she's one of —"

"Yes," Addax said. "So stop delaying and let us through, all right?"

The sentries flapped aside, both of them examining Sunny intently as she and her escort flew past them. In all of Sunny's fantasies about fulfilling the prophecy and saving Pyrrhia, she'd never imagined there'd be quite so much *staring.*

And she certainly hadn't counted on getting locked up as often as she already had been.

As they swooped down toward the thick, forbidding walls of Burn's stronghold, Sunny thought with a shudder that this might be the worst prison so far. Scarlet's palace had had gladiator fights, but at least she hadn't kept the dismembered parts of her enemies on display.

"And it isn't exactly easy to cut off a dragon's head," Sunny remembered Starflight saying, *"even if it's already dead."* They'd been reading in the study cave. He'd rolled out the scroll and tapped the drawing of the stronghold. *"You have to be pretty brutal to get through the scales and everything else."*

Sunny also remembered that the outer walls had been added by Burn after Queen Oasis died. *They look solid and thick and imposing . . . but useless for keeping out dragons who can fly. The only creatures they'd really keep out for certain are scavengers.* A scavenger had killed Burn's mother, after all. *Is Burn afraid of them?* From what Sunny had seen of her, it was hard to imagine that Burn was afraid of anything.

Addax led the way as they spiraled down onto the hot white stones of an enormous courtyard that encircled the old palace. Long, squat buildings had been constructed along the inner side of the walls; they appeared to be extra barracks for soldiers. Small gatherings of armed SandWings were visible in each direction, either cleaning weapons, sparring, or sleeping.

In the center of the courtyard, opposite the palace entrance, stood an odd kind of monument: a tall black obelisk surrounded by a circle of sand wider than a large dragon's wingspan. Words were carved into the sides, with the letters all painted in gold, but Sunny couldn't read them from where she was.

The old palace within the walls was a lot more elegant than the parts Burn had added. There were slender towers and windows as tall as dragons and high pavilion landing platforms topped with domes and spires. Shapes were carved all over the stone — lizards and desert birds and suns, mostly, as far as Sunny could see at first glance. It made the palace look for a moment as though it was crawling with life or shimmering with heat — an unsettling illusion of motion, probably intended to make visitors uncomfortable.

The doors were open to the huge front entrance of the palace, and Sunny realized with a start that a dragon was standing just on the edge of the sunlight, staring out at her from the shadow.

Her heart plunged as she thought, *Burn*, and then the dragon moved and she glimpsed black diamond shapes on the scales. With an even stronger burst of fear, she thought, *Blister? How could Blister be here?*

And then the dragon stepped into the light and she realized he was male, and not one of the three SandWing sisters after all.

He still looked horribly like Blister, though. He had the same narrow face and lidded dark eyes, the same black patterns on his pale yellow scales. His poisonous tail barb slithered along the stones behind him and his sharp claws made a tapping sound as he advanced toward them. He wore a cluster of keys and pouches and bells on chains around his neck that clinked and jingled slightly as he walked. Some of them were plain iron, while others flashed with jewels or gold plating.

Addax bowed his head respectfully.

"Smolder," he said, "I've brought a gift for Queen Burn."

"I see," Smolder said. Sunny felt a little better; his voice didn't have the oozing, creeping, sinister quality of Blister's voice. He sounded just . . . normal, like one of her friends. "Who are you?" he asked her, and she liked that, too, that he spoke directly to her instead of over her head as though she was nothing but a piece of treasure.

"My name's Sunny," she answered. "Who are you?"

"I'm . . . the brother," Smolder said, and something in his expression said he had many thoughts about that, but wouldn't risk going into detail.

"Burn's brother? The only one?" Sunny asked, trying to remember what she'd read about the SandWing royal family.

"There used to be three of us, but the other two made the wrong dragons mad." He grimaced.

"The wrong dragons meaning your sisters," Sunny guessed. "So you're on Burn's side?"

"I'm here, aren't I?" he said, and it occurred to her that that wasn't much of an enthusiastic yes.

"Where is Queen Burn?" Addax cut in abruptly.

"She is not at home at the moment," Smolder said. He spread one wing and beckoned Sunny toward the main entrance. "She's out looking for a certain quintet of young dragons."

Sunny stopped, looking up at him with a shiver. If Burn was searching for her friends instead of fighting battles, she must really want to destroy them.

"Wait," Addax said. "I want to see her — I mean, this is my prisoner — she's one of the ones in the prophecy —"

"I know. I'll take it from here," Smolder said firmly. "You can wait in the barracks until she returns." He nodded at the courtyard. "Don't worry, you'll get all your pardons and your reinstatement." He flared his wing across Sunny's back and ushered her forward again.

"But . . . my reward . . ." Addax's voice trailed off as Sunny and Smolder stepped out of the bright sunlight into the cool shadows of a vast hall, big enough for a hundred dragons. Far overhead, large fans shaped like dragon wings beat the air, and Sunny spotted a few small dragons pulling on ropes to keep them moving. Tapestries woven in blues and golds and white covered the walls, echoing some of the same patterns in the stonework outside, and airy white curtains billowed at the long windows. A heavy table ran down the middle of the hall, loaded with food, and Sunny heard her stomach grumble.

"Take anything you like," Smolder said.

"No, thank you," Sunny answered politely. It seemed unlikely that the entire table of food was poisoned, but she didn't intend to make killing her any easier than it already would be. She tilted her head to study the tapestry closest to her and realized that the odd pattern of rust-colored spots on it was actually dried spatters of blood.

"The food is for the soldiers," Smolder said, sounding amused. "I promise it's safe to eat."

"I'm not hungry," Sunny said. "Um . . . when do you think Burn will be back?"

Smolder shifted his wings in a shrug. "I never know. She prefers not to discuss her plans." He lifted his claws and studied them thoughtfully, shaking out sand that was caught between his scales. "The real question is what to do with you. On the one talon, I assume she'd rather find you alive when she gets back, so she can kill you — or interrogate you and then kill you — herself. On the other talon, if I lock you up and you somehow escape, which I'm sure you'll try to do, I'll be in far worse trouble than if I just kill you right now. But on the third talon, if I successfully keep you captive, she should be quite pleased. It's a risk, though. You're guaranteed not to escape if I kill you."

"But on the fourth talon," Sunny said hurriedly, "how will Burn find my friends if she can't ask me questions? Or use me as a hostage? Think about how valuable I am alive."

"Hmm," Smolder said with a little smile. A tiny brown mouse crept out from under the table and made a dash for the nearest wall. Smolder flicked his tail toward it, but stopped at the last minute and let the mouse vanish into one of the cracks. He looked back at Sunny. "All right, you talked me into it. You can live for now, but I'd appreciate it if you'd keep your escape attempts as feeble and ineffective as possible."

He started toward a doorway at the far end of the hall and Sunny followed, wondering if that was supposed to be funny. Smolder had this odd way of talking that kind of made everything he said sound like a joke. But then, Sunny's life and death didn't seem particularly hilarious, at least if you asked her.

There were five doors leading off the main hall, plus a staircase that led up to a balcony with two more doorways. Sunny considered trying to memorize the layout of the palace, but as soon as they stepped through into the dark, winding passage beyond, she knew it would be hopeless.

The corridors of the old palace crisscrossed and twisted almost as often and confusingly as the streets of the Scorpion Den, and they were sometimes barely wide enough for two dragons to squeeze past each other. Short flights of steps kept taking them up to new levels and then down again, and every other turn brought them to a spot that looked exactly like something they'd just passed. Sunny almost wondered if Smolder was messing with her head, except that he seemed to be calculating something under his breath and barely paid attention to her as they walked.

The stone floors were worn smooth with the passage of many dragons, and the walls and ceiling were flat and usually bare as well, so Sunny felt as if she was walking through long, narrow boxes. It was eerie and claustrophobic, with no space to fly, except for the occasional glimpses of sunlight from the upper levels. And three times they passed open, sunlit courtyards, where dragons were lying with their wings spread wide, soaking in the heat.

I haven't seen any treasure, Sunny realized. *No gold talonprints, no pearl-studded pools — not even anything like the beautiful flowers that decorate the RainWing village, unless you count the tapestries. I wonder if that's because the SandWing treasure is really all gone. Or perhaps sparkly things aren't Burn's style.*

She spotted a few carved statues of SandWings here and there, most of them with their wings tilted back as if they were about to take flight. After their experience in the

Kingdom of the Sea, Sunny had to admit that all statues made her a bit nervous. Any of them could be animus-touched, enchanted to do something sinister.

"I think I should put you in the weirdling collection," Smolder said after a while, as if they'd been discussing her placement the entire walk. "It's as safe as the dungeon, but more comfortable. Also more psychologically destabilizing."

"What?" Sunny said.

"The idea that you might actually belong somewhere like that," Smolder said. "It's driven a few dragons insane."

"Oh," Sunny said. "Sounds charming."

Smolder rumble-chuckled and turned a corner, finally leading her out of the labyrinth into one of the inner courtyards. This one was surrounded on three sides by colonnades and balconies, with a pit of sand in the middle. Sunny slid her claws through the sand as she followed him, thinking, *What if this is the last time I ever feel sand under my talons?*

The far wall of the courtyard was curved, and when Sunny looked up, she realized that it was actually a windowless tower of red sandstone soaring up toward the sky. It had grooves stretching the whole length of it, like claw marks, and bands of carvings, all of hideous dragon faces. There were no holes in the tower apart from one door at the bottom, and Sunny was seized with a fierce, desperate longing to stay as far away from it as possible.

But of course this was where Smolder was taking her, and of course she had no choice.

He unlocked the door with a plain silver key from a chain around his neck, picked up a bucket of water that had been waiting outside, and led her into the dark interior.

At first she thought her eyes were dazzled by the sun, but as they adjusted, she realized that the flashes of light around her came from small mirrors embedded in the walls, which caught the reflections of bronze oil lamps dangling at various heights on long wires from the ceiling far above.

A winding ramp led from the floor around and around, up to the top of the tower. And here was Burn's notorious, disturbing collection on display. Spaced at intervals along the ramp were the exhibits. Sunny caught glimpses of claws and misshapen tails and melted scales and thought with a shudder, *I'm one of them now.*

Right at the bottom of the ramp was a wingless white dragon, its mouth twisted open in a roar of fury.

Sunny jumped back, nearly knocking Smolder over, before she realized the dragon was dead. And then that was actually worse, because it clearly *had* been alive, once, before Burn slit it open, let the life pour out, and then stuffed it so she could display it.

Is that going to be me?

Instead of saving the world — am I going to end up stuffed and mounted on a pedestal?

The fear that flooded through her made her want to lie down, cover her head with her wings, and scream for days.

Trust in the prophecy, she told herself fiercely. *I can't die here. The dragons of Pyrrhia are counting on me.*

But Morrowseer's voice was still there, whispering, *"The prophecy isn't real,"* and as hard as she tried, Sunny couldn't quite find that faith that had once chased out every fear.

The white dragon wasn't entirely wingless, she realized. It had little stubs on its back that had never grown into wings. There was something eerily sleek and snakelike about it. The most truly horrifying part was the look on its face.

"Isn't it creepy?" Smolder said in her ear, and she jumped again. "Someone brought him to Burn ten years ago, claiming he was the forbidden offspring of a SandWing and an IceWing. Which is the right thing to say to her, even if it wasn't true — and who knows if it was — because she has, let's just say, some pretty strong opinions about tribe purity and not contaminating SandWing blood with cross-tribe breeding."

"Oh," Sunny said faintly. She thought of Starflight, who felt a million miles away right now. On her list of reasons why they probably wouldn't work out, she hadn't thought to include "contaminating SandWing blood."

"SMOLDER!" a voice bellowed suddenly from overhead. "I HEAR YOU DOWN THERE. If you don't bring me more water *right now*, I *swear* I will catch that scavenger of yours and *EAT HER.*"

Sunny's heart plunged through the floor. She stared at Smolder in shock.

She knew that voice.

Queen Scarlet of the SkyWings was alive — and she was Burn's prisoner, too.

CHAPTER 10

"Queen Scarlet is *here*?" Sunny whispered to Smolder. "Everyone's looking for her! There are dragons who think *we're* holding her captive!"

He scratched his nose with one claw and sighed. "My sister likes to keep a close eye on her . . . things," he said. "The SkyWing queen is a bit of a problem right now. Although mostly she's a problem for me, the unlucky dragonsitter." He glanced up at the dark ceiling way above them, then peered around the floor.

"Flower!" he shouted suddenly. "Flower!" He lifted a small bell from around his neck and rang it, letting the tinkling noise echo across the dark space.

Something pitter-pattered on the ramp above them, and after a moment, Sunny picked out a tiny figure scurrying down.

That's not a dragon, she thought with surprise.

It was a scavenger — alive and upright and chattering like a squirrel, bold as you please, right in the middle of the SandWing palace. It jumped down the last level to the floor and darted over to Smolder. For a grim, worrying moment,

Sunny expected him to rip the scavenger's head off or offer the whole creature to her for dinner or something.

Instead, the SandWing prince rested his front talons on the floor and the scavenger clambered right onto one of them, sat down, and resumed chattering a little louder, along with some vigorous paw waving.

"Oh my gosh," Sunny said, momentarily distracted from Queen Scarlet. "It's so cute." The scavenger looked kind of like a bigger, less hairy version of the sloths in the rainforest. It ran on its back two legs with easy balance, and its slender paws had no claws on them. A thatch of dark fur covered the top of its head and ran down like a mane onto its shoulders. It had a square of white fabric tied around itself that looked suspiciously as though it had been hacked off one of the main hall curtains, plus a sort of pouch bag made of the same material.

"I know, isn't she?" said Smolder. "That's what I've been saying. I have to watch her carefully, though. Several dragons would be perfectly happy to eat her if they caught her alone. This is one place I figure she's safe." He lifted her up to his snout and the scavenger leaned forward to bump noses with him.

"Where did you get her?" Sunny asked. "And why do you call her Flower?"

Smolder reached around and set the scavenger on the back of his neck, where she grabbed on to his spikes and balanced as he started up the ramp. Sunny trailed behind him, wondering if this might be a good time to make a run for it, but she was pretty sure the tower door had locked behind them.

"We had some scavenger visitors about twenty years

ago — you may have heard about that," Smolder said in his sarcastic voice. "This is the one who didn't escape."

Twenty years ago? It took Sunny a moment to realize what he must mean.

"Wait — visitors, plural?" Sunny asked. "I thought it was just one scavenger who killed the queen and stole the treasure." They passed a fish tank glowing with a greenish light that seemed to be coming from the sea creatures themselves. There were fish with bulging eyes and extra flippers, seahorses with fangs, snails that oozed purple ichor, and an octopus kind of thing with at least twenty arms that was busily occupied with crushing up seashells and dropping them into its black beak of a mouth.

"Nope," said Smolder. "Three scavengers. Two escaped with the treasure, but we caught this one trying to hide just outside the palace. Burn was going to put her head on a spike on the wall and eat the rest, but I decided I wanted to keep her. And at the time, I had other dragons to back me up." He took a deep breath and folded his wings back into a tent over the scavenger for a moment, before tucking them into his side again.

"Blister argued that a scavenger head on a spike wouldn't impress anyone — in fact, it would just remind everyone of Mother's embarrassing death," he went on. "Blaze thought Flower was cute, too, and wanted to see if we could get another scavenger and breed them to make more pets. And my brothers said I should get to have one thing I wanted, now that Mother wasn't around to keep making me unhappy."

He paused, and Sunny glanced up at him. She got the feeling it wouldn't be a good idea to ask any questions about Oasis.

"SMOLDER!" Queen Scarlet bellowed again, and a burst of fire lit up the tower from an upper level.

"Coming!" he called politely, then carried on talking to Sunny as if there were really no hurry at all. "Anyway they voted to let me keep her, and by now Burn is used to her. I was going to call her Stabby — she was pretty fierce with this little sword she was carrying, before we took it off her. But then she found a tapestry with some flowers on it and kept pointing to them, and then to herself. So I think she wants me to call her Flower, although all her chattering noises sound the same to me."

Sunny glanced at another glass exhibit case as they walked by, and then really wished she hadn't. Inside were lots of *parts* of dragons — webbed SeaWing talons, a few tongues with three forks instead of two, half a wing that was speckled purple and gray unlike any dragon's she'd ever seen, a coil of tail with strange lichens growing on it, and a number of oddly bent teeth and claws.

She shuddered and dragged her focus back to Smolder and Flower.

"I've never heard of an animal choosing its own name before," she said. "But then, I've never heard of anyone keeping a scavenger as a pet either. The only pets —" She stopped and clapped her front talons over her mouth in horror. She'd nearly mentioned the RainWings and their pet sloths, which could have given away exactly where her friends were.

Stupid stupid stupid, Sunny, she scolded herself. *Be more careful about what you say.*

"The only pets?" Smolder echoed, giving her a curious look.

"The only pets I've ever heard of are kept *by* scavengers," Sunny said quickly.

"Ah, yes," said Smolder, and for the first time his voice was affectionate instead of sardonic. "Flower likes mice, and she's always feeding any birds that dare to come down into the courtyards." He lifted one of his claws and the scavenger patted it, as if to reassure him she was still there.

"Does she . . . understand you?" Sunny asked.

"Of course not, but she's very clever," he said. "I trained her to come when I ring this bell, and I taught her to draw, so she can draw pictures of anything she needs."

"She can *draw*?" Sunny said, fascinated. She'd learned to write and draw with a paintbrush that was more than half this scavenger's size. "With what?"

"She made herself this adorable tiny paintbrush. She likes to make things," Smolder said proudly. "She's also made all these cute little costumes for herself, don't ask me why. It's like how birds build nests, I think — all instinct, but really endearing. Although Burn complains that she's worse than moths, leaving holes in all our curtains. I'd call it resourceful, if anyone asked me."

Resourceful? I'll say, Sunny thought, remembering the burnt-out village as well. She gave the scavenger an appraising look, and the scavenger stared back at her with those dragonlike brown eyes, deeper and wiser than you'd expect.

What's going on in that tiny head? Sunny wondered. *Her brain can't be any bigger than a grapefruit. But maybe it works in mysterious ways. Maybe scavengers are cleverer than they seem.*

Another dragon suddenly loomed out of the shadows, but Sunny was able to stop herself from flinching away this time. It was another stuffed specimen, this time a MudWing with striated red lines along his outstretched wings. He had no claws, no teeth, and a puzzled expression.

"Three moons," Sunny said. "What happened to him?"

"The seller said his egg was animus-touched," Smolder said. "Or rather, animus-cursed. Some kind of vengeance thing, maybe. Who would want a dragonet without claws or teeth? How could he live? He was destined to end up here eventually."

Like me, Sunny thought despite herself. *Weird-looking, no other use for me.*

Stop that. You have a real *destiny.*

She tilted her head at the sad, stuffed dragon. *Animus-touched? Could that be what happened to my egg? Did some dragon do this to me before I was hatched? Deliberately?*

But who, and why?

Her mind flashed back to the questions Thorn had asked the NightWings. She was looking for a NightWing named Stonemover . . . that sure sounded like an animus name. *What if he did something to my egg?*

She was so preoccupied with this question that when they came within sight of an orange dragon, she assumed it was another stuffed specimen and barely glanced at it.

But then the dragon lunged at them with a furious hiss, and Smolder backed up in a hurry, nearly knocking Sunny off the winding ramp. She dug her talons into the cracks in the stone as her heart tried to leap out of her chest.

"Sssssssmolder," Queen Scarlet hissed. "Finally."

Coils of smoke wreathed around her horns, but they couldn't hide what was underneath — how the side of the SkyWing's face was melted into a hideous dark mess, revealing a glimpse of her jawbone underneath and pulling one of her yellow eyes down and out of proportion with the rest of her face. The rubies that had been embedded in her scales were gone above that eye, and so were all her earlier adornments — the golden chain mail, the medallions, the rings on her claws, the rubies on her wings. The only jewels left were the tiny rubies above her good eye, which glittered malevolently in the dim light.

The last time they'd been face-to-face, it had been through the bars of a cage. Sunny had been the prisoner and Scarlet had been one of the most beautiful, powerful dragons in Pyrrhia.

No wonder she hates us, Sunny thought. *But Glory did this to her to save the rest of us. We'd all be dead by now otherwise.*

"Here's your water," Smolder said, setting the pail down on a claw-scratched *X* on the floor.

The queen snatched at the pail, and Sunny realized that the *X* marked the very limit of her reach. Heavy chains kept her from moving any farther.

On the other side of the *X*, littering the floor around Scarlet's claws, were shards of shattered glass and puddles of glowing green slime. Here and there in the puddles lay the corpses of peculiar insects — Sunny could see oddly bulging caterpillars, nine-legged hairy spiders, and a bright blue dragonfly whose back bristled with sharp needle spines.

"When are you going to clean this up?" Scarlet snapped at Smolder, her snout dripping as she came up for air from the bucket. "There's slime on my beautiful tail and I keep finding bits of horrible bugs in between my scales."

He snorted. "Perhaps you should have thought of that before smashing up your host's prized collection." He nodded at something lumpy glittering in the shadows behind her. "Burn is going to be especially upset about her NightWing. They're not exactly easy to replace."

Sunny realized that Scarlet must have been chained up near a stuffed NightWing, which she had then clawed and shredded in a fit of rage. Sunny shuddered.

Scarlet lashed her tail. "I'll get to the rest of her toys, too, once I'm free."

"Scarlet," Smolder said patiently, "we're not keeping you prisoner, we're keeping you *safe*. If you were in your own kingdom right now, you'd be dead. You're in no condition to fight Ruby for the throne."

"That's *Queen* Scarlet to you," she said fiercely. Her gaze moved to Sunny, and then she swiveled her head to stare with her good eye. Sunny took an involuntary step back behind Smolder.

"I know her," Scarlet growled. "That dragon is *mine*."

"I am not," Sunny retorted. "I'm not anybody's."

"I know where your RainWing friend is," the queen snarled, pacing to the end of her chains and glaring at Sunny. "As soon as I am free, she is *dead*."

"Then I hope you stay locked in here forever," Sunny snapped.

"I have friends, too," Scarlet hissed. "I won't be here much longer."

Sunny looked up at Smolder, but his expression was more tired than worried. "Come along," he said to Sunny. "We have to fly around her. I know it's inconvenient, but I'm not taking responsibility for unchaining her — Burn can move her when she gets here, if she wants to."

He spread his wings and soared over Scarlet to the next level up, with Flower clinging tightly to his neck. Sunny followed, a bit nervously, her wings brushing the walls as she tried to stay as far out of Scarlet's reach as possible.

They landed close to the top of the tower, where the light was dimmest, and Sunny saw with a sinking heart that there were chains just like Scarlet's here, waiting for her. They lay collapsed on the ground like dead snakeskins, and they clanked horribly as Smolder picked them up.

Sunny curled her tail around her talons and looked at them for a moment, breathing deeply to calm herself. She looked up and met Smolder's eyes.

"Do I really have to stay here?" she asked quietly.

Smolder hesitated with the chains draped across his front talons. Flower looked from him to Sunny, then slipped off his back. To Sunny's surprise, the little scavenger came right up and patted Sunny on the side of her neck. She didn't have to be able to talk; the gesture said clearly, "Don't worry, you'll be all right" — as clearly as if the scavenger had had a tail to twine around Sunny's.

"It's not like I have much choice," Smolder said. "I can't imagine what else to do with you."

"It's just . . . really dark," Sunny said. Her scales were practically crying out for the sunlight right beyond these walls. But more than that, the thing she couldn't bring herself to say, was that she could already tell that being in here too long would carve out her soul one miserable moment at a time, until she'd be as empty and hopeless as one of the stuffed dragons.

"I know," Smolder said, and Sunny sensed the first hint of possible compassion in his voice. She wondered if it was partly because Flower felt sorry for her.

"Tell you what," he said after a pause. "I'll think about it tonight and see if I can come up with something else tomorrow. If not, I'll take you out for a bit at midday, at least let you stretch your wings in the sun, as long as you promise not to escape. Deal?"

"Sure," Sunny said. "Thank you." It wasn't much, but it sounded like the best she could hope for.

He clamped the chains around her ankles, locking them with another one of the keys around his neck. Sunny turned her head away, unwilling to watch herself made a prisoner yet again, and spotted a large box tucked against the wall not far away, at the very end of the spiraling ramp.

"What's that?" she asked.

"Something new for Burn's collection," Smolder said, glancing up at it. "The dragon who came by to sell it claims it's something rare and priceless and that Burn will definitely want it, but that it might die as soon as we open the box. So I'm leaving it closed until Burn gets here, and she can decide what to do with it."

"You don't even know what it is?" Sunny asked. "What if it's an empty box?"

"Then I'll get yelled at," Smolder said, "but he'll get hunted down and killed, so I doubt he'd risk it. Dragons have tried to trick Burn before — sewing odd animal parts together, dyeing normal insects strange colors — and it has always proven to be a very bad idea. Besides, he haggled so hard over the price, he nearly refused to give it to me. It must be something pretty unusual. Also, it keeps making this strange high-pitched hissing noise."

He gave her a sharp look as he snapped the last chain on. "Don't get any ideas from Scarlet's bad behavior. My sister has reasons to keep the SkyWing queen alive. She has a lot more reasons to make you dead . . . so don't add to them."

Sunny nodded, not trusting herself to speak. This was the nightmare — the situation she and her friends had always feared. She was in Burn's clutches now, and she couldn't think of any possible way she might escape.

"I'll be back before you know it," Smolder said. He dipped his wing toward the scavenger. "Up, Flower."

The little creature looked up at Sunny with her thoughtful brown eyes, then patted Sunny's side again and sat down.

Smolder tipped his head sideways and peered at her. "Flower? Come along." He rang his bell and held out his claws.

Flower shook her head firmly and put one paw on one of Sunny's front talons.

"She wants to stay with you," Smolder said. "That's funny. Flower is usually extremely cautious around any dragon who's not me." He narrowed his eyes at Sunny. "If I leave her with you, will you be careful with her? No knocking her off the ramp, no stepping on her, and definitely no eating her."

"I wouldn't eat her!" Sunny protested. "I barely even like meat, except sometimes a lizard here or there. And I think she's being really sweet." There was something comforting about the idea of having someone with her in this dark tower, apart from Queen Scarlet — even if it was a scavenger.

"Well," Smolder said, fidgeting. "If you promise to be careful. Flower, are you sure?"

Flower kept her paw on Sunny and stared back at him without moving.

"All right." He sighed. "See you soon."

He lifted off the edge and flew in a gentle spiral down to the bottom of the tower. Sunny leaned out and saw the shaft of sunlight that spilled into the room as he opened the door — and then saw it disappear again as the door slammed behind him. The weight around her ankles felt suddenly even heavier.

She rested her head on her front talons with a sigh, curling her tail in close. Flower immediately tucked herself into the curve of Sunny's side, reached into her bag, and pulled out a scrap of scroll paper and a lumpy stick of charcoal. In the dim light, she started to sketch, and Sunny, peering over her shoulder, saw a dragon's face appearing in rapid strokes. *Her* face, in fact.

"That's amazing," Sunny said. How could an animal create art like that?

Flower glanced up and did something with her mouth that looked exactly like a dragon smile. Sunny found herself smiling back, despite her fear and her worry. At least she wasn't alone.

"Little SandWing," Queen Scarlet's voice hissed softly from below her. "You think Burn is what you have to worry about right now. She's not. *I* am. I'll be free soon . . . free . . . and I'll be coming for all my enemies. . . . Think about *that* while you try to fall asleep . . . what I'm going to do to your friends when I get my claws on them . . . how messy and thrilling it's going to be. . . ."

Sunny closed her eyes and covered her ears, but the whispers continued inside her head.

What if Burn comes tomorrow? What if she kills me right away?

What if I never get to find out the truth about my mother and my egg? Never get to spend more time with her?

What if the prophecy is fake? What if I really have no destiny — other than to end up here? What if nobody is going to end the war or save the world?

And worst of all . . .

What if I never see my friends again?

CHAPTER 11

Somehow, eventually, Sunny slept, which she knew because she woke up to find Flower tugging gently on her tail and Smolder unlocking her chains.

She sat up slowly and stretched her wings, which still ached from all the flying she'd done in the last several days.

"What's happening?" she asked Smolder.

"Oh, I thought we'd go for a walk," he said wryly.

Sunny squinted at him. "Are you joking? Or is that just your voice? Can other dragons tell when you're joking? Because I can't figure it out."

He threw back his head and laughed. "I have heard that before," he admitted. "There was someone who used to tease me about it. She told me she was going to assume that everything I said was a joke, since that would simplify things. You can do that, too, if you like."

"All right," Sunny said. Smolder wasn't exactly the sinister prison guard she would have expected from Burn's brother. She much preferred this oddness instead, even when it was unsettling.

The last chain clattered to the floor and Smolder held out one talon so Flower could climb up onto his back again.

"Make sure to steer clear of Scarlet," he reminded Sunny, who didn't need reminding. "She's in a foul mood today."

"I HEARD THAT," Scarlet roared.

Smolder rolled his eyes at Sunny and dove off the edge. She followed, catching a glimpse of the smoking orange queen as they whisked past. Scarlet sent a blast of flames into the air right behind them; Sunny felt the heat crackle along the scales of her tail and saw Flower press herself closer to Smolder's back.

Outside, it was early morning — barely sunrise, Sunny realized. *Smolder didn't leave me locked up very long; he didn't even wait until midday to come get me. Maybe he's secretly kinder than he wants me to think.* The light slanted low across the courtyard and small brown birds hopped along the top of the walls, gossiping cheerily. The air smelled like roasting lizards and the sand was still cool under her claws as she followed Smolder to an archway on the left.

"Where are we going?" she asked.

"I have been investigating a mystery for the last twenty years or so," said Smolder. "Occasionally I ask other dragons what they think. Invariably, they disappoint me. But you seem unusual — more unusual than most — so I figured I'd try again. Ever hopeful, that's me."

"Twenty years?" Sunny said. "I hope it's not a very urgent mystery."

Smolder chuckled, then said, "Well, it rather is. But it's been resolutely impossible to solve nonetheless." He led the way through a room of pillars, all of them carved with swirls that looked like dragon tails, and into a long hallway lined with sparkling rust-colored tiles in a spiraling pattern. Sunny brushed one of the tiles with her wing, thinking that it was the first beautiful thing she'd seen in this palace.

The hallway slanted down and down and down until Sunny was sure they were underground, and finally it ended in a room with four locked doors.

Smolder walked to each door and opened them with large brass keys from around his neck, revealing four rooms of roughly equal size, with thick stone walls and plain gray stone floors. All of them were completely empty.

"The rumors about the SandWing treasure were never entirely accurate," he said as he did this, twisting the keys in his claws. "We were very wealthy, yes, but we weren't quite stupid enough to keep it all in one place. *Almost* that stupid, but not quite. We kept only our most prized possessions in our treasure rooms — along with a backup stash of rubies, diamonds, and gold in case we ever needed it. So it wasn't our entire wealth or a palace full of treasure that went missing. Only the contents of these four rooms . . . but they contained quite a lot."

He held up a talon for Flower to climb onto, then set her carefully on the floor in front of the treasure rooms. She looked even smaller next to the massive rooms. Sunny realized that Flower was probably small enough to squeeze under the doors.

The scavenger put her tiny paws on her hips, tossed her head fur back, and looked for all the world like she was bored of this dragon game.

"So here's what I'd like to know," Smolder said. "How did three scavengers about this size — two, actually, once they lost this one — manage to carry *four rooms' worth* of treasure off into the desert?"

Sunny studied the little scavenger in front of her. It was actually a very good question. Flower was only about as tall as a full-grown dragon's head. She had no wings and miniature, practically useless paws.

Well, maybe not that useless, she thought, remembering the sketch of her face from the night before.

"Could they have built something to carry it?" she said, crouching to examine Flower's paws. The scavenger squeaked at her. "I saw the ruins of one of their villages on my way here. Their dens look like real houses, and there was an iron bell in the wreckage, too. So they're good at making things . . . maybe they made some kind of wagon to carry it in?"

"A wagon would have left tracks across the sand," Smolder pointed out. "The only tracks we found were hoofprints — three horses, galloping flat out. You tell me how they could do that with more than two bags of gold on their backs, let alone all of this."

"Oh, you found prints?" Sunny said, stepping into the first room and peering around. "Didn't you follow them?" She moved to the second room, which was the same as the first, except perhaps with a little more sand on the floor.

"*Follow* them!" said Smolder. "If only we'd *thought* of that."

"Aha," Sunny said. "That was definitely sarcasm."

He gave her a crooked smile. "Well, look. There was a lot of confusion when we first found the queen's body. We all heard her roaring in the middle of the night — it must have woken every dragon for miles. That's what brought us outside the palace, thinking something terrible had happened. All we found at first was Mother, lying there, dead. Had one of her daughters killed her? Why not in a proper duel? Who else would dare kill the SandWing queen? Who else *could* — and why wouldn't they admit to it? The first clue we found was this little creature, trying to hide by burying herself in a dune. She was injured and, of course, had no treasure on her, apart from a cute little claw-sword thing."

Smolder reached into the bag around his neck and, somewhat startlingly, produced a banana. He handed it to Flower, who sat down and began peeling it with expert little twitches of her slender paws.

"That's when we realized scavengers were involved, so we knew they must have come here to steal treasure. Burn was so furious. We finally found the horse tracks," Smolder went on. "But they had at least two hours' head start by then. We caught up shortly before they reached their forest home — and then Burn decided we should *let* them reach their forest home." His eyes were dark, watching Flower. "Once they led us right to it . . . we burned it to the ground."

"Yikes," Sunny said. *That's a lot of scavengers to wipe out just because three of them did something stupid.*

"Burn said we had to stamp out the vermin before they began to think they could do something like that again,"

Smolder pointed out, as if he guessed what she was thinking.

"So after you burned the village . . ."

"We searched for the treasure in the ashes. No sign of it anywhere — not a single jewel or gold nugget. We tried hunting down the few scavengers who'd escaped the fire, but some of them must have slipped through our claws — and one of those must have the treasure, even now, twenty years later."

Sunny started pacing from room to room. Something wasn't right about this story. A lot of things weren't quite right about this story. That much treasure — how could it disappear into thin air? How could *scavengers* make it disappear into thin air?

She stopped and looked down at Flower again. The brown eyes looked back at her curiously.

"Are you *sure* the scavengers killed Queen Oasis?" Sunny asked. "It wasn't maybe just really bad luck that they were there at the same time as some other killer?"

Smolder nodded. "I thought of that. But it was a scavenger-sized spear in Mother's eye. And — this part is a little weird — they cut off her tail barb and took it with them. We never found that either, but there was a trail of venom drops and dragon blood beside the horse tracks."

Sunny wrinkled her snout. "Why would they *do* that?"

"Why do scavengers do any of the inexplicable things they do?" Smolder tossed another banana to Flower. Sunny wondered if the scavenger had any idea they were talking about her.

"Hmm," she said, studying the rooms. Now that she was here, looking at the space and at a scavenger at the same time, the original story sounded more and more ludicrous. It was crazy enough that scavengers had managed to kill a dragon queen. But then they also stole all her treasure? Without getting caught and eaten?

Her wings twitched with a sudden idea. Maybe the question wasn't *How did they transport all that treasure.* Maybe the real question was *What else could have happened to it.*

"Wait," she said. "When did you check these rooms? When did you see how *much* was missing?"

"Oh." Smolder breathed a plume of smoke and squinted at her. "When we returned from burning the den. I remember flying back and thinking that the scavengers couldn't have gotten much if we couldn't find any trace of it. And then Burn led the way down here to do an inventory . . . and we found everything gone. I never figured out how Flower unlocked the doors either."

Sunny lashed her tail so hard it smacked into one of the doors, sending a shiver of pain through her scales.

"That's *it*, then," she said excitedly. "Someone else took it while you were out hunting the scavengers. Who didn't go with you to chase the scavengers and burn the den?"

"Lots of dragons," Smolder said. He frowned thoughtfully at the open doors. "Blister and Blaze both stayed here."

"Then of course it was one of them!" Sunny said. "The scavengers probably didn't even get anything before Oasis caught them. They don't have your treasure. One of your sisters does."

Smolder was already shaking his head. *"No,"* he said. "No, that's not possible. It must be scavengers, or this war would be over already."

Sunny met Flower's eyes, then looked back at him. "Over? How do you figure?"

"There's — I'm not supposed to talk about it."

"You can't do that!" Sunny said, flaring her wings. "You can't tell me half of something and then not tell me the rest!"

He wrinkled his snout, looking faintly amused again. "You *are* my prisoner, remember?" he said. "It's a royal SandWing secret, I'm afraid."

"Oh, aren't you fancy," Sunny said. "All right, I'll figure it out."

"Don't do that," Smolder said with a hint of alarm in his voice.

"A royal secret involving your treasure that would end the war if someone had their claws on it already. Oh!" Sunny said. "I bet it's something animus-touched. Is that it? That must be it. Oooh, is it some kind of enchanted treasure that's like, oh, if you're holding this, you're the SandWing queen? So a scavenger must have it, because if a dragon had it, she'd be queen and the war would be over. Interesting."

Smolder stared at her with unfathomable black eyes for a long moment.

"That's . . . not it?" Sunny finally asked, nervously.

"That was unsettling," he said.

"It was just logic," Sunny said. "My friend Starflight would have figured it out faster." She stopped and curled her tail around her talons. *If only Starflight were here. Or Clay, or any of them.*

"Well," he said, "I suppose you're likely to be dead by the end of the week anyway. Just remember that if you tell anybody, we'll have to kill them, too."

"Aren't you cheerful," Sunny said crossly. "What is it anyway? The SandWing scepter?"

He shook his head. "I'm not telling you that."

"The Lazulite Dragon?" Sunny racked her brain, trying to remember what famous pieces of treasure were mentioned in the scrolls.

"Stop guessing!"

"The Eye of Onyx!" Sunny said, and from his expression she knew that was it. His face wasn't quite the emotionless mask that Blister's was.

"Well, that's why the scavengers must have the treasure," Smolder said quickly, as if hoping she hadn't noticed. "If Blister or Blaze had it, one of them would be queen instead of hiding in another kingdom. If *any* SandWing had it, they'd be ruling the desert already."

Sunny shrugged. "So the scavengers managed to get something — and happened to get the most important thing. Someone else still took the rest of it. I bet you anything."

"Hmmm." Smolder narrowed his eyes. Smoke billowed from his nose, writhing around his horns. "In that case, we'd still have to find the scavengers and what they stole."

Sunny didn't have an answer for that. She had a feeling "find the scavengers" meant "burn down more dens," and it made her feel sorry for the squishy little creatures, especially if they were all as cute and clever as Flower.

"Smolder!" a voice called. "Smolder!"

Talons scrabbled on stone as a snub-nosed SandWing came pelting down the long sloping hall. He started calling out as he ran toward them, his voice traveling across the distance.

"We're under attack!" he yelled. "Help! General Sandstorm is already dead! No one knows what to do! It's chaos! We're all going to die!" He skidded the last several steps toward them and nearly tumbled into one of the treasure rooms. Sunny jumped out of the way of his flailing tail.

"Who's attacking?" Smolder said sharply, grabbing the messenger and steering him back up the hallway with one brisk motion. "IceWings or SeaWings?"

"I don't know! It happened so fast! It was like they rose straight out of the sand."

"Maybe it's Queen Scarlet's friends," Sunny said anxiously, scooping up Flower and hurrying behind them. Smolder gave her a look as if he'd forgotten she was there. "Remember? She said someone was coming to rescue her — what if this is them?"

The messenger let out a horrified squeak. "Then we're *definitely all going to die!*"

"Stop that," Smolder said, giving him a quick shake. "There are enough SandWing soldiers here to fight off any invasion." He held out his talons and Sunny passed Flower to him. Smolder set his pet gently in a side room with no windows. "Stay," he said sternly, pointing a claw at the little scavenger.

Flower put her paws on her hips and chattered something indignant at him, but he ignored her and swept on up the corridor.

"I don't have time to lock you up again right now," Smolder said to Sunny. "But I'm still watching you. If you try to escape while we're fighting, you'll end up back in that tower and you're never coming out again."

"I get it! You're menacing!" Sunny shouted at him. "Now what are you going to do about Queen Scarlet? You should send more guards to watch her *right now*. *She's* the one you should worry about escaping. At least *I* won't *murder everyone* on my way out!"

Smolder's stern expression wavered for a moment as he looked down at her. "I think I should be offended that you're obviously more afraid of my prisoner than you are of me," he said. "But I suppose I'll worry about that later. You!" he shouted at a pair of guards running by. "Find four more soldiers and take them to guard Burn's weirdling tower. *With your lives*, you understand?"

They nodded, about-faced, and took off toward the tower.

"Thank you," Sunny said, more than a little surprised that he'd actually listened to her.

Now they could hear roars and snarls and the clash of claws outside, along with the sound of shouts and running talons all over the palace.

"Watch her," Smolder said to the messenger, pointing to Sunny.

An unearthly shriek tore through the morning air and Smolder hurtled into the nearest courtyard, then up into the air. The black diamonds on his wings flared like crows taking flight as he soared higher, then banked sideways and shot toward the outer wall.

Sunny ran into the courtyard behind him and spread her wings.

"Wait," the messenger protested. "Where do you think you're going?"

"To see what's happening!" Sunny said. "I want to know who's winning, don't you?" *Because if it's Scarlet's "friends," then I need to get out of here, no matter what Smolder thinks I've promised him.*

"Um," the messenger said, twisting his tail between his talons. "But . . . I'm not sure. . . ."

"Come on!" Sunny launched herself into the sky and heard the scramble of his claws behind her as he followed.

She aimed for the highest point of the palace that she could see: a spire with an open pavilion platform at the top. The corners of the roof were carved like dragon wings open in flight, and wind chimes on each side glittered and whispered in the faint breeze. In a few moments her claws touched down on white stone and she took a fluttering step for balance. Spread out before her, to the south of the stronghold, was the battle.

Sunny squinted, her eyes adjusting to the light of the rising sun as she searched for distinctive colors — perhaps the blues and greens of SeaWings, or the white and pale blue of IceWings, as Smolder expected — or perhaps the reds and oranges of loyal SkyWings come to rescue their queen.

But there was something strange about this battle. Sunny couldn't see any unusual colors down there — nothing but the tan, pale yellow, and off-white scales of SandWings.

SandWings fighting SandWings.

Was it Blister's army attacking? But it didn't look like a whole invading force. In fact, if Sunny had to guess, she'd say there were only about thirty dragons attacking the stronghold, against about a hundred defenders.

And then she saw a flash of sunlight catch on a gold arm bracelet, and she leaned forward with a gasp.

That's Thorn.

Now that she'd spotted her, it was unmistakable. The wiry, pale yellow dragon was deep in the thick of the fighting, slashing at SandWing soldiers with her talons and stabbing her tail as she rose into the air, then dropped below two warriors, then hurtled up to smash into another.

Sunny scanned the rest of the attackers and picked out Six-Claws, then Qibli, fighting as close to Thorn as they could.

This wasn't another army, or one of the SandWing sisters. The stronghold was being attacked by the Outclaws.

My mother came to get me, Sunny thought, her scales humming with joy. *Six-Claws must have told her the truth instead of the lie we came up with.*

But then she took another look at the battle, and her heart sank.

Five SandWing soldiers lay dead on the sand, but the Outclaws were still outnumbered almost four to one. Smolder was shouting orders as he shoved soldiers into formations, tightening the defenses so a bristling wall of spears was ready to ram the scattered attacking dragons. One wave of SandWings piled into Six-Claws, who staggered back with a roar, losing height so his bloodied tail swept the sand below him. Sunny watched in horror as seven soldiers encircled Thorn, cutting her off from her allies.

The Outclaws came to rescue me — and it's going to get them all killed.

CHAPTER 12

Sunny paced from one end of the pavilion to the other, her heart pounding. Her eyes hurt from staring at the battle, as if she'd been trying to change the outcome with the power of her eyeballs.

Don't die trying to rescue me. Please, please, please don't die.

It was almost killing her to watch as her mother dodged flames and claws and deadly tails. A giant SandWing slammed into Thorn's chest and tried to drive her down onto the sand. Thorn slashed at his snout and darted away. But another soldier attacked from behind her, stabbing his venomous tail down toward the center of her spine.

Sunny shrieked with fear, and the messenger behind her nearly fell off the spire.

"What?" he yelped. "What is it? Who's dead?"

At the last moment, Qibli barreled into the soldier and knocked him away. Sunny wasn't sure her mother had even noticed how close that had been. *She's not careful enough,* Sunny thought anxiously, standing up on her back legs and flapping her wings.

"What's happening?" the messenger said plaintively, craning to see around her.

"It's my mother," Sunny said. "She's here to rescue me."

The SandWing scrunched his snout at her. "Are you sure? That doesn't sound like any mother I know."

"Well, that's just sad," Sunny said, trying to listen to him and watch the battle at the same time. "Even your own mother?"

The other dragon made a noise that sounded half chuckle, half snort. "My parents sent me to Burn's army to toughen me up. They said this way I'd end up as brave as a real soldier or else dead, and either of those would be an improvement."

"What's your name?" Sunny asked. Down below, in the battle, Six-Claws seized two soldiers and smashed their heads together, then whirled to slash another one's throat with his tail.

The messenger hesitated. "Am I allowed to tell you that?"

"Why not? My name is Sunny."

"I know," he said. "All right. My name is Camel."

Sunny flicked her wings open and shut, brushing against the wind chimes. Camel seemed like a normal, nervous dragon. Someone she could be friends with in another life. Maybe he'd listen to reason.

"Do you have any dragonets?" she asked.

"Not yet, but my partner and I have three eggs hatching next month," he said proudly.

"So you can be a different kind of parent than yours were," Sunny said. "The kind that takes care of his dragonets. The kind who would attack a stronghold full of soldiers to protect them," she added hopefully. She didn't know much about parents in general, but she knew what *she* would do if she had dragonets and any of *them* were in danger.

"Hmm," said Camel, looking even more anxious. He swished his tail and gazed down at the battle — the blood on the sand, the sprawled bodies, the flashing claws.

Maybe this isn't the right approach for this dragon, Sunny thought.

"All I'm saying," she continued, "is that I can't stand here and watch my mother die trying to save me. Please, please, let me go help her." She leaned toward the wide-open blue sky, imagining how she would dive in and drag all the soldiers away from Thorn.

"Oh," Camel said uncomfortably. "Oh, no, no. I can't do that. If Burn finds out, she might take my eggs away. That wouldn't be good parenting, would it?"

Sunny sighed. "I guess not," she admitted fairly. "But maybe I can stop the fighting, so nobody else has to die."

Camel hesitated again, looking down at the battle, and Sunny wondered if his partner was one of the ones out there fighting. "How?" he asked. "I mean — you're not —" He glanced at her harmless tail and away again quickly.

Not exactly scary. Not exactly big. Not even a little bit useful.

He was kind of right. What did she think she could really do if she joined in?

Is there another way to stop them? A Sunny way?

She stared down at the battling dragons, racking her brain.

And then something moved under the sand.

Sunny leaned forward, staring intently. Not far from one of the fallen soldiers, a patch of sand rippled as though something were buried underneath it.

Something, or some*one*.

Sunny had the horrible feeling for a moment that the ghost of Queen Oasis herself was about to come bursting out of the sand to attack the dragons.

But the head that popped out was not a SandWing's. It was followed by shoulders and wings that glowed coppery orange in the bright sunlight. The dragon wriggled the rest of the way free and began swarming across the sand toward the stronghold walls.

Sunny gasped.

She recognized those scales — like hers, they were a color unique to only one dragon in Pyrrhia, as far as anyone knew.

It was Peril. It had to be. Peril, the SkyWing who had helped them escape from Queen Scarlet's palace.

Well, first she had pretended to help them escape, and then she'd betrayed them, and then she'd nearly killed Clay, but in the end she'd done the right thing, although sometimes it was hard to remember that. But without her, the dragonets and Kestrel might have been trapped in the Sky Palace until Scarlet figured out a "thrilling" death for each of them.

Sunny's heart sank, thinking of Kestrel and how she'd died under Blister's claws in the Kingdom of the Sea. How would Peril react to the news of her mother's death?

But more important, what was she doing here? And why was she clearly trying to sneak into the palace?

Peril reached the walls and glanced back at the battle, but the fighting was too fierce for anyone to notice her. She spread her wings and launched herself over the wall, landed neatly in the courtyard, and darted into the palace.

Sunny inhaled sharply as an awful thought struck her. *Surely not.*

"Did you see that orange dragon?" she asked Camel. "I have to follow her. Come with me, so it's not like I'm escaping from you."

"Um," Camel said. "But wait, shouldn't I —"

Sunny didn't hear the end of that sentence; she was already in the air and winging toward the courtyard that held the weirdling tower. She could see the dark red crown of it looming over the rooftops.

Her talons came down with a thump in the sandpit and she glanced around at the tower door, but it was still closed, and, she hoped, locked. Not that a lock on a wooden door would be much use at stopping Peril and her fiery talons. The six SandWing soldiers arranged outside wouldn't be able to stop her either. They looked curiously at Sunny, but held their positions.

Camel flapped down behind her and landed on the wall, as far from the tower as he could get without losing sight of Sunny.

She waited a moment, trying to calm down her heartbeat. *Maybe I'm wrong. Maybe Peril isn't here to rescue Scarlet. I mean, why would she?*

But then she heard talons clattering over stone, and Peril came running into the courtyard.

The SkyWing skidded to a stop when she saw Sunny. Her flame-blue eyes went wide through the wisps of smoke that rose from her scales.

"Hi, Peril," Sunny said, hoping she sounded more friendly than terrified.

Peril twitched nervously. "She said not to let you guys stop me." Peril glanced around the courtyard, peering into the shadows with a hopeful expression. "Is, um — I mean, are you all here?"

"No — sorry," Sunny said. She knew who Peril was really looking for. "Clay's not here, but he worries about you."

"Did he say that?" Peril asked. She touched her front talons together — the same way she had after Clay had taken her talons in his, when they had said good-bye, Sunny remembered. "That he worries about me? What did he say exactly?"

"Um," Sunny said, trying to remember the last time Clay had mentioned Peril. They'd been a little busy lately, escaping from the SeaWings and invading the NightWing island and running from volcanoes. But he had said something about her one night in the rainforest, after Starflight had disappeared. Clay and Sunny had been curled together near Kinkajou, the little RainWing dragonet who'd been injured in the contest where Glory became queen. She was asleep, and it was Sunny's turn to watch her; Clay was keeping her company.

"He said, 'I wonder where Peril is right now,' " Sunny said. " 'I hope she's all right. There's that new queen in the Sky Kingdom —' and I said, 'Ruby,' and he said, 'Right, her.

I hope she's taking care of Peril and not making her fight anymore.'"

Peril waited a moment, and then said, "That's it?"

"Well, then his stomach started growling, and he had to go look for something to eat," Sunny said. "But he wants to see you again. I'm sure of it."

"I bet you've had all kinds of adventures together," Peril said a little bitterly.

"It's been really scary," Sunny said. "It seems like every dragon we meet either wants to kill us or lock us up." She glanced around at the tower and sighed. "Case in point."

Peril looked down at her talons. The sunlight gleamed on the gold veins in her wings.

"What about you?" Sunny asked. "Um, have you . . ." She didn't know how to finish that sentence. *Have you stopped killing dragons? Have you found a safe way to live around others? Have you by any chance come here to rescue a dragon who really wants to kill me?*

"The answer is, she's not," Peril said sharply. "Ruby. Is not taking care of me. She ordered me out of the Sky Kingdom as soon as she took over. She said if I ever set claws in the Sky Palace again, she'd find a way to kill me, and I'd better believe it. She said I was dangerous and unpredictable and she didn't want me near her subjects." Her voice broke and she coughed, ducking under one wing.

"Oh, Peril, I'm so sorry," Sunny said.

"Don't feel sorry for me." Peril lifted her head and frowned. "I *am* dangerous. That's, like, the whole entire point of me."

"That's not true," Sunny said. "You can be whatever you want to be. I mean, I could say, *well, I have no barb on my tail, I guess I'm just harmless and useless and should sit in the corner covering my head whenever there's a fight.* But I don't want to be useless and I'm not going to do that, not if dragons I care about are in danger." She glanced at the sky, wondering anxiously how the battle was going and whether Thorn was still all right. "Um, speaking of which . . . I could really use your help right now."

Peril shook herself, copper scales flashing. "I can't help you. I have to rescue Scarlet while everyone is distracted with that battle outside."

Sunny felt a cold shiver of fear run through her scales. She had still hoped maybe that wasn't why Peril was here. "But why?" she cried.

"I've been waiting days for a chance like this, when I could get her out without fighting anyone," Peril said. "So you can tell Clay, I'm trying really hard not to kill anyone." She hesitated, looking at the guards behind Sunny, between her and the tower. "I'm *trying*," she said again.

"No, I mean, why would you help her?" Sunny asked. "After everything she did to you?"

The breeze picked up into a quiet wind, scattering grains of sand across Sunny's claws and bringing her the heavy, scaly smell of fear from the SandWings behind her. They hadn't moved from their spots, but they stood tensed and ready with their weapons. Sunny guessed at least some of them knew who Peril was from visits to the Sky Kingdom with Burn.

"I know Scarlet's not perfect," Peril said. *Understatement of the year,* Sunny thought. "But she didn't kill me when she could have, when anyone else would have, when I was a dragonet. And she didn't throw me out. She treated me like I was special."

"She lied to you," Sunny pointed out. "About Kestrel, and about the black rocks she said you had to eat so you could never leave her. She was using you, not taking care of you."

"She took better care of me than my mother did," Peril flared. "And from what I saw of her, Kestrel isn't the nicest dragon in the world either, right?" She hesitated again, then said tentatively, "Have you seen Kestrel? Do you know where she is? I wonder . . . I've been wondering if I should have gone with her when she asked me to."

Sunny's heart sank. She didn't want to deliver this news. *But I can't lie to her literally twenty seconds after I just accused Scarlet of so much lying. I don't know how she'll react. But I have to tell her the truth.*

"Peril," she said softly. "I'm really sorry, but . . . Kestrel's dead."

Peril stared at her for a long moment, her odd eyes glowing blue and black, and then slowly, like a mountain crumbling, she collapsed to the stones and covered her face with her talons. "No, no, no," she said. "I sent her away. I said we'd find each other again."

"I know," Sunny said, wishing she could wrap her wings around Peril the way Clay had. But Clay was the only dragon she knew who could touch Peril without dying. "I know. Oh, Peril, I'm so sorry. Listen," she said desperately. Her anxiety about the battle outside was making every scale on her wings feel like jumping off and flying away. "Listen, I'm like you. I thought my mother didn't want me either. But I just found out that's not true, just like you — my mother wanted me the way Kestrel wanted you. Except I'm so afraid she's going to die before I get to know her, and that's why I need your help, *please*, Peril. She's attacking the palace right now trying to rescue me, and you could save her. I'm sorry, I know it's awful to throw all that at you at once, but I really need you."

Peril pressed her talons into the stone and sat up. She took a deep breath, exhaling smoke in a cloud around her wings. Finally she looked down at Sunny, with an expression as though she was trying to find any small part of herself in Sunny's eyes.

"Tell me more," she said. Her legs trembled as if they might not keep holding her up, but she listened intently as Sunny explained about Thorn and the Outclaws.

"All right," she said at last, when Sunny paused for breath. "I'll stop the battle. But then I'm setting Scarlet free, so don't try to get in my way."

"But —"

"That's the deal," Peril said stubbornly. "I've already lost one mother. Scarlet is what's left, so she's the best I can do."

Sunny curled her tail around her talons. She was very worried about this plan, but there wasn't time to keep arguing. And what could she say? *Having no mother would be better than having that mother?* What did she know about it, really?

"Thank you," she said instead. "I trust you," she added. She wasn't sure she really did, but she wanted to. "I know you can do it without hurting anyone."

"Um," Camel said unhappily from above them. "I really think I shouldn't let this happen."

"You can't stop her," Sunny said to him as Peril shot into the sky. "And your job is to watch me; that's all Smolder said. I'm not going anywhere, see? Well, except back up to the pavilion to watch. Come on." She followed Peril up and watched the shimmering copper scales flash toward the battle outside the walls.

From the high pavilion, Sunny could see two more corpses lying below the battle, but after a heart-stopping moment, she realized that neither one was Thorn or Six-Claws. She stared at the battle intently until she finally spotted her mother, grappling claw to claw with a soldier.

Smolder was there, too, not far from Qibli, shouting orders and darting around the formations. He was one of the first to spot Peril as she approached. Sunny could tell because he froze very suddenly, staring in the direction of the SkyWing.

The soldiers around him turned to see what he was looking at. Three of them took one look at Peril, shrieked, and fled into the desert, their shadows flickering rapidly across the dunes until they vanished in the direction of the Scorpion Den. Sunny guessed they had been to Burn's palace and seen what Peril could do.

She'd never seen what Peril could do, not to another dragon. She'd been trapped in her cage while all her friends were in the arena at the Sky Palace, so she'd missed all the fighting. But Clay had told her about it — the melting scales, the black talonprints burning into her victims, the scorched smell — and it sounded terrifying. She hoped she wasn't about to see it now.

Gradually the Outclaws stopped fighting, too, and fell back, until there was a wide circle of dragons around the clear space of sky where Peril hovered.

Sunny's sharp ears caught some of what Peril was saying to them, but not all of it. Something about taking over the fortress, something else about surrendering.

She saw Smolder start forward as if he were going to argue with Peril. *Oh, please don't,* she thought anxiously. It was strange to admit it, but she actually liked him. She definitely didn't want him to die or get his scales melted.

But several SandWing soldiers grabbed him and pulled him back, shaking their heads and pointing to the smoke that rose clearly from Peril's wings.

Thorn said something, and Peril gestured toward the stronghold. With a sort of grateful bow, Thorn flew past her, followed by all her Outclaws.

"Hooray!" Sunny cried, flapping her wings with excitement. "Race you to the courtyard, Camel!" She leaped off the tower and soared down toward the stones where she'd first landed in the stronghold.

Thorn had just set down and was turning to issue orders to her dragons when Sunny catapulted to a stop in front of her and threw her wings around her mother.

"By all the snakes!" her mother yelped. "Sunny!" She lifted Sunny off her talons and spun her around. "Never mind!" she shouted at the Outclaws over Sunny's shoulder. "Found her!"

Sunny felt giddy and weightless, like a tent with its pegs pulled up, flying loose in a sandstorm. "You came to get me," she said breathlessly.

"Of course I did, beetle," her mother said, stepping back and looking around. "Six-Claws told me everything. I spent seven years looking for you; I wasn't about to lose you after only ten minutes of conversation." She grinned with all her teeth. "Besides, I've always wanted to invade Burn's stronghold. I take it she's not here."

"Luckily," Sunny said. "I doubt she'd have surrendered as graciously as Smolder did."

"We should do the tour quick before she comes back, then," Thorn said cheerfully, as if she hadn't been scales away from death a few moments earlier. "What do you think that is?" She put one wing over Sunny's shoulders and steered her toward the black obelisk Sunny had noticed before.

Their claws sank into the sand around the monument, which was white and clean as if it were swept every day. As they got closer, Sunny could read the words carved and painted in gold on the side of the pillar.

HERE LIES

QUEEN OASIS

MOTHER OF QUEEN BURN

HER BONES NOW BELONG TO THE SANDS OF TIME

"Yikes," Sunny said, suddenly realizing what it meant. She scrambled sideways, off the sand, pulling Thorn along with her. "Queen Oasis is *buried* under there! Right below us!"

"Probably where she died," Thorn guessed, looking up at the walls Burn had added after she took over. "This would have been right outside the original palace, where the scavengers attacked her." She peered at the inscription again. "That's more poetic than I would have expected from Burn. Very impressive."

The sound of wingbeats overhead made them both look up as the SandWing soldiers came flapping back into the courtyard. With them were Peril and Smolder, who spiraled down to land beside Thorn.

"I'm going to be in so much trouble," Smolder said to Sunny with a sigh. "Burn might actually kill me this time. Losing you and Scarlet in one fell swoop? That's probably worse than anything my brothers ever did."

"I'm sorry," Sunny said.

"Sorry enough to stay our prisoner?" Smolder asked hopefully.

"Who is this hilarious dragon?" Thorn asked her.

"This is Smolder, Burn's brother," Sunny said. "Smolder, this is Thorn, my mother. She's the leader of the Outclaws. And this is Peril."

Thorn half bowed again to Peril. "Our lucky angel," she said.

Peril nodded, looking a bit uncomfortable. Sunny guessed she wasn't used to gratitude, and that she'd certainly never been called an angel before.

"Perhaps *I* should move to the Scorpion Den," Smolder said gloomily. "Thorn, was it? Hmmm." He gave her a thoughtful look, as if he'd heard of her somewhere before.

"I need to kill the dragon who betrayed me," Thorn announced. "His name is Addax. Please produce him."

"Oh, no, don't," Sunny blurted. "I mean, don't kill him, please. He only — he just — he had his reasons, and look, I'm all right, aren't I?"

Her mother tilted her head at Sunny, looking surprised and concerned. "Don't you want to punish him? Aren't you angry?"

Am I? Sunny glanced at the barracks of soldiers beyond Smolder. Somewhere in there, Addax had been reunited with his family. And somewhere in there, he was probably hiding right now, knowing what might happen to him next.

"Punishing him won't make anything better," Sunny said. "It'll probably just make someone else angry and vengeful and lead to more awful things. I'm really all right. Let's leave him and get out of here."

Thorn brushed Sunny's wing with hers and nodded. "All right, if that's what you want. Mercy is yours to grant. I have one more question for this dragon, though." She turned to Smolder. "You've lived here a long time. Can you tell me if you have any NightWing prisoners?"

Smolder shook his head. "No. I'm afraid my sister doesn't keep most of her prisoners. Alive, I mean."

"You had one NightWing, though," Sunny offered. "In Burn's collection, didn't you? The stuffed one that Scarlet destroyed?"

"What?" Thorn said. Her wings went very still. "What do you mean, stuffed?"

"It's sort of a hobby for Burn," Smolder said with an embarrassed expression. "If she finds a dragon she wants for her collection, she'll usually kill him and stuff himself. . . . I know, it sounds pretty horrible."

"It *is* horrible," Sunny told him bluntly. "It's one of the worst things I've ever heard, ever."

"Where?" Thorn said to Smolder in a cold voice. "Show me this murdered NightWing. Right now."

CHAPTER 13

As Smolder led them through the labyrinth of the palace again, Sunny noticed that Peril kept her wings pressed as close to her body as she could. *Afraid of setting something on fire,* she guessed, feeling sorry for the SkyWing.

"Mother," she whispered, "why do we care about this NightWing?"

"Hopefully we don't," her mother answered cryptically.

They crossed the sandpit to the tower. The six SandWing guards jumped aside with a relieved expression when they saw Smolder.

Sunny heard Peril take a deep breath. *Time for her to face Scarlet,* she realized. *And us, too, since we'll have to get past her to see the NightWing.*

They could hear Scarlet roaring as soon as they opened the door. "Who's down there? Smolder, I hear your stupid keys clanking. If you —" She cut off abruptly and Sunny looked up. She could see yellow eyes glinting through the smoke as Scarlet peered down at them.

The silence that followed as they wound their way up the ramp was more unsettling than the shouting. What was Scarlet thinking? What would she do when they reached her?

The former queen of the SkyWings sat with her tail curled around her talons, glaring fiercely at them. Smolder stopped in front of her, but she ignored him, fixing her malevolent gaze on Peril instead.

"What are you doing?" she growled.

"Rescuing you," Peril muttered, staying behind Sunny.

"This is an odd way to go about it." Scarlet swept her tail in an arc, knocking glass shards over the edge to shatter on the floor far below. "Such an interesting group of friends you've brought with you."

"Where is the NightWing?" Thorn demanded.

Smolder pointed wordlessly at the shadowy lumps behind Scarlet.

"Don't go near her," Sunny warned her mother as Thorn started forward. "She's really dangerous."

"That's true," Scarlet hissed.

Thorn paused, then faced the prisoner. "Show me the NightWing's face."

"Looking for someone?" Scarlet said, sounding amused. "Now why would I help you?"

"Because I'm telling you to," Peril interjected abruptly. "Do it if you want me to get you out of here."

Queen Scarlet rose up on her back legs, spreading her wings so she looked majestically powerful despite her disfigurement. "It sounds to me like you've forgotten who your queen is," she snarled at Peril.

"It sounds to *me* like you've forgotten who has the scale-melting talons here," Peril snapped back.

Scarlet hissed and more smoke poured from her snout to envelop her horns. "Don't you threaten me. I don't take orders from anyone."

"Then you can rot here," Peril said hotly, turning around so fast that Sunny had to jump out of the way of her tail.

She'd only taken three steps when Scarlet cried, "Wait! Wait."

Peril stopped, breathing deeply, but didn't turn around.

"The NightWing," Thorn said with quiet authority, pointing.

Scarlet growled deep in her throat, then picked up something from behind her and threw it as hard as she could at Smolder.

He caught it and then tossed it to Thorn with a yelp.

It was the NightWing's head.

Thorn looked down at the dragon head in her talons with an expression of pure horror, but it quickly melted into relief. She gently set the head down on the stone and stepped back.

"Is — is everything —?" Sunny asked.

"A stranger," Thorn said. "Nothing to worry about." She rubbed her forearms. "Let's go back to the sunshine."

"Peril," Scarlet said, a low rumble in her throat. "Where are you going?"

"I'll be back to let you out once Sunny is far away from here," Peril said, looking over her shoulder at the imprisoned queen. "Don't try to argue with me. I know what you want to do to her and I won't let you." She set off down the ramp as fast as she could, and Sunny followed, feeling grateful and anxious in equal parts.

"I know what *you* want, and it's not going to work!" Scarlet shouted after her. "He's never going to love you! You can keep trying to save his friends, but no one will ever love you except me! I'm the only one who accepts you the way you are! You'll always be a monster to everyone else!"

Peril threw the door open, leaving scorch marks on the wood, and dashed out of the tower.

Sunny caught up to her outside, where the SkyWing was curled up small in the middle of the sand, rubbing her claws together.

"She's wrong," Sunny said to Peril's back. She hesitated, glancing back at Smolder and Thorn as Smolder relocked the tower. "Don't let her make you hate yourself. I can't promise you anything about Clay, but I think — I mean, if I know him at all, I can tell you the way to his heart is by helping his friends." *Although I cannot picture him with you. The kindest dragon in Pyrrhia . . . and someone who's killed who knows how many dragons? How could you ever deserve him?* She didn't say any of that out loud, though. If she was being perfectly honest, she'd have to admit to herself that she'd never think anyone was worthy of Clay.

Peril sniffed and then nodded.

"And *I* don't think you're a monster," Sunny added, thinking, *You've been monstrous, but maybe you can change. I have to believe you can change.* "You're a dragon like anyone else. You can remake yourself however you want to."

Peril snorted. "Easy for you to say."

Not really, Sunny thought. *My friends think they know who I am, too, no matter how much I try to show them I'm more than that.*

"You don't have to set Scarlet free," Sunny reminded her. "You could come with me instead."

Peril tossed her head, folding her wings back. "Don't worry about me. I'm fine."

Which means "I don't want any more sympathy right now," Sunny thought.

She turned back toward the tower as her mother and Smolder approached.

"I think we have something that belongs to you," Smolder was saying to Thorn. "If you don't mind waiting, I'll go check Burn's library."

Thorn gave him a suspicious look and he chuckled. "Or you can come along, but it's rather a mess, is all." He glanced at Peril. "Lots of papers everywhere."

"I'll wait here," Peril said sadly. She drew her tail in close to herself, leaving a moon-shaped swathe in the sand.

"Lead on," Thorn said to Smolder. Sunny joined them, and they headed into yet another twisting set of corridors, these ones lined with flickering diamond-shaped mirrors that caught the sunlight from small holes in the roof and walls.

"Mother," Sunny said as they walked. "What's going on? I thought you hated NightWings. Why did you think you might care about that one?"

Thorn stopped and waited until Smolder was far ahead, picking through his keys with a bright, brassy jingling sound.

"I don't hate all NightWings," Thorn said quietly. "I mean, I'm not fond of them, and I don't trust them, as a rule. But I'm looking for one in particular, an animus dragon named Stonemover."

"Because he did something to my egg?" Sunny guessed. "Is that why?"

"Not exactly. Well, ha — I guess in a manner of speaking," Thorn said, glancing up at the skylights with an odd half smile.

Sunny stared at her. She had a pretty good idea what that look meant. "He isn't," she whispered.

"You wondered why you don't look like a regular SandWing," Thorn said.

"So it's because —" Sunny's claws trembled with shock. Of all the theories she'd ever imagined . . . yes, this one had crossed her mind, but of all the tribes she'd wondered about, never this one, never, never this one.

"Yes, Sunny," said Thorn, her voice falling like drops of water into the stillness between them. "It's because you're half NightWing."

CHAPTER 14

"But the NightWings are awful!" Sunny cried. "I don't want to be anything like them!"

"So don't be," her mother said. She started walking again, and Sunny hurried to keep up. "No one's making you be awful. And didn't you say you're friends with one?"

"Starflight is different," Sunny said.

"So was Stonemover," said Thorn. "At least, I thought so. It's been a long time."

Sunny's scales seemed suddenly too large, or maybe too small. Everything felt wrong, as if she was wearing someone else's wings. Half *NightWing,* by all the moons. "Please tell me about him. I want to know everything. I mean, I think I do. Do I? How did you fall in love with a NightWing, of all the tribes?"

Thorn folded her wings back and ducked under a low archway. "Eight years ago, I met a dragon, out in the sands not far from here, actually. His scales were like the desert sky at night and he was always nervous, in a sweet, worried way, like no other dragon I'd ever met. Remember, I grew up in the Scorpion Den. There you have to be tough and cutthroat all the time, or you're dead. I liked the way

Stonemover fidgeted and the questions he was always asking, and I liked that he wasn't pretending to be scarier and meaner than he really was. He was just himself. And he was very smart."

"He sounds a lot like Starflight," Sunny said. She wondered if that meant anything. If she was like her mother, did that mean she would end up in love with a dragon who was like her father? Was that her type? Was that her destiny, her and Starflight together?

She had many thoughts about that but no idea how to sort them out.

"He gave me this," Thorn said, touching the moonstone around her neck. "I asked him why he was here, and he said he was trying to save his tribe. I liked that, too," she went on. "He really, really cared about saving his tribe. I'd never seen loyalty before, because there was nothing like the Outclaws back then, not in the Scorpion Den. He said he was doing something essential that nobody else could do."

"Oh!" Sunny gasped. "The tunnels! He must be the animus who built the tunnels!"

Thorn looked at her curiously. "You know about that? Wait, tunnels, as in multiple tunnels?"

"Two of them," Sunny said, "as far as I know. Those are the only ones I've been through anyway."

"You *have* been around," Thorn said with a hint of admiration in her voice. "I only knew about one tunnel. He was here every day for a while, trying to pick the right spot and working up the energy to create it. So I kept coming back to bother him, and finally I guess he fell for me, too."

Who wouldn't? Sunny thought. "But," she said, "didn't anyone care that you were from two different tribes?" *If Burn thinks it's wrong, I'm guessing she's not the only dragon who feels that way.*

What if it were me and Starflight? She realized she didn't really know what dragons in the outside world thought about inter-tribe relationships. It had never come up in any scrolls, and the guardians under the mountain had never talked about it — but they never talked about families or love at all.

"No one knew except Six-Claws and my friend Armadillo," Thorn admitted. "Stonemover was my secret. Of course, I didn't have a whole lot of other friends back then."

"If they knew now," Sunny said slowly, "would you lose the Outclaws?"

Thorn stepped in front of Sunny and put up her wings to stop her in place. "Listen to me," she said. "I don't tell everyone about my past because I like my privacy, and there isn't much of that when you lead a band of outlaws. But I'm not ashamed of you or of where you came from. If other dragons have a problem with it, that's their problem. It's not against the law to be with a dragon from another tribe. It just . . . hardly ever happens, that's all. Usually each tribe keeps to itself. Which makes you rare but not illegal or taboo or horrifying or anything like that. Don't ever let any dragon make you feel like you shouldn't exist. You understand?"

Sunny nodded. She thought dragons should be allowed to love whoever they fell in love with, but at the same time, she couldn't help thinking, *Look at me, though . . . no natural*

weapons, no powers, scales that mean I don't fit into any tribe . . .
I'm kind of a walking argument for avoiding inter-tribe
relationships, aren't I?

Her mother looked as if she could read Sunny's thoughts
on her face. She brushed her front talons over Sunny's head
and horns and cupped her snout. "Sunny, you are perfect the
way you are."

"So what happened to Stonemover?" Sunny asked. She
didn't want to think about her weird looks anymore, at least
for a little while.

"He disappeared." Thorn let go of her and blew out a
breath with hints of fire in it. "I came back one day and he
was gone. Morrowseer was there instead. He said it was my
fault, whatever had happened to Stonemover, and never to
look for him or try to speak to him again. Pompous worm-
faced snob-head camel turd."

"Mother!" Sunny said, nearly shocked into laughing.

"That's what he was," Thorn growled. "Morrowseer. I
dream about wringing his neck all the time." She sighed, and
her claws scratched across the stone as if they were frus-
trated, too.

"We didn't like him much either," Sunny admitted. "So
that was it? Didn't you ever see Stonemover again?"

"No, but of course that wasn't it," Thorn said, turning to
walk on again. "I looked for him everywhere. I went through
the tunnel, but it led to the rainforest — isn't that odd?
I thought it would lead to their hidden kingdom, but no. I
searched the whole place, but there were no NightWings
there, only some very sweet, rather bewildered RainWings.

Very confusing. I never understood how that would save his tribe."

"I'll explain it to you later," Sunny said. "Did he know about me?"

"No," Thorn said. "We were fighting, a little bit, when I found out I was with egg. I planned to tell him once he apologized. But he'd gotten very strange and cold, so maybe he wasn't going to."

"That's what happens to animus dragons," Sunny said. "Whenever they use their magic, they lose a little bit of their soul, or something like that. They get meaner and colder and a little more crazy. From what I've heard anyway."

Thorn stopped again and stared down at her, worry filling her dark eyes. "I didn't know that. That's what was happening to him? I wonder if he knew. . . . He must have known. Why didn't he tell me?" She flicked her tail thoughtfully, furrowing her brow.

"So then —" Sunny prompted her.

"So then I was afraid the NightWings would come after your egg if they knew about it. That's why I buried it in the desert; that's why I asked Dune to help me look after it. I had no idea he was with the Talons of Peace — and even if I had known, I wouldn't have guessed that would make him steal my egg. Would you?"

"Here we are," Smolder called, and they realized he'd stopped in the tunnel ahead, next to a dark wooden door. He selected a delicate gold key and unlocked it, then had to shove hard to get the door open.

Sunny realized why as they squeezed inside behind him. He wasn't kidding about the mess. Piles of scrolls had toppled over to block the door, and there were papers and glass paperweights and small carved onyx lizards scattered all across the small, square room. If there had ever been any system of organization, there was no way to tell now.

"This is not Burn's favorite place," Smolder said, stepping around the piles gingerly and still knocking over several more with his tail. "I can't guarantee she's ever been in here, in fact. And our mother wasn't the most organized dragon in the world either. I tried once to put it all in order. As you can see, I was wildly successful."

"Hmm," Sunny and Thorn said, the same noncommittal noise at the same time.

Smolder gave them an amused look. "And while I was organizing, I discovered that we have a system for intercepting messages that go across the Kingdom of Sand. Well, Queen Oasis had a system. Again, I'm not sure Burn knows or cares about it. But we have dragons who pose as messengers and other dragons who are instructed to attack real messengers, and so a fair percentage of the letters sent in our realm come here instead. Presumably so that we can scan them for hints of rebellion or assassination schemes, which, clearly, we are keeping careful track of around here." He waved his claws at the disaster-strewn library. "I guess that's how it seemed like my mother always knew everything. I keep it going in case we need it one day, even though no one has time to review all this. In any case, I thought I saw one marked 'Thorn.' Which I carefully filed somewhere useful, I'm sure."

Smolder dug his talons into a pile of scrolls and Sunny realized with a start that there was a desk there, underneath the drifts of paper. "Help me look?" he suggested.

Thorn and Sunny waded in and began peering at scrolls and mini scrolls and thick papyrus notes with scrawls of black ink on them. Sunny's wings toppled over a stack of thin, scraped stone tablets that turned out to have messages carved on them as well.

"Are you sure about this?" Thorn asked after they'd searched for a few minutes. "Maybe you remembered wrong. Or maybe it wasn't anything important."

"Maybe," Smolder said, lifting a bowl filled with dried leaves and peering at the papers underneath. "I'm pretty sure I remember it looked important, though."

Sunny wished she had time to read everything in here, or a way to bring it all back to Starflight. *So many scrolls. So many scraps of dragons' lives, moments and messages caught in between sent and never received. I wonder if the world would be different if some of these letters had gotten to where they were supposed to go.*

Claws scrabbled on the stone in the hall outside, and Smolder went to the doorway to poke his head out.

"What is it?" he called as two guards rushed by.

"A wing approaching from the northeast," one of them called back. "Might be Burn."

Sunny's head snapped up and she flapped her wings at her mother. *We have to get out of here.*

"Oh, great moons, at last," Smolder said. "Sorry about this, you two."

"Sorry about what?" Sunny asked, turning toward him just as he jumped out of the room and slammed the door on them.

"NO!" Thorn roared.

Sunny leaped over the scrolls and grabbed the door handle, but she could hear the key turning in the lock already. She threw herself against the wood, but it was solid and only bruised her shoulder.

"Smolder, don't do this!" she shouted through the door. "Don't give us to Burn! Please!"

"I can't let you waltz out of here," he said, his voice faint and muffled. "I saw what Burn did to my brothers. I know how to stay alive. Like I said, I'm sorry."

Sunny pounded on the door. "At least give us a fair chance to fight her! Smolder!"

But she could hear his tail slithering away into the palace.

He was gone.

Leaving her and her mother locked in, trapped and waiting for Burn.

CHAPTER 15

Thorn picked up an onyx lizard and hurled it across the library. "Blood-red eggs and fireballs!" she shouted. "I'm going to flay that dragon alive!"

"Won't your Outclaws save us?" Sunny asked, wading through the papers to the desk. She ran her talons all over it, but there were no drawers and no place for a hidden extra key.

"If they're smart, they'll fly for the hills the moment they hear that Burn is coming," said Thorn. "They'll expect me to run and meet them at the Scorpion Den. Act smart, stay alive, stick together but don't be an idiot — those are our basic rules." She picked up a scroll and ripped it furiously down the middle.

"All right, so we do that," Sunny said. "We figure a way out of here. I know we can." She twisted to look around the library, searching for anything she could use to pick the lock. Not that she had any idea how to do that, but she'd read about someone doing it in a scroll once.

There were no windows, so no way to call out for help. The light came from a small chandelier of hanging oil lamps high above them. The ceiling was tall but made of solid stone. The door was the only way out.

"What about your SkyWing friend?" Thorn said. "Might she guess what's happened and come looking for us?"

Sunny shifted her wings and shook her head. "I doubt it. If she hears Burn is coming, I'm sure she'll free Scarlet and run, too." She stepped back and stared at the door. The *wooden* door. "But if she could burn down this door, we should be able to do the same thing, right?"

"Wait!" Thorn cried as Sunny drew in a breath. She spread her claws at the mess around them. "It's not safe. If you set the door on fire, it could spread to the papers in here. The whole room could be in flames in a heartbeat, and we'd burn to death before we made it out."

That was a horribly good point. Sunny guessed that that had occurred to Smolder as well. He was more cunning than he looked, perhaps as cunning as Blister. He'd also cleverly found a way to separate them from Peril.

"Well," Sunny said, "I suspect I'd rather burn to death than end up stuffed in Burn's collection. But I think I can do it carefully — I'm pretty good at aiming small flames. Let me try, all right?"

Thorn hesitated, then nodded. Sunny was pleased. She was pretty sure her friends wouldn't have trusted her to do anything this risky.

She swept papers away from the door with her tail until it was surrounded by a half circle of clear stone floor. Then she leaned forward, opened her mouth, and hissed, letting fire build up in the back of her throat. It felt fierce and hot, like she'd swallowed the sun, and she never liked using it for long. Aiming carefully, she breathed a small jet of flame in an arc around the lock.

The thick wood turned black where the fire touched it, and smoke curled from the gash left behind. Nothing burst into flames . . . not yet anyway.

Sunny did the same thing again, trying to trace the same line, over and over, four more times, until she saw a glimmer of light on the other side. She jammed her claws into the blackened wood and twisted them around, digging and slashing until the whole lock came loose and thumped into her talons.

"I did it!" she whispered to her mother as the door swung a few inches open.

Sunny turned and found her mother holding a folded square of thick papyrus paper, with the word *Thorn* scrawled across the front in black ink.

"There *is* a letter for me," said Thorn curiously. "He wasn't lying about that part. How odd." She flipped it over and opened it.

"Mother, we really have to go," Sunny said, but her voice trailed off as she saw the expression on her mother's face. "Mother? Thorn?"

"It's from him," Thorn said, glancing up at Sunny. "From your father. Listen: 'Dearest Thorn. I can't keep doing this. I can't use my powers for the NightWings any longer, or I'll lose myself completely. So I'm running away, and I'd like you to come, too. Meet me at Jade Mountain. I'll wait for you as long as I have to. I love you. Stonemover.'" Her voice trailed off.

"Jade Mountain!" Sunny cried. "There's supposed to be a dragon who lives there — maybe it's Stonemover! Oh, maybe he's still waiting for you, after all these years! Isn't that romantic?"

"That frog-faced blob of camel spit!" Thorn shouted abruptly, making Sunny jump. She crumpled the paper in her front talons, threw it to the ground, and smashed it with one of her feet. "All these years? He's alive, he's not a prisoner, and he's known exactly where I was this whole time, but he never once came to look for me or tried to contact me?"

"Well," Sunny faltered, "maybe he thought you got his letter but didn't want to be with him."

"So send me another letter!" Thorn cried. "Try a little harder! Don't be a jerboa-head!" She stomped past Sunny and into the hall, checking in both directions. "Come on, let's run for it. I saw a courtyard this way."

They bolted down the long stone corridor and swerved to the right at the end. Sunny could see a patch of blue sky up ahead, beyond a wall of dark red columns. She started to unfold her wings as she ran.

"The prisoners!" a voice shouted behind her. "Prisoners escaping!"

Sunny's heart plunged.

"Uh-oh," Thorn muttered. They skidded up to the courtyard and found several SandWing soldiers milling about there, preparing their weapons as if they were getting ready for battle.

The soldiers all turned and stared at them.

"Go!" Thorn shouted, flaring her wings. Startled, Sunny hurtled into the sky. One of the soldiers roared and leaped after her; she felt the wind of his talons slashing just short of her tail. She twisted away and looked back in time to see her mother blast the soldier in the face with a burst of flames. He shrieked and plummeted to the ground.

The other soldiers were slower to react, and faster to catch on fire when Thorn blasted the rest of them as well.

She soared up out of the shrieking and mayhem and smoke and circled Sunny. "What are you waiting for?" she called. Thorn banked around and headed for the main court-yard. Sunny followed close behind her.

"I hope they'll be all right," Sunny said, glancing back at the flames.

"I hope *we'll* be all right," Thorn said. "Oh no! Moonlickers! Six-Claws, you idiot!" She swerved suddenly sideways and Sunny saw what she was aiming for: a cluster of battling SandWings on the stones below, with Six-Claws and Qibli in the center of it.

She heard Six-Claws roar, "Where is Thorn?" And then Thorn snatched a loose brick from the nearest wall and lobbed it past his head, clocking the dragon behind him in the snout.

"I'm right here, snails-for-brains!" she bellowed. "Let's go!"

Without a moment's hesitation, Six-Claws and Qibli and twenty other dragons leaped aloft, kicking off their opponents and swinging their deadly tails wildly behind them.

"Where are the others?" Thorn called to Six-Claws as they all veered south, flying as fast as they could.

"Fled already," Six-Claws said tersely. "Cowards."

"Following orders," Thorn reminded him. "As you should have done."

"We weren't leaving without you," he growled.

"Yeah," Qibli piped up. "I didn't trust that Smolder dragon. I knew there'd be trouble! Didn't I say so? Can't trust a royal, that's what I always say."

"Because you've met so many royal dragons in your life, have you?" Six-Claws demanded.

Thorn shook her head, but didn't argue, saving their breath for flying.

Sunny risked a glance back, but nobody was chasing them yet. She guessed the stronghold was disorganized chaos right now, with no one sure whether they were still in a surrendered stalemate, whether Peril was still lurking around to kill them all, whether it was really Burn on her way, or whether Smolder was still in charge.

She could see the wing of dragons in the distance, approaching the stronghold — too close, only minutes away from finding out what had happened — and she was pretty sure the hulking shape in the lead was truly Burn.

Her eyes scanned the horizon. Had Peril made it out safely? Or would Peril always be safe, because no one could get near her with talons like hers?

She spotted two small shapes winging away to the north, glinting orange and gold in the sunlight. Peril and Queen Scarlet, now free. Sunny shuddered. If Queen Scarlet really did know where the dragonets were, how long did they have before she came for them? What kind of revenge had she planned, all those nights in the horrible tower?

A feeling of dread climbed into her chest and squeezed; for a moment she couldn't breathe.

Clay — Tsunami — Glory — and poor wounded Starflight.

"Mother!" she called, beating her wings to catch up to Thorn.

Thorn grinned toothily at her. "I've been called lots of things in my life, but that's the strangest and the best at the same time."

Sunny brushed her mother's wingtip with her own. "I have to return to my friends," she said. "I need to warn them — I'm afraid they're in danger, now that Queen Scarlet is free."

"Probably," Thorn agreed. She hesitated. "Couldn't I send a messenger instead? I wanted to bring you back to the Scorpion Den — I still haven't heard about your life and what you've been doing all these years."

"I know," Sunny said. She wished she could stay with her mother, with those warm strong wings close by to keep her safe. For the first time, she could imagine life without the prophecy. She could be a normal dragon, living in the Scorpion Den with her mother instead of worrying about saving the whole world. But prophecy or not, her friends were her real life, her whole life. She couldn't leave them in danger. "But this is really important. I'll come back to you soon. Or — you could come with me?"

Thorn sighed and shook her head. "There might be retaliation from the stronghold. I have to fortify the Den, prepare my dragons, make sure everyone's safe."

That was true. Thorn had risked a lot, bringing her Outclaws into this dangerous rescue mission. Sunny touched her wingtip again. "Thank you for coming to get me."

"Always," Thorn said fiercely.

"I'll see you soon," Sunny said, tilting her wings.

"Sunny!" Thorn called. "Be careful!"

"I will," Sunny called back, already soaring toward the mountains.

"No, I mean —" Thorn swooped out of the formation for a moment, catching up to her and circling her in the air. "I mean, if you go see your father. I know you're thinking about it." She nodded at the line of mountains, where the jagged peak of Jade Mountain towered darkly over the rest. "Be careful with Stonemover. If all that is true about being an animus . . . well, I saw him do a lot of magic. We don't know how much soul he has left."

"Are you going to go see him?" Sunny asked.

"Someday," Thorn said with a small flicker of anger in her eyes. "Apparently he's in no hurry, so I'll take care of my dragons first."

"I should do that, too," Sunny said. "With my dragons, I mean."

Thorn smiled at her. "See you soon, daughter."

Sunny watched as the Outclaws soared away across the desert, all their wingbeats together stirring up small sandstorms below them. Then she oriented herself toward the mountains again and flew, beating her wings as fast as they would move.

She couldn't use the tunnel to the rainforest; she couldn't risk the trip past Burn's stronghold to get to it. It would be safer, if longer, to go over the mountains. But she should have a head start on Peril and Scarlet, who had flown the other way and who didn't know about the tunnels. *I hope,* she thought. *I don't think there's any way they* could *know.*

Her breath seemed to come more easily with every wing-beat, even as the forest and the mountains came closer and closer. She was leaving the desert — but she was going back to her friends at last.

— CHAPTER 16 —

The plan was to go straight to the rainforest.

As tempted as Sunny was by the idea of meeting her father, she was more worried about her friends. She needed to get back and warn them, fast.

But the weather had other plans.

A gale-force wind howled down the mountains that night, carrying with it the worst storm Sunny had ever been caught in. Not that she'd encountered many, living in caves her whole life — but there was that one hurricane in the Kingdom of the Sea, and Sunny was pretty sure this was worse.

Or maybe it only felt worse because she was alone and caught outside with no shelter and rapidly becoming very, very wet.

The rain pelted in her eyes and dragged down her wings, while the wind kept trying to slam her into the cliffs, and the whole time, thunder roared as though the clouds were playing drums on the mountaintops. Lightning cracked terrifyingly close to her wings, and Sunny thought, *I won't be able to save anyone if I end up as a fiery heap in a ravine.*

She veered toward the peak of Jade Mountain, the one solid thing she could identify in the driving storm.

Will he be there?

Will he want to meet me?

Will he be scary, or awful, or dangerous? Will he be like Orca, the crazy animus SeaWing who killed all those dragonets?

She wished she had Clay or Tsunami with her. That would have been better, if she could have gone back to the rainforest first and gotten one of them to come along, so she didn't have to meet her mysterious, powerful, potentially homicidal father alone.

But the storm drove her on as if it had talons of its own, dragging her up the mountain with shrieking fury.

Soaking wet, exhausted, and shivering with anxiety, Sunny finally crash-landed in a cave high up on the mountain's south side. She stumbled to a stop, scraping her scales painfully on the rocky floor, and shook out her wings in a flurry of droplets.

It was dark inside, and Sunny thought it was unlikely that she'd have accidentally wandered into the exact cave where her father lived. Surely there were other caves all over the mountain. But the darkness made her uneasy, and cautiously she breathed out a plume of fire.

Nothing. An empty stone cavern loomed around her, not that different from the ones she'd grown up in. She breathed more fire, letting it warm her from the inside, and searched the cave until she found a thick branch that had been swept inside by the storm. She set it ablaze and held it up to use as a torch.

The flickering light revealed a gap in the rocks in the back corner. When she investigated, she found a sort of natural tunnel that seemed to lead farther into the mountain, to a cave system that probably ran all the way through it.

Sunny hesitated, leaning against the stone wall. Should she rest here and fly on in the morning? Maybe she could leave unnoticed and come back when she had reinforcements.

But how could I get this close to my father and not try to see him?

She thought of Peril and Kestrel, and how Peril had thought they'd have more time to get to know each other. *You never know what might happen.*

That decided her. Holding up the torch, she slipped into the gap and started down the rocky slope beyond.

She wandered for what felt like a long time, marking the walls with her claws whenever she came to a fork in the tunnels. She found caves dripping with stalactites, clambered over rocks like giant bubbles, flew over a dark pool with no ripples where her torch reflected eerily across the glassy surface.

It felt familiar, being underground like this. She wondered if other dragons — especially other SandWings — would be more unnerved by these surroundings. But this was so similar to the small, enclosed world she grew up in. She almost expected to turn a corner and find the study cave, with the map spread against one wall and scrolls piled in the corner and her friends arguing over who would play Blaze when they acted out the history of the war.

And then . . . she stopped in a narrow passageway with a low, craggy ceiling.

Was that breathing?

She held her own breath and listened.

It sounds like breathing.

Air rasped quietly somewhere, in and out, as if something large were sitting concealed in shadows . . . not too far away . . . maybe even watching her.

Sunny's scales crawled and she clutched the torch closer. *Do not panic. Listen.*

After a long moment, she realized that the breathing was even and rhythmic. *That's not the sound of something lurking; that's the sound of a dragon sleeping.*

She crept up a passageway toward the noise. *I think it's this way.*

Sharp edges of rocks caught on her tail and stabbed at her feet as she climbed. Closer . . . and closer . . .

The torchlight flickered suddenly, dipping and swaying, and then Sunny felt it as well: a gust of wind, whistling down the tunnel from far away.

She lifted the torch higher and saw that the tunnel widened into a cave only a few paces ahead.

At first, as she edged closer, the cave looked empty . . . but then the firelight reflected off something black and glossy in the shadows against the back wall.

Scales. Black scales, rising and falling in sleep. It was a NightWing for sure.

Sunny stopped and stared at the slumbering dragon.

Is that my father?

He was bigger than Thorn, but not enormous, nowhere near the size of Morrowseer or Burn. Deep lines were etched into his face, so he looked as if he were in pain even in his sleep. His talons were curled awkwardly into stiff shapes and his tail flopped heavily along the ground behind him, barely moving as he breathed, as though it were made of stone.

Sunny took a quick breath in, and then stepped closer.

It wasn't just his tail. Other parts of the dragon — his back legs, his shoulders, the edges of his wings — looked heavier and thicker than a normal dragon's scales.

Like he's actually turning into stone. Is that possible?

She lifted the torch and peered at the section of tail closest to her. The black scales looked like dark pebbles here, sinking into the skin beneath.

She was so preoccupied, studying this odd phenomenon, that it took her a moment to realize that the dragon's eyes had opened, and he was staring back at her.

"Oh!" she gasped, jumping back. "I'm sorry! I didn't — I mean — I didn't mean to wake you — I was — the storm —"

"I don't bite," he said in a deep, serious voice.

"Oh," Sunny said again. "Well. That's good. You mean you don't bite other dragons, right? Like me? Are you being reassuring?"

He blinked slowly at her. "I don't bite . . . other dragons."

"Great," said Sunny, not feeling very reassured. It was unsettling how he hadn't moved a muscle of his body as he spoke to her; even his jaws seemed to hinge very slowly open for him to talk. "So . . . hi. I'm Sunny."

He didn't answer.

She waited a moment, then said, "Are you Stonemover?"

That seemed to surprise him a little, if the tiny flicker of movement in his brow meant anything. "Yes."

It is *my father. It's really him. He's still alive and right here in front of me.*

And he doesn't look crazy and homicidal. He just looks . . . sad.

Stonemover blinked again. "How did the Talons find out my name?"

"I'm not from the Talons," she said. "Do the Talons come here? Oh, right, Kestrel said we could send her a message through you. I guess that would be useful when you're an underground movement and never know where you'll have to hide."

"True," he said. "After all, I am not going anywhere."

"Oh," Sunny said, glancing at his scales. "Because — what happened to you?"

"You are nosier than the Talons," he observed, but without any anger in his voice. "It is my animus curse."

"Really?" Sunny said. "This happened to you when you used your magic? I thought you'd lose your, you know, soul or something, not . . . this." She waved her claws at the petrified scales weighing him down.

"I turned the magic on itself," he said. "The curse appears in my scales now instead of taking my soul." He sighed through his nose, a sad, windy sound with drifts of smoke. "Too late anyway."

"Too late for what?" Sunny asked.

"My soul." He managed to turn his head a fraction toward her with an eerie creaking sound. His dark eyes were as still and unreadable as the underground cave lake. "The things I have done."

"You mean like building the tunnels," Sunny said, and now there was a definite flash of surprise all the way through his eyes. Then it faded, and his eyes narrowed as he examined her from horns to talons. It might have been scary once, his expression, except that the rest of him was so pathetic and sad. He could hardly even move. Sunny didn't feel afraid of him at all.

"*Who* are you?" he asked.

"I'm —" Well, this felt awkward, just throwing it out there midconversation. But how else could she tell him? Was there an easy, not shocking way to break this kind of news? "OK. The truth is, I'm your daughter. Thorn is my mother. I only just found her, just — wow, just yesterday — no, two days ago — and she told me about you and —" Sunny talked on, not sure what to think of the expressions darting across Stonemover's face: confusion, suspicion, hope, dismay, maybe anger? "And I wanted to meet you — I hope that's — I hope you — well, I know it's weird, because she never got a chance to tell you about me, so —"

"We had eggs?" he rasped.

"You had me," Sunny said. "An egg, one dragonet. Just me." She looked down at her talons. "Mother wanted to tell you. But she never got your note. She didn't know you were here until she found it yesterday. She's been looking everywhere for you."

Her father sighed through his nose and closed his eyes. "I thought she'd given up on me."

"She might have now," Sunny said, trying to prompt more of a response. Why didn't he care more? Why hadn't he tried harder? She felt a wave of sympathy for her mother. "Why didn't you go look for her?"

"I'm not the right dragon for Thorn," he said. "Perhaps I never was."

"*She* obviously thought you were," Sunny pointed out. "She really worried about you."

He sighed again. *He sighs a lot,* Sunny thought, wishing she could poke something into his nose to make him stop. "There's nothing I can do. I did all the wrong things . . . a long, long time ago . . . and nothing can change that."

Something suddenly scrabbled in the dark nearby and Sunny nearly leaped onto Stonemover's back in terror.

But when she swung the torch around and then down, the light reflected off tiny little eyes and pointed ears and wet russet fur.

It was a fox, sauntering into their cave as bold as anything. Sunny realized it had come down another passageway, and she could feel the wind coming from that direction as well. *The passage must lead to an exit out to the mountainside.* The fox carried a dead squirrel in its jaws, and it gave Sunny a scornful look, as if it certainly didn't expect her to dare pick a fight with someone as tough as him.

"Shoo," Sunny said sternly. "Go find yourself another cave."

"Oh, this is dinner," Stonemover said. He hinged his jaw open, and to Sunny's wonder, the fox trotted over and dropped the squirrel right into his mouth. It stepped back and gave Sunny another haughty look as Stonemover began to chew.

"Wow," Sunny said. *Are foxes intelligent, too, like scavengers? What if all animals are smarter than we think they are? Is there going to be any prey left that I won't feel bad about eating?* "How did you train it to do that?"

Stonemover waited until he'd swallowed, and then he said, "I didn't. I enchanted him."

Sunny frowned at the fox. "You mean with animus magic? That only works on *things*. Not animals."

"Turns out it works on animals," said Stonemover, "if you're desperate and try hard enough."

She folded her wings in and shivered. "That's creepy."

"Dinner doesn't mind," he replied, and it took her a moment to figure it out.

"You call the *fox* Dinner?" she said.

"Why not?" His shoulder moved an infinitesimal amount, the smallest of shrugs.

"Because that's peculiar," she said. "And really creepy for him, if he knew what you were saying."

"I didn't think about it," he said. "I've never introduced him to anyone before. Anyway, I only enchanted him to bring me food every few days; he still has a fine ordinary life as a fox, I'm sure."

As if in answer to this, Dinner shook himself vigorously, scattering water all over Sunny, and then trotted out of the cave again.

"I mean," Stonemover concluded, "I had to do something, or I would have starved."

"Hmm," Sunny said. She didn't like the thought of any dragon using magic to command a living thing. *Would animus magic work on something bigger than a fox?*

She didn't want to follow that thought to its possible conclusion.

"I can't believe I have a daughter," Stonemover said, and Sunny felt a little warmer toward him, hearing the sadness in his voice. "I used to dream — I would think about what our dragonets might look like, if Thorn and I ever — but I thought it was too late."

"I bet you didn't picture me," Sunny said ruefully. "I don't have the SandWing tail barb and I also don't have any cool NightWing powers. I always thought maybe I looked weird because of the prophecy, somehow, but —"

He would have sat up if he could, she could tell. His head twitched a little closer to her. His breath smelled like squirrel. "Prophecy?"

"About the dragonets saving the world and stopping the war," Sunny said. "You know. You must know."

"Yes," he mused.

"I'm one of them," she said. " 'Hidden alone from the rival queens,' that's me. It's kind of a long story."

"But —" he started, and paused.

And then Sunny *was* scared, because the look in his eyes was the look of news she knew she didn't want, and it was righteousness and pity and truth-is-the-important-thing and she didn't want it, she didn't want him to say it.

"Stop, don't," she blurted, but at the same time he said:

"But don't you know? The prophecy isn't real."

— CHAPTER 17 —

"Hmm," Stonemover said, studying her expression. "You did know. You know it's fake."

"Well, I've heard that," Sunny said. The walls felt as if they were tilting in toward her. She curled her claws and twitched her tail, avoiding his eyes. "That's what Morrowseer said. But why should we trust him?"

Stonemover managed to look faintly amused. "Morrowseer wouldn't make himself seem any less powerful if he could ever avoid it. He must have been forced to tell you the truth, for some reason."

"He was manipulating us, like always," Sunny said. "But just because I don't like him doesn't mean the prophecy couldn't be real."

"Oh, little dragon," Stonemover said, and she got the feeling he'd already forgotten her name. "I promise you the prophecy is not real. I was there when they came up with it. I was also there when the NightWing scribes were ordered to write more about our so-called powers, building them up in every scroll, every story. Queen Battlewinner planned that carefully. But no NightWing has had any power to see the future or read minds in over a hundred years, if anyone ever did. That is the truth."

Sunny wanted to throw things and yell like her mother did when she was angry. "NightWings," she growled. "You guys make it really, really hard to like you. Why are you telling me this? You obviously haven't told the Talons, or everyone would know."

"Because I suspect I am dying," he said with a dry cough, "and someone should know. If not my own daughter, then who?"

"Well, hooray," Sunny said. "Lucky me." She tucked her tail around her talons and hunched her wings up. After a moment, she said, "Really? Are you really dying?"

"I'm always dying," he answered, which also made Sunny want to poke him in the nose. She honestly had no idea why her mother had ever liked this dragon.

But at least he's telling me the truth. That's more than I can say for most of the grown-up dragons I've ever known. She tried to push down the bitterness she felt about NightWings and all their lies; she tried to look at just Stonemover, her father, and see him as his own dragon, not one of a tribe.

He's really sad.

Imagine if I had been born with animus powers into a terrible place like the NightWing island. The queen must have used him from the moment they found out what he could do. He never had a choice about what to do with his life.

Maybe nobody does.

Even though I want to end the war so badly, maybe there's nothing I can do.

The prophecy was really fake. Her life was really a lie.

She was really not special, and she was really not destined to save the world.

She looked at her father, whose eyes had closed. His breathing was starting to slow down, as if he were falling asleep again.

"Can I stay here tonight?" she asked.

"Please do," he said quietly.

Sunny blew out the torch and curled up in a ball in the warmest corner of the cave, across from Stonemover's petrified scales. She rested her chin on her front talons, feeling like her own scales were made of stone, too, heavy and exhausting to lug around. She wished she could wake up back in the cave under the mountain two months ago, before any of this had happened, when she still believed in the prophecy, their destiny, a wonderful future, and perfect parents waiting out there for all of them.

Her eyes closed, and her sadness drifted away into sleep.

Sunny was back in the stronghold, wandering through Burn's weirdling collection, except instead of a tower, it had become an endless maze of increasingly creepy oddities. Every time she turned a corner, a new disturbing thing lurched toward her.

She realized Flower was sitting on her shoulder, holding on to her neck like one of the rainforest sloths and chattering quietly to herself.

This was comforting only for a moment, and then a headless gray dragon suddenly loomed out of a shadowy doorway, tottering at her and splattering blood from its claws.

Sunny leaped aside, pressing her back against the wall. She closed her eyes.

Stop. Stop. Don't be scared. This is just a dream. You're safe now, far away from Burn.

She imagined the bright rolling sand of the desert, trying to change her dream surroundings by force of will. After a few moments, she felt the warmth of sunlight on her face, and she opened her eyes.

It had worked. She was standing on the desert sand . . . and right in front of her was a scavenger.

Sunny started back with a yelp of surprise, and so did the scavenger. But it didn't turn and run, and it didn't scream. It just stood there and blinked at her with enormous brown eyes.

She reached up to her shoulder. Flower was still there. This scavenger in front of her was not Flower — Sunny had never seen it before.

Aw, Sunny thought. *It's so cute.* She guessed it was female, like Flower, although this one seemed smaller and younger. Seeing Flower . . . that's probably why she was dreaming about scavengers, although it was surprising to dream up one she'd never seen before. A long, dark mane flowed from the scavenger's head down to the middle of her back, and she had the same adorable little nose and monkey features as Smolder's pet, including the long, thin, clever paws with no claws on the end.

Sunny tilted her head at the scavenger's paws. Wait. She was holding something — something about the size of an orange, which caught the desert sunlight with a shimmer of blue.

While Starflight had been trapped with the NightWings, he'd found a way to communicate with his friends by dropping into their dreams using an old animus-touched sapphire called a dreamvisitor. Apparently there were three of them out there in the world somewhere, and he had found one on the NightWing island. Glory had explained it to Sunny and Clay and Tsunami, rolling her eyes as if she couldn't believe they'd forgotten that one sentence in one scroll they'd studied years ago. Sometimes she could be as bad as Starflight, although nobody would ever dare tell her that.

Sunny took a step toward the scavenger, but she didn't even flinch back. Instead, she took a step toward Sunny, holding out her free paw. She pointed at Flower and chattered something.

Am I not dreaming? Is this real?

Could a scavenger possibly have a dreamvisitor? How would it have gotten a dragon jewel like that?

She inhaled sharply, flaring her wings. *The only possible way: by stealing it. From the queen of the SandWings, twenty years ago.*

"Where did you get that?" she asked, flicking her tail at the jewel in the scavenger's paw.

The scavenger looked down at the dreamvisitor. Her eyes widened, and the desert sand behind her suddenly went blurry. Sunny caught a glimpse of black shapes around her, towering against a background of trees in moonlight.

With a muffled yelp, the scavenger gave Sunny a fierce look, clutched the sapphire to her chest, and vanished.

"Wait!" Sunny shouted. "I need that treasure!" She pounced on the spot where the scavenger had been, digging frantically in the sand. But of course it was gone, popping out of her dream as abruptly as it had popped in. And there was no way to get her back — the scavenger was the one who had the dreamvisitor, and therefore controlled where she went and who she saw.

But why would she visit me? And how? I thought you could only visit the dreams of dragons you've met before.

Or seen . . . she must have seen me somewhere, sometime while we were traveling around Pyrrhia. Although I'm sure I didn't see her.

Sunny sat down, sweeping her claws through the sand.

So if I can figure out where, maybe I can find her — and the stolen SandWing treasure.

She closed her eyes and concentrated, trying to bring back those blurry dark shapes that she'd glimpsed behind the scavenger, just for a moment. They'd looked familiar. And there had been trees, too — so it wasn't the Kingdom of the Sea, or the Sky Kingdom. Were there scavengers in the rainforest?

The trees didn't look tall enough.

Sunny's eyes snapped open. *The forest between the mountains and the desert. Where I saw the ruins of the old scavenger den.*

The little scavenger was in the ruins.

Which means now I know where to start looking.

Ice Kingdom

Sky Kingdom

Burn's
Stronghold

Under the Mountain

Kingdom of
Sand

Scorpion Den

Jade Mountain

PART THREE

THE EYE OF ONYX

— CHAPTER 18 —

It was still raining when Sunny woke up the next morning. She could hear the pitter-patter at the far end of the passageway, and the breeze that gusted toward them smelled damp and fresh. But it came along with dim morning light, and the wind wasn't as cold or fierce as it had been the night before. She felt sure that the worst of the storm had passed.

She stood up and stretched, reaching her wings as wide and high as they would go and pressing her talons out in front of her.

Everything felt less awful again, somehow.

Her father was still asleep. Sunny hesitated, half tempted to leave without saying good-bye, but she couldn't do that to him.

"Stonemover?" She picked up the burnt stick she'd used for a torch and nudged a part of his shoulder that didn't look entirely made of stone yet.

"Mmmph?" he answered. His eyes slowly peeled open.

"I have to go," she said.

"Already?" He sighed, this time long and smoky so she had to step back to breathe. "Can't you stay? It's really . . . quiet here."

Really lonely, you mean, she thought.

"I'm sorry," she said, then added with a burst of excitement, "I think I've figured out how to end the war. I mean, I think I found a clue, sort of. At least I have an idea."

Stonemover's eyes were dark and puzzled. "But . . ." he said. "But why? The prophecy isn't real, remember?"

"That doesn't matter," she said. "I'm not doing it because a prophecy told me to. If I can stop the war, I think I should. It would be nice if someone else would take care of it, but maybe that's what everyone else is hoping, and maybe someone just has to do it."

"Hmm," said Stonemover. "Somehow I suspect it won't be that easy."

"Maybe it will be," Sunny said brightly. "I'll find the Eye of Onyx and give it to one of the queens, and that's all it'll take."

"Ah," said Stonemover. "That'll never work."

"I thought you might say that," Sunny said. "Don't worry, I'll come back and tell you all about it when it totally *does* work." She smiled at him, and she thought she saw the slightest movement of a maybe-smile twitching around the corners of his mouth.

"I wish —" he said, then stopped.

I don't even know where to begin with wishing, Sunny thought. *I wish the Talons hadn't taken me? No, because then I wouldn't have grown up with my friends. I wish I'd been born looking like a real SandWing? No, because then I wouldn't be me, and I wouldn't want to be anyone else.*

Maybe I wish the prophecy were real.

I wish I knew for sure that this would work.

Sunny shook out her wings. "Just wish me luck," she said. "I'll see you soon."

She could sense Stonemover watching her gloomily as she headed up the passage, toward the light and the quiet rain. She wondered what her mother would think of him now, how much he had changed since they knew each other.

None of my friends got to know both of their parents. I'm lucky they're both still alive — and I'm lucky they're not that bad.

But now that I've met both of them, I know which one I want to be like.

I'm not going to sit in a cave and mope because things aren't the way I want them to be. I'm going to go make them happen, the way Thorn started the Outclaws and searched for me. If she'd given up, how would we ever have found each other? She'd have been just another dragon in the Scorpion Den, and maybe our paths would never have crossed.

The passage ended in a shallow cave overlooking the mountain range below. The sun was rising in the east, which was also the direction of the rainforest. But the forest with the scavenger was to the west.

Do I have time? What if Scarlet gets to the rainforest before I do?

Sunny hesitated with her claws gripping the ledge and her wings outspread. Maybe Scarlet had been bluffing about knowing where the dragonets were. How would she guess they were in the rainforest, if no one else had found them there? Maybe she was only trying to scare Sunny.

Well, she did a good job of that.

Too bad I don't have the Obsidian Mirror anymore. It'd be useful to know what Scarlet is doing. Maybe I should go warn my friends and then come back.

But what if the scavenger leaves the ruins? This could be my only chance to find the Eye of Onyx and stop the war.

It was a detour, but she had to risk it.

She leaned forward and plummeted down the mountainside, soaring west toward the scavenger ruins and, she hoped, the missing treasure.

The burnt village was easy to spot from the air: a dark gash, stark and black against the surrounding greenery. Sunny spiraled toward it, studying the trees with her sharp eyes and looking for any movement that might be a scavenger.

Nothing so far, but it was late afternoon and Sunny wasn't even sure whether scavengers were normally nocturnal or preferred the day.

She landed lightly in a cloud of ash that smelled like a wood fire. The ruins were still and deserted, and Sunny wondered uneasily if she had been wrong. What if the scavenger wasn't here? Or what if she'd been here but was now gone, and Sunny had missed her?

Think positive.

She paced the entire perimeter of the den, searching every structure with even half a wall still standing. Every noise made her freeze and listen, her head cocked to the side, but it was always squirrels in the nearby trees or other little creatures scurrying in the underbrush. Which reminded her that she was hungry, so she caught a mouse and ate it, sitting on the old bell platform at the center of the village.

Well. There was no one here now, but that didn't mean she should give up. Maybe the scavenger would return later. Except she probably wouldn't if she spotted a dragon prowling through the ruins . . . but then again, if she'd stolen the treasure from the SandWings, that meant she had to be fairly bold and reasonably stupid.

Still, Sunny decided to hide, just in case.

She found a tree with thick, overlapping leaves and wide branches and settled into the crook of the trunk, keeping a sharp eye on the burnt village. From here she had a good view of most of it, and she spent the rest of the day watching and waiting.

By nightfall, as one of the moons climbed cheerily up the sky, Sunny had begun to doubt herself again. *I should just go. I don't have time to sit here — I have to get to my friends in the rainforest.*

Besides, if she comes during the night, I won't be able to see her anyway. If only I could see in the dark like Tsunami.

She dug her claws into the bark, forcing herself to be patient. If the Eye of Onyx was nearby, it was worth waiting for. Once she had that, she'd have a way to end the war.

Which won't stop Scarlet from wanting to kill us, of course.

She stared hard at the village, now a shadowy mass of odd lumps and pointy shapes, overlaid with the silvery moonlight.

Was that —?

Something was moving in the forest outside the ruins. A small light bobbed up and down not far from the ground, blinking in and out as it went behind trees and bushes.

Now her ears could pick out the sound of footsteps. They were very quiet, but here and there a twig snapped, and she recognized the noise of paws brushing through leaves.

Softly she unwound her tail from the branch and slithered down the trunk. She crept silently through the dark village toward the light as it left the trees and floated toward a set of collapsed stone stairs, if Sunny remembered right from her earlier tour of the ruins.

There were two of them.

Two scavengers, one of them with short, fluffy hair — but the other one's hair was long and she moved in a quick, confident way. Sunny was sure it was the same scavenger from her dream.

She waited until they climbed onto the steps and sat down. They were warbling in low tones that sounded like some of the rainforest monkeys, and the one with the long hair sometimes waved her paws as if she were drawing a picture in the air.

Flower did the same thing, Sunny remembered.

Now, the trick would be to approach them and get the treasure without scaring them off — and without getting attacked. They didn't *look* like they were carrying any sharp little weapons, but you never knew with scavengers, according to the scrolls. And if these two had stolen the treasure, that meant they'd killed Queen Oasis, so they could be very dangerous.

She paused in the shadows for a moment, considering, and finally decided a direct approach was the only option.

"Don't run away," she said, stepping out in front of them and spreading her wings.

Both scavengers yelled with fright and promptly tried to run away.

Sunny leaped into the air and landed in front of the scavenger from her dream. That was the one she wanted. "I *said*, don't run away!" Sunny barked, even though she knew the scavenger couldn't understand her. "Hey! Come back!" She flung her tail out and tripped the little creature as it bolted in another direction. "I won't eat you, I promise!" She pounced and managed to trap the scavenger between her front talons.

The second scavenger suddenly came running out of the ruins and threw something at her. This turned out to be the tiny lamp they'd been carrying, which bounced off Sunny's scales but left a stinging burn where it hit.

"OUCH!" Sunny roared. "All right, I *might* eat you if you keep doing that!" She swept her tail around and knocked the second scavenger over, then picked up the first scavenger and hopped a step back, growling.

The scavenger between her claws was kicking and wriggling and being generally impossible. Sunny was trying really hard to hold it gently, but it was like hanging on to a moonbeam.

And the other scavenger was already struggling back upright, probably to attack her again.

Sunny looked around and spotted a building that hadn't burned as badly as the rest of them. Two of the walls still stood, forming a corner made of heavy round stones. The walls were as tall as Sunny's head — too tall for a little scavenger to jump off, unless they were more like frogs than Sunny thought they were.

She deposited the first scavenger on top of the wall, then whipped around, seized the second scavenger, and stuck him up there as well. They both made little yelping sounds and clung to the stones.

"There," Sunny said. "Now you *can't* run away." She sat down and folded her wings back. "So. Where is the treasure?"

Their big eyes stared back at her. Sunny reached for a branch, set it on fire, and stuck it upright in the ground, so she could see them better.

The scavenger from her dream pointed at Sunny and chattered something at the other scavenger. *If she were my pet, I could give her a name,* Sunny thought. *Maybe something like Holler, for all that noise she was making. And the other one could be Fluffy, for his hair.*

She smiled. Holler and Fluffy. Totally cute. But also maybe totally responsible for this whole war, if they were the ones who stole the treasure. They looked a little small to be treasure thieves, but then, all scavengers were too small to be trying something that idiotic.

"The dreamvisitor," Sunny said, cupping her front talons together as if she were holding a jewel. "The one you had in my dream. Where is it?" She tilted her head.

Holler and Fluffy started arguing, or at least, it certainly looked that way, raising their voices and barking at each other, waving their paws.

Sunny watched this for a moment, then stuck her claw between them and said, "All right, you're adorable, but that's enough. Dreamvisitor? Treasure? Now?" She rested her open talons between them.

Holler hesitated, looking at Fluffy, and then reached into a pocket of the fabric that was draped around her. She pulled out the sapphire and dropped it into Sunny's palm.

"Whoa," Sunny said. She hadn't actually expected that to work. She raised the jewel to her eye and studied it. It certainly looked like the animus-touched gems from the scroll.

"Thank you," Sunny said to Holler. "Where's the rest?"

Holler blinked at her.

"Um," Sunny said. She took the jewel and put it on the ground, then drew a large circle around it in the ashes and mimed adding more jewels to the circle. Then she spread her wings around it and waved at the imaginary pile of treasure. "The rest of the treasure. That you stole. Where this came from." She picked up the dreamvisitor and waved it again.

Fluffy indicated the imaginary treasure and barked something at Holler. Holler ignored him, pointed over Sunny's shoulder, and said something to her in what really sounded like an imperious tone of voice, if it wasn't too crazy to think about scavengers trying to order dragons around.

Sunny narrowed her eyes at Holler. Now that she had a moment to think about it, she could see that both scavengers were smaller than Flower. They didn't seem entirely full-grown. Scavengers reached their full size before twenty years, didn't they? So if the treasure had been stolen twenty years ago — surely it couldn't have been these two who took it.

But there was the dreamvisitor, real and heavy in her claws.

Fluffy began chattering vigorously at Sunny. Holler grabbed his shoulder and tried to stop him, but he fended her off. He pointed at the imaginary pile of treasure and then at himself and then at Sunny. *That. Me. You.* And then he mimed picking something up and giving it to Sunny.

Is he offering to bring me the treasure? Sunny's hopes rose.

Holler stamped her foot and snapped at him. He put his paws on his hips and yapped back.

"I have an excellent idea," Sunny announced. She gently scooped her claws around Fluffy and lifted him off the wall onto the ground. He yelled and flapped around a bit until she let him go and stepped back, and then he stopped, watching her warily. "You go get the rest of the treasure, and when you come give it to me, you can have Holler back." Sunny tapped Holler lightly on the head.

This took a while to sink in. Sunny pointed to the forest, held up the dreamvisitor, pointed to Fluffy and Holler, in several different combinations, until finally Fluffy took a few steps toward the trees, calling up to Holler. She yapped back at him, and he bobbed his fluffy, shaggy head, then hurried off into the darkness.

"I hope this works," Sunny said to Holler. "I'm not actually going to eat you or anything, even if he doesn't come back."

"Yibble yibble yibble," Holler said to Sunny, or at least, that's what it sounded like.

"You're very cute, but you're all a lot of trouble," Sunny said.

"Yibble! YIBBLE YIBBLE!" Holler shouted, pointing over Sunny's shoulder again.

Or maybe she was pointing *at* Sunny's shoulder. Where Flower had been sitting in Sunny's dream.

"Oh," Sunny said, thinking of Glory's sloth. "Do you want a ride? Are you sure?" Sunny flicked her tail. "You won't be scared?"

"Yibble!" Holler demanded.

"All right," Sunny said, scooping her up. Holler shrieked, with a little more terror than Sunny thought was necessary, considering she'd asked for this. As Sunny set her on her shoulder, Holler grabbed Sunny's neck and balanced herself across her scales, making startled yelping noises.

"Hold on tight," Sunny said, swinging her head around to check that Holler was firmly in place. She spread her wings and leaped into the sky.

It was a clear, starry night; all the clouds from yesterday's storm had blown away, and two of the moons were half full in the sky overhead. The rustling leaves below them looked like waves rippling on the sea.

Sunny soared up in a long arc, swooped down across the forest, and veered back around again. The scavenger was quiet on her back, which was much preferable to shrieking.

I hope Fluffy understood me, Sunny thought. *I hope he hasn't gone to get a pack of other scavengers with pointy things.*

Imagine if he really does come back with the missing treasure! I could be moments away from holding the Eye of Onyx.

The Eye of Onyx, and power over the whole Kingdom of Sand.

Sunny shivered from horns to tail and felt the scavenger clutch her neck tighter.

Whoever holds the Eye could be queen. Even I could be queen. That would be one way to end the war — none of the three sisters wins, and I take the throne. Sunny, queen of the SandWings.

Of course, that would leave three dragons with a single unified mission: kill me.

It was scary, but it gave her an eerie thrill to think about, too. What if that was her real destiny — to rule the SandWings?

She glanced down at the forest and saw movement near the torch she had lit. Fluffy was back! She tucked in her wings and dove toward the ruins, landing with a thump right in front of him.

Fluffy jumped back with a yell. His eyes widened when he saw Holler on Sunny's shoulder, and he launched into another shouting fit, practically hopping up and down. Holler slid off Sunny's back and joined in.

Sunny wasn't interested in their little monkey squabble, though. She was interested in the bulging canvas sack that Fluffy was clutching.

Reaching over Holler's head, she deftly lifted the sack out of his paws. She turned toward the firelight and, fidgeting with excitement, emptied the contents of the sack onto the ground.

Gold coins and jewels tumbled out and bounced through the ashes, clinking and clattering into a small pile. Most of the jewels were tiny — none as big as the dreamvisitor — and barely worth stealing. The biggest object was a statue of a dragon carved from blue stone, with emeralds for eyes. *The Lazulite Dragon,* Sunny guessed, remembering the scrolls about the missing treasure.

She sifted through the pile, her heart sinking. She knew the answer at first glance, but she dug through it all, examining every coin, just to be sure she was right.

She was.

The Eye of Onyx was not there.

CHAPTER 19

"This isn't all of it!" Sunny cried, whipping around to face the scavengers. "Where's the Eye? Why isn't it here?"

They stopped chattering immediately and jumped away from her, holding their paws up in the air. Fluffy pointed at the sack and yibble-yibbled frantically.

"You must have it! Where else could it be?" Sunny started pacing back and forth. She could feel smoke rising from her snout, and she knew she was probably scaring the scavengers, but they didn't run away. "I need the Eye of Onyx. It's my one chance to end the war!" She stopped and faced them again. "How am I supposed to end the war without it?"

"Yibble?" Holler said tentatively. "Yibble . . . yibble?"

"Well said," Sunny said to her. "That's very helpful." She sat down and frowned crossly at the pathetic pile of treasure.

"Ribble yibble," Fluffy said to Holler.

"Urble YOBBLE," she snapped back.

"Someone else must have it," Sunny said, thinking aloud. "If you had it, you'd have brought it to me, because you were worried about Holler. You wouldn't keep the one thing I need, when I'm sure scavengers prefer shiny little things like all of this. So you don't have the Eye of Onyx, which means it's . . . somewhere else in Pyrrhia."

She sighed, and then stopped herself mid sigh so she wouldn't sound like Stonemover.

Her first theory was probably right, and some other dragon had stolen most of the treasure. Perhaps they had the Eye of Onyx and didn't realize what it was or what it could do. But that didn't help Sunny, who had no way to track down the real thief.

She felt something touch her talon and looked down. Holler was standing in the curve of Sunny's wing, patting her talon in a way that seemed to say *"don't worry"* and *"it's not the end of the world."*

"You're brave *and* cute," Sunny told her. "I wish I could keep you. If Glory can have a sloth, I don't see why I can't have a scavenger or two." She glanced at Fluffy, who was edging closer, glancing up at her warily. "But it's too dangerous. I'd feel terrible if one of you got hurt."

She gave Holler a thoughtful look. These small, breakable scavengers were brave enough to fight or ride a dragon who could eat them in three bites.

Could I be that brave? Like, for instance . . . could I try to stop a war? Even if I don't have a magical jewel or a mystical prophecy to back me up. Even if my friends decide not to help. Could I still do it?

Isn't it important enough?

Why shouldn't I try? So what if there's no foretold destiny saying I have to. Shouldn't I do it anyway, just because I want to?

But how? She tapped her claws on the ground, thinking.

"Yibble robble fnob?" Holler said. She pointed to Sunny's shoulder again.

"Sorry, Holler. I don't have time to take you for another ride," Sunny said regretfully. "I have to go." She shook out her wings and reached to scoop all the treasure back into the sack. She was a little bit tempted to let the scavengers keep it, but she had a feeling she could find some use for it — giving it back to the SandWings, perhaps.

"I'm going to find my friends and see if they'll help me," she informed Fluffy and Holler. "And then . . . then I've got a war to stop."

She patted them each gently on their heads before gathering her wings to take off. As she sailed into the sky, she looked back and saw them waving. She wondered if she'd ever see them again. Maybe she could come back and look for them after the war was over.

The weather was with her this time, and she flew through the mountains much faster than she had on the way out, when she'd had to stop every time the NightWings rested or ate. She always ate light, so it didn't take long for her to pause, catch and eat a squirrel or a lizard once a day, and keep flying.

So it was only two days later when she cleared the mountains and saw the rainforest ahead of her, illuminated by the rising sun beyond it. It looked so vast and green and peaceful. Sunny found herself caught by a moment of longing, a wish that she could just dive into those leaves and stay there forever. There would be enough to do, helping Glory rule the rainforest and organize the NightWings. It was beautiful and there was always enough food, and the RainWings were easygoing dragons to share a tree with.

The war would come here eventually, she told herself. *Even the RainWings aren't safe — we already know that from what the NightWings did to them. And between Scarlet and the three sisters looking for us, we probably aren't safe anywhere either.*

No hiding in caves. That's my promise to myself. No hiding at all. When the world is all wrong, I'm going to be a dragon who does something about it.

Her nerves started to get the better of her the closer she got to the RainWing village, though. She kept picturing her friends' faces — doubtful, kind but condescending, all "really? *you,* Sunny?" and "that *is* sweet, but now let's be serious." Her stomach was doing flips and spirals by the time she spotted the treehouses on the outskirts in the early afternoon, and she was almost tempted to turn around and fly away again.

What if they're mad at me? she suddenly thought with another stomach lurch. *What if everyone's furious at me for running off?* It had occurred to her to use the dreamvisitor while she was traveling, but she'd decided against it — she wanted to explain everything to her friends face-to-face.

A movement distracted her from her thoughts — something shifting, out of the corner of her eye, but when she looked she couldn't see anything but dangling vines and bright orange flowers. Immediately she ducked and rolled, so the tranquilizer dart shot right past her and thudded into a tree trunk, startling several shiny blue frogs.

"It's me!" Sunny shouted, twisting to wave her claws at the leaves around her. "It's Sunny! I'm Queen Glory's friend!" She held out her talons and spread her wings wide, hoping one of the hidden RainWings would remember her.

A face materialized on a nearby branch, his scales shifting from brown and green to dark purple. The dragon blinked a few times, looking more wary than most RainWings Sunny had ever met.

"The queen *was* looking for a little gold dragon," said a voice behind Sunny, and another dragon emerged, this one shifting to the clementine orange of the flowers. "This could be her."

"Shouldn't we knock her out anyway?" asked the purple dragon. "Just to be safe? You know the queen keeps telling us to be more careful."

"She means about the NightWings," said the orange dragon blithely. "This one's not a NightWing. I'm sure she's fine."

On the one talon, Sunny certainly didn't want to be shot with a dart. She wanted to be wide-awake when she saw her friends again. On the other talon, she was afraid she could imagine this exact conversation if, say, a smoldering vengeful SkyWing happened to show up in the rainforest looking for them. "Oh, she's not a NightWing? Well then, let's take her straight to the dragonets, no worries."

"I am Glory's friend," she promised them, deciding to worry about Scarlet later. "I need to see her."

"The queen . . . let's see, she might be in the audience treehouse," said the orange dragon thoughtfully.

"Or the healers' hut," said the purple dragon. "She's there a lot."

"Or visiting the NightWing camp."

"Or checking on the progress of the school."

"Or reviewing —"

"All right," Sunny interrupted. "I'll just look for her. Thank you."

They both flicked their tails and bobbed their heads, and their scales immediately began shifting back to camouflage as Sunny flew on.

The healers' hut, she decided. *So I can see Starflight.*

But before she got there, she spotted the mahogany-brown scales of a MudWing stretched out on one of the sleeping platforms.

"Clay!" she yelped happily. She barreled up to him and nearly flung her wings around him before she realized it wasn't Clay at all. It was some other MudWing dragonet, who jumped back with a startled expression and hid something behind his wings.

"Whoa," Sunny said, skidding to a stop on the wood. "Who are you?"

"Who are *you*?" he responded rudely.

Sunny usually liked everybody, at least at first, but something about this dragon immediately rubbed her the wrong way. "Where's Clay?" she asked.

"How should I know?" he demanded.

Sunny frowned at him, then turned to fly away. If he didn't want to be helpful, she didn't need to bother with him.

"Hey!" he called. "Come back!"

Sunny ignored him. She had noticed the angle of the sunlight and realized that it was the RainWing sun time, when most of them would be sleeping high up in the treetops, recharging their scales. She wondered if Glory was up there, too, or if she ever let herself sleep.

Just then she spotted the healers' hut — and coming out of it, opening his wings to fly, was Clay, definitely Clay this time, every wonderful brown scale of him.

Sunny dove into his wings, nearly knocking him backward, except that he was big enough to catch her. He made an "oof!" noise and then realized who she was.

"Sunny!" he roared. "It's you! You're alive! You're all right!" He seized her and swung her around, her tail flying out behind her, and then quickly put her down. "*Are* you all right?" he asked anxiously. He touched her wings and checked her talons. "We thought something terrible had happened to you. We've been searching and searching. Come, come in." He dragged her into the hut before she could say anything. "Starflight! Sunny's back!"

Two black dragons turned their heads in unison toward the door. Sunny recognized Fatespeaker, the NightWing who had been one of the alternate dragonets, raised by the Talons in case they needed a spare set to fulfill the prophecy. She was crouched beside a nest of leaves, where Starflight was lying with his wings spread out.

Sunny flinched at the sight of the burns all along Starflight's dark scales. Some kind of silvery ointment glistened over the wounds, and she saw a little of it on

Fatespeaker's talons as well, as if she'd been helping to put it on.

"Sunny?" Starflight said in a hoarse voice. "Really?"

Sunny realized with a stab of guilt and horror that Starflight's eyes were covered with a mask of leaves, carefully plastered in place. "It's me," she said, hurrying over to his side. She nudged his shoulder gently with her snout, trying to share her warmth with him. "I'm here."

Starflight let out his breath. "Are you all right?" he said anxiously.

"Better than you are," she tried to joke.

"I told him you were fine," Fatespeaker interjected in a helpful voice. She patted the edge of the leaves where Starflight lay. "I had a vision! I mean, it was fuzzy, but I was pretty sure you were fine."

Starflight coughed awkwardly, as if he'd been trying to avoid talking about Fatespeaker's visions for days. Sunny remembered what Stonemover had told her — that no NightWing had had prophetic powers or mind reading for generations. So was Fatespeaker lying? Or did she believe her own wild stories? She didn't seem cruel enough to deceive Starflight about whether Sunny was all right — but then, Sunny didn't really know her at all.

"I'm sorry I wasn't here to take care of you," Sunny said, touching one of Starflight's wings gently.

"*I* took care of him," Fatespeaker said.

Sunny felt a flash of something odd. Like she wanted Fatespeaker to shush and go away. *Jealousy? But wouldn't that mean . . . that I like Starflight the way he likes me?*

Did she? It would be nice if she could love him back. It would make him happy — and she did care about him. Plus he was a real hero — he'd just saved the entire NightWing tribe from extinction.

We don't have time for mushy romance right now anyway, she told herself sternly. *Whatever's going to happen with me and Starflight, whatever we are — we'll figure it out after we stop the war.*

She glanced around the room and noticed that Webs was still there, asleep in a corner, although the venomous scratch on his tail looked almost completely healed. There were a few RainWings as well, four with injuries that might have happened during the attack on the NightWing island, and two others whose breaths rattled in their skinny chests as they slept. Sunny guessed they had been prisoners and were still recovering from their treatment at the talons of the NightWings. She could see spots on their snouts and ankles where iron bands had rubbed the scales raw.

The only other dragon occupying a bed was the SkyWing, Flame. He'd grown up with Fatespeaker among the Talons of Peace, as another possible alternate for the dragonets. She could tell that the healers had applied the cactus-milk antidote to the wound that slashed across his face, but it would still leave a nasty scar. She wondered if his face had looked that furious before he was injured; she suspected yes. He was awake, glaring around the treehouse with trails of smoke coming out of his nose and ears.

"So where were you?" Clay asked, bumping Sunny's wing

with his own. "Tsunami thought maybe you'd been kid-napped, isn't that crazy?"

"Well, I kind of was kidnapped," Sunny admitted. Starflight and Fatespeaker both gasped. "But I got away. Except then I got caught again, and then I was a prisoner in Burn's stronghold for a while."

"What?" Starflight tried to sit up and nearly fell off his bed. Clay's eyes were wide and shocked.

"I'm here now, though, aren't I?" Sunny said. "It all turned out fine. I've taken care of myself. Mostly," she added honestly. "It was a little crazy. But I should tell you all at the same time. Where are Tsunami and Glory?"

Tsunami was drilling RainWings in evasive maneuvers, although apparently what that actually meant was a lot of yelling things like "Pay attention!" and "Leave that toucan alone!" and "Why are you pink? Stop being pink!" and "THREE MOONS, ARE YOU EATING AGAIN?"

Sunny half hoped that meant she'd be all yelled out, but of course it didn't. Tsunami had *plenty* of yelling energy left for Sunny.

"Where have you BEEN?" she roared. "Do you know how WORRIED we've been? How could you DO that to us? I was so sure the NightWings did something to you that I nearly threw them all back to the volcano! We've had search parties out every day, but not ONE SIGN of you ANYWHERE! Not even Deathbringer, well, he said he smelled you over to the west, but who trusts him, NOT ME IS WHO. I haven't slept in days, Sunny! DAYS!"

She grabbed Sunny and wrapped her wings around her in a fierce hug. Sunny felt her own anger melting and realized she'd been furious with Tsunami ever since overhearing the conversation in the Obsidian Mirror. *She may not take me seriously,* Sunny thought, *but she really does love me.*

"I'm sorry," Sunny said, muffled, into Tsunami's shoulder. "But I swear I was doing important things. I'll tell you all about it. Where's Glory?"

"Checking on the NightWing camp," Tsunami said, relaxing her grip on Sunny but keeping one wing around her. "She is kind of awesome with them. All scary and tough and royal, like a real queen. Do *not* tell her I said that."

Sunny grinned up at her. "Are they behaving?"

"For the most part," Tsunami said. "They were all absolutely starving, so just giving them enough food is making them a whole lot happier and easier to deal with. Glory's letting them hunt and eat as much as they want, except for the sloths. Those are off-limits, apparently. I guess being a giant sucker for cute furry things is a RainWing genetic defect."

"I wouldn't eat them either," Sunny pointed out.

"Well, but that makes sense," Tsunami said. "You practically *are* a cute furry thing."

Sunny debated getting riled up about this, but Tsunami was already turning to one of the RainWings — all of whom were staring nosily at Sunny — and ordering him to fetch Glory.

"Tell her to meet us in the healers' hut," she said. "And NO DAWDLING. If you stop to admire so much as one beetle I will seriously bite you."

"All right," the RainWing said affably and flew off in a way that probably counted as a hurry for a RainWing, but was only marginally faster than your average snail.

"I swear," Tsunami muttered through her teeth. "Sunny. You'll probably be shocked to hear this, but I don't think I'd make a very good RainWing."

Sunny laughed. "I missed you," she said, and meant it.

It wasn't long before they were all gathered around Starflight's bed. Sunny felt a rush of joy as Glory swept into the room. Here were all her friends, all together in one place like they were supposed to be.

"Sunny," Glory said, and the relief in her voice was matched by the bright yellow of her scales. She even reached out and squeezed Sunny's front talons, which was more affection than Sunny would have expected from her. "Thank goodness you're alive. Because now I can totally behead you. Starflight, what's our official policy on beheading right now?"

"Our constitution says no beheading Sunny," he said loyally.

"Let's amend that," Glory said, flicking her tail. "To *I can behead anyone who worries me half to death like this*."

"I know you're probably mad," Sunny said. Glory's ears and wings were starting to shade more red than yellow. "OK, definitely mad. But there were — lots of — stuff happened, and —"

"It had better be wildly important 'stuff,' " Glory growled. "You know what I don't need in my first week as queen, in addition to a whole new tribe of pretty much the worst, most unhealthy, most annoying dragons ever? I *don't* need to also be *freaking out* because one of my best friends has disappeared. I *don't* need to be using my best dragons on patrols searching for you when they should be helping me run a brand-new experimental two-tribe kingdom."

"That's me," Deathbringer said, poking his head in from outside. Sunny jumped. She still wasn't used to seeing any NightWings in the RainWing village, apart from Starflight. "When she says her 'best dragons,' she's talking about me."

"I am *not*," Glory said, a little too indignantly, Sunny thought. "Quit stalking me."

"This is not stalking," he objected, sliding into the room as if he were perfectly welcome. "This is protecting you."

"Nobody invited you to this private conversation," Tsunami said bossily.

"Hey, I'm just making sure the queen is safe," he said, spreading his wings.

"*The queen* can take care of herself," Glory pointed out. "Out of the two dragons in question, *the queen* happens to be the one with camouflage scales who can shoot venom. What can you do again? Sit in the dark, is that it? Guess what, I can do that, too." Inky black spilled across her scales and she looked down her snout at him.

"I can stop dragons from killing you," he said. "Three assassination plots so far, Your Majesty. No one's better at stopping assassins than the world's best assassin."

"You poor dragon," Glory said. "If only you had a shred of self-esteem."

"What?" Sunny cried, dismayed. "NightWings have tried to kill you? Three times already?"

"So he says," Glory observed. She didn't look remotely scared or even ruffled. "Apparently he's my bodyguard now. Not that anyone asked him to be, ahem."

"It's true, I did have to fight my way past a whole pack of volunteers," he mused mockingly. "Oh, no, wait. It's just me. The only dragon who cares if you live or die."

"He's just trying to make his list look longer than mine," Glory said to Sunny. "We're keeping track of who has saved who more often. I say it doesn't count if you have to save me from your own dragon-murdering self, and he says I shouldn't get credit for sending him away before the IceWings got him."

Sunny couldn't help but notice that Deathbringer was apparently allowed to know where the RainWing village was, and to roam around it freely. So whatever she said about him, Glory really must trust him, certainly more than any other NightWing.

"If you two are quite finished jabbing at each other," Tsunami said, rolling her eyes, "I'd like to hear what Sunny's been doing for the last week."

"Me too," Clay said fervently, sidling up beside her. Sunny twined her tail around his, relieved that at least one of her friends wouldn't be mad at her, no matter what she'd done or how worried he'd been.

"Well," she said, "I found my parents. And I met Burn's brother. And I saw Peril again, and Queen Scarlet is alive, oh, and she's maybe coming here to kill us, although I hope she doesn't really know where we are, although she said she did."

Glory cleared her throat quietly, but everyone turned to look at her anyway.

"Um," she said. "So. Yes. Actually, she does know where we are." She squinted at the skylight, rubbing the back of her head. "She maybe visited me in a dream. With a dream-visitor. And saw where I was. So. Yes."

"That seems like something worth mentioning!" Tsunami yelled.

"I was going to tell you all," Glory said huffily, "but then Starflight disappeared and I became queen and I got a little . . . busy."

"Anyway," Sunny interrupted before the two of them could start one of their interminable arguments. "So she was in Burn's stronghold, but she's not anymore."

"Could you start at the beginning?" Starflight asked. "I'm a little confused."

"Me too," Fatespeaker chimed in. *As if anyone asked you,* Sunny thought, then felt incredibly guilty for thinking it.

"All right," Sunny said. "It started with these three NightWings grabbing me. . . ."

CHAPTER 20

"And so," Sunny finished, "I decided we shouldn't wait any longer. Maybe we'll never find the Eye of Onyx, but we can still choose a queen and end the war. Someone has to, and I think it should be us."

She paused and looked around at her friends, whose faces ranged from disbelieving to astonished to terribly worried.

"I can't believe all of that happened to you," Starflight said in a low, shaken voice.

"And we weren't there to protect you," Tsunami said, exchanging a glance with Clay.

"She did all right," Glory said unexpectedly. "Stealing the Obsidian Mirror, that was crazy-brave. Crazy *and* brave, I mean. And talking Peril into saving Thorn — well, that would have made *me* nervous."

"Also, confronting scavengers," Deathbringer chimed in. He gave a little shudder out to his wingtips. "No, no, no, thanks. Not for me."

"You're scared of scavengers?" Glory asked, amused.

"NO," he said. "They just . . . give me the heebie-jeebies, that's all. With their . . . eyes and paws and . . . *faces*."

"That's pretty cute," Glory said. "The big bad assassin terrified of itty-bitty scavengers."

"One day I'll throw a sword-waving scavenger at you and see how tough *you* are," he bridled.

"But, Sunny," Clay interjected, "we can't stop the war. The prophecy isn't true, remember?"

"So?" she said. "If there had never been a prophecy, would the war have to go on forever? No. It has to end sometime. I vote right now."

"But it doesn't have to be us," Starflight said, then immediately added in almost a mumble, "Maybe it has to be us." He reached up to the leaves on his eyes, remembered they were there, and lowered his claws again.

"No!" Fatespeaker said, grabbing Starflight's talons. "It doesn't have to be you! It especially doesn't have to be *you*! You've done enough."

"Sunny's right, though," he said. "Why shouldn't it be us? Maybe everyone else is waiting for the prophecy and so they don't realize they could end the war themselves. And think about all the dragons who need this war to be over."

"My brothers and sisters," said Clay. "If they're still alive."

"Anemone," Tsunami said. "So she doesn't have to use her animus powers and lose her soul."

"All the SandWings," Glory added. "They need a queen and a unified kingdom."

"So will you help me?" Sunny said, picking nervously at a vine of small, star-shaped red flowers that snaked through the window.

"Well, even if we did, what's the plan?" Tsunami said practically. "Pick a queen and then send Deathbringer to kill the other two?"

"Yikes," Deathbringer said, flaring his wings. "Give me the easy job, why don't you."

"Oh, if only we knew Pyrrhia's *best* assassin," Glory mused teasingly.

"No, no," Sunny said, flapping between them before they could go too far down that road. "No killing."

"It would be almost impossible," Tsunami mused. "I assume dragons have tried before."

"What if we got an animus to enchant something?" Starflight suggested. "That was Blister's plan to use Anemone, and it was a smart one. Enchant a spear to go kill Burn, or perhaps we could put her life essence in a tree and set it on fire, or something like that?"

"We're *not* making Anemone do that!" Tsunami snarled.

"Are you serious? Can an animus dragon really do those things?" Fatespeaker asked. "That's absolutely terrifying."

"It's a little more complicated than that, but basically," Deathbringer answered her. "And yes, it's terrifying."

"*No*," Sunny said again. "We're not going to kill them!"

"I agree with Tsunami," Clay said. "We can't ask Anemone to use her powers. That would be awful for her."

"I wasn't thinking of Anemone," Starflight protested. "I was thinking of Sunny's father, Stonemover. He's sort of beyond hope anyway, isn't he?"

Is he? Sunny closed her mouth to think about that. She had a feeling that if he used his magic again, that would be it for Stonemover. Especially if he used it for something as massive as killing two dragons. But would it be worth it? To save the rest of Pyrrhia? Would he do it?

Could she bring herself to ask him to do it? He was disappointing, but he was still her father. Didn't she want to get to know him better?

"With either of those options, we'd have to pick which sister we want to be queen," Glory said. "And they're all terrible."

"Blaze seems nice," Clay said optimistically.

"Blaze is a dizzy idiot who'd be dead by day two," Glory said. "I say Blister. She's evil, but she's smart, so she'd probably rule the kingdom fine, and if we're her allies she'll leave us alone. I think. Well, maybe not. OK, probably not. But at least we'd know where she was."

"Wait," Sunny said. "I don't want to kill any of them."

"Burn is the least awful," Tsunami argued. "She's mean, but she's not scheming. We'd see her coming if she tried anything on us."

"Mean and brutal," Starflight reminded her. "Remember the murdered dragons in her collection. And the SkyWing egg she smashed — just an egg, not even a dragonet yet. As long as she's alive, I don't think we're safe." He paused, then added, "I don't think Sunny will be safe."

Sunny leaned over to brush his wing with hers.

"So how do we decide?" Clay said. "Who do we choose and who — and how — I mean, are we really going to —"

"No!" Sunny said. "Listen, for once, please —" But Tsunami, Glory, Fatespeaker, and Deathbringer all started talking over her at once, arguing about the sisters and how to get rid of them.

Sunny clapped her talons over her ears and shouted:

"Stop! I SAID STOP!"

Everyone blinked at her in the sudden silence.

"No," she said again, more firmly. "We are *not killing any of them.* We're not using magic to do something underhanded. We are going to get all three of them in one place, and then we will either have a competition, like the RainWings have, or we'll let all the SandWings decide."

"Let the SandWings decide?" Tsunami said skeptically. "What?"

"Like when we decide things together," Starflight said, understanding immediately. "By voting. Or talking it out. Like the NightWings, or Queen Coral's council."

"All the SandWings?" Glory said. "I don't see how that could work."

"They'll never agree to it," Deathbringer said, shaking his head. "The sisters. They haven't been in one place together in over eighteen years. They certainly won't put the decision about the throne in the claws of their future subjects."

"Well, that's what we're going to try," Sunny said stubbornly. "I think we can get them all together, especially if you guys help me. But if you don't, it doesn't matter. I'm doing it anyway." She settled her wings back and looked at her friends defiantly.

There was a long pause. Sunny could imagine what they were thinking, what they were about to say. *"Oh, Sunny. It's a sweet idea, but it'll never work. You have too much faith in the goodness of dragons. You're so naïve and ridiculous. Why don't you work on a project here in the rainforest instead, like counting bananas or something? Your crazy ideas and obsession with the prophecy is just —"*

"All right," said Clay. "I'm in."

Sunny's heart leaped. She beamed at him.

"Me too," said Starflight, struggling to his feet. "It's worth a try. I want it to work."

"But you need to rest!" Fatespeaker protested.

"We need to be safe," Starflight said, "and we won't be safe, and neither will our friends and all the dragons who count on us, until the war is over."

"I agree," said Glory. "I'll help, too. Although I can't leave my dragons here for long, not with the NightWings so close by and not settled yet."

"The NightWings are your dragons, too, now," Deathbringer pointed out. Sunny caught the way he looked at Glory and thought, *What he really means is: I am yours, now and forever.*

Is that how Starflight feels about me? She glanced at him, with his sad bandaged eyes and determined expression. *I don't . . . I don't think that's how I feel about him. I mean, I love him . . . but not like that.*

"Fine!" Tsunami said. "Fine, yes, of course I'm in. It's never going to work, but I'll do it. Whatever *it* is. So. Then. What are we doing?"

Suddenly they were all looking at Sunny; even Starflight's face was tilted in her direction.

You wanted their attention. You wanted them to listen to you. You'd better earn this.

"We start by sending a message to Burn, Blister, and Blaze," she said firmly. "We start with Blister — and we get to her through the Talons of Peace."

CHAPTER 21

"This is awesome," Tsunami said. "I'm so excited. Going to see my very favorite dragons in all of Pyrrhia."

"Are you being Glory now?" Sunny asked. "Queen of Sarcasm?"

"I can be sarcastic, too! She doesn't get to be queen of *everything*," Tsunami grumbled. She tilted her wings to do another sweep over the shoreline. They were on the eastern outskirts of the Mud Kingdom, on the edge of the Kingdom of the Sea. Below them, the ocean rushed up onto the beach and then back, wave upon white-topped wave. The sky was gray from edge to edge, and the air was wet with something that couldn't decide if it was mist or rain.

It was dreary. Sunny missed the hot, dry desert. You couldn't even tell it was almost the middle of the day; the sun was well hidden behind those ranks of clouds. Her wings felt unpleasantly damp as she circled around behind Tsunami.

"Where is that blasted MudWing?" Tsunami muttered, scanning the beach.

"I wish we hadn't had to bring him," Sunny said. "I'm

not convinced he really knows where he's going. I wish we could have brought *our* MudWing instead."

"*Our* MudWing doesn't know where the Talons of Peace camp is," Tsunami pointed out. "Ochre supposedly does."

Ochre was the disagreeable MudWing Sunny had met in the rainforest; it turned out he was one of the alternate dragonets as well. So he'd grown up with the Talons of Peace and had agreed to go back to them and guide Sunny and Tsunami there.

The other two options, Flame and Fatespeaker, had had slightly more violent reactions. Fatespeaker had declared passionately that she wouldn't leave Starflight's side — she said he needed her, which gave Sunny another jealous twinge — and added that the Talons never particularly liked her anyway.

Flame, on the other talon, had thrown an entire bowl of mangoes at them and roared that he wasn't letting anyone see him with his face all destroyed, least of all the Talons who'd just handed him over to the stupid NightWings in the first place.

So they were stuck with Ochre. Which had meant three days of travel with a dragonet whom Sunny liked less and less. He was like the not-funny, not-adorable opposite of Clay, constantly hungry but in a pushy way instead of a sweetly embarrassed way. He'd even made himself a sack out of leaves with a handle of vines that he could hang over his neck, and he'd filled this with half the fruits in the rainforest, as far as Sunny could tell. That way he could eat and fly at the same time, dripping bright yellow and purple juice all over his brown scales and spattering the ground below them. And, incidentally, refusing to share, not that she wanted anything from a bag he'd drooled all over anyway.

"Besides," Tsunami added, "Glory still needs Clay back at camp, to help with the NightWings. Especially if Queen Scarlet is on her way."

"I don't understand why she hasn't come after us yet," Sunny said with a shiver. She glanced down at her own small necklace, a pouch containing the dreamvisitor. They'd been using it for the last few days to check in with her friends back in the rainforest, but so far everything was quiet there. It made Sunny's scales feel wriggly and oversized, not knowing where Scarlet was and what she was plotting.

Tsunami followed her gaze to the dreamvisitor pouch. "We could have avoided this whole trip," she pointed out.

Sunny shook her head. "It's not safe. If we used the dreamvisitor to contact Blister — or even the Talons of Peace — or to check on Scarlet — they might catch a glimpse of the rainforest and realize where we are. Like I figured out where the scavenger was when she dreamvisited me. Or Glory said she caught a glimpse of the weirdling tower behind Scarlet, too. We couldn't risk it."

"I know," Tsunami sighed. "So here we are, looking for the Talons of Peace. My —"

"Your favorite dragons," Sunny finished for her.

"I don't trust them," Tsunami added.

"That's why you're here," Sunny agreed. "Because you think otherwise they might grab me and do something nefarious."

"Trapping us in an underground cave for six years comes to mind," Tsunami muttered.

Sunny squinted at a dark shape winging out of the fog up ahead. "That's Ochre, right?"

"And there's someone with him," Tsunami said, snapping her head up and frowning fiercely. "A few someones." As the group of dragons came closer, she hmmphed with surprise. "I've seen that dragon before," she told Sunny. "The one in the lead, the SeaWing with the black spirals on his scales. I saw him meeting with Riptide, the very first time I saw Riptide in the Kingdom of the Sea. I didn't realize at the time that he was with the Talons of Peace."

"He's flashing something at us," Sunny pointed out. The SeaWing's glow-in-the-dark scales were lighting up in some kind of pattern.

Tsunami growled. "If he's with the Talons, he should know that I don't understand Aquatic, since he was proba-bly one of the squid-heads who made the decision not to teach it to me. Maybe I should go over there and thump him and then pretend I misunderstood what he was saying."

"I think he's just suggesting we land," Sunny guessed, since all the approaching dragons were now veering down toward the beach.

"Well. Sure. I could have figured that out," Tsunami said. "But he didn't have to rub my snout in it, did he?" She flapped on ahead and Sunny followed.

They landed on the sand, which was wet and clumpy between Sunny's claws. Across from them were Ochre and five dragons from the Talons of Peace: an IceWing, a

SkyWing, a SandWing, and two SeaWings — one of them green with black spirals on his scales, the other sky-blue with dark blue horns.

Wait, Sunny thought. *I know that other SeaWing. . . .*

"Riptide!" Tsunami cried.

The blue dragon's whole face lit up. "You're alive!" he said, stepping forward.

"That's far enough," said the other SeaWing, flaring one wing in Riptide's way.

"Of course I am," Tsunami said to Riptide, ignoring the green dragon. "What are you doing with these —"

Sunny kicked her as hard as she could. *Remember why we're here, Tsunami. No insulting the dragons we're asking for help.*

Tsunami glared at her, but she seemed to get the message. "With the Talons of Peace?" she finished.

"Queen Coral threw me out," Riptide said sadly, furrowing lines in the sand with his claws. "She considered killing me, or imprisoning me again, but she said I'd fought bravely in the battle at the Summer Palace. So she let me leave with my life. And I didn't know where else to go — I thought the Talons might know where you were, but . . ." he trailed off.

"But we had no idea," said the other SeaWing in a clipped, cold voice.

Tsunami gave him an incredulous look. "You're not seriously mad at *us,* are you? Because no. I am mad at *you*; that's how this works."

"This is Nautilus," Riptide interjected quickly. "The leader of the Talons of Peace."

"For now," growled the SkyWing, flicking her red tail back and forth and glowering through a trail of smoke. "Do you have the other dragonets?" She jerked her head at Ochre, who was munching his way through a banana and eyeing the seashells around his claws as if he was wondering whether they might be edible, too.

"We don't 'have' them," Tsunami said.

"But we know where two of them are," Sunny added. "Our friends helped them get away from the NightWings."

"They didn't want to come back here, though," Tsunami said. "We offered."

The SkyWing scowled at her. "Which two?"

"Is Viper one of them?" demanded the SandWing.

Uh-oh, Sunny thought. She shook her head, but before she could answer, the IceWing hissed, "There's a dragon coming this way."

They all turned and saw someone flying over the cliffs around the beach, high above their heads. The sun caught on red scales and all the dragons on the sand tensed. *Is it a SkyWing scout? One of Ruby's soldiers, or someone working for Burn?*

Or Queen Scarlet? Sunny thought worriedly before she realized this dragon was smaller and a different color.

He was also clearly heading toward them, as if he'd been watching them for a while.

"That looks like Flame," said the SkyWing, squinting. "But it can't be. What's wrong with his face?"

"It might be Flame," Sunny said, glancing at Tsunami. "He could have followed us. Maybe he changed his mind about coming back."

"Maybe he just didn't want to fly with us," Tsunami said. "Or with *him* anyway." She flipped her tail at Ochre.

"Flame?" called the SkyWing. *"Flame?"*

The dragonet was soaring down toward the sand now; when he heard his name, he faltered in midflight and nearly crash-landed on the dunes.

"Mother?" he called back, wobbling upright again.

The SkyWing shoved past Sunny and Tsunami and caught Flame as he dropped toward her. She let out a roar at the sight of his face.

"What happened to you? Who did this?" She wrapped her wings around him and pulled him close.

Flame seemed to collapse into her, burying his head in her neck. Sunny heard muffled sobbing and felt a wrenching stab of pity for the SkyWing dragonet. She'd only ever seen his mean, prickly, grouchy side, but clearly he could be someone else with someone who really cared about him.

I miss my mother, she thought, wishing she had large warm wings wrapped around her right then. *I guess I've always missed her. But I miss her even more now that I know her.* Thorn was so far away, on the other side of the continent. Sunny folded back her wings and lifted her chin. *I'll see her again soon. As soon as this war is over.*

"That's Avalanche," Riptide said quietly to Tsunami, nodding at Flame's mother. "She's a spy, so she normally lives in the Sky Palace, and she left Flame here to keep him out of the war." He hesitated. "She was away when Morrowseer came and took the dragonets. She was furious when she came back and found him gone. She nearly killed Nautilus."

Nautilus shifted uneasily on his talons. "Some dragons don't understand the things we have to do for peace," he said, but not in a way that sounded like he meant it. "Do — do I want to know what happened to the others?" he asked.

"Fatespeaker is fine," Sunny said, "but we don't know what happened to Squid, and Viper is dead."

The SandWing across from her snarled and raised his venomous tail. "How?"

"An accident in the Night Kingdom," Tsunami answered. "Viper was fighting and fell into some lava. It was her tail that did that to Flame's face."

"We need Morrowseer," Nautilus growled. "Several of us would like to have words with him. Words and teeth and claws."

"And tails," added the SandWing. He looked angry but not devastated. Sunny wondered if he was an uncle instead of Viper's father, or something like that.

"Morrowseer is dead, too," Sunny said. "So we need your help."

"Oh, *really*," said Nautilus. "Suddenly the wonderful independent dragonets need *us*?"

"Don't be a rotting tooth," Tsunami said to him. "If you want this prophecy fulfilled and this war stopped, you'll help us, so shut up."

He opened and closed his mouth a few times, then settled for flashing something with his luminescent stripes that Sunny guessed she wouldn't want translated.

"We need to send a message to Blister," she said. "You're the only ones we could think of who might be able to reach her."

"She's looking for *you* pretty seriously," Riptide said. "You probably just have to stand out in the open for a day and she'll land on you."

"Right, sure," Tsunami answered. "Except we're trying to do this in a not-ending-up-dead way."

"Fair enough," he said. "Good idea. I support that plan."

"What do you want us to tell her?" Nautilus asked. "*If* we can get in touch with her and *if* we agree to do this."

Sunny looked him in the eye, knowing perfectly well that he'd do anything she said, if it meant a chance at peace. He may have made some terrible decisions over the last seven years, but she believed that he did care about one thing very much, and that was ending the war.

"Tell her to meet us on the tenth midnight from tonight," she said. "In the entrance courtyard of the stronghold in the Kingdom of Sand. If she doesn't show up, she forfeits her chance to be queen."

"This is it?" the SandWing demanded. "You're fulfilling the prophecy and choosing a queen? It's Blister?"

"Come along and see," Sunny offered. "Anyone who wants to. Bring all the Talons of Peace. If it goes the way it should, you won't be fugitives anymore. If Blister shows up and everything goes as planned, then the war will be over."

"We'll think about it," Nautilus said, but even he had an unmistakable undercurrent of excitement in his voice.

"It's important you tell her," Sunny insisted. "We don't know how else to reach her."

"We're not, like, friends with her," Riptide said. "Just so

you know. It's not like the Talons of Peace are working with her, I swear."

"But you can find her?" Tsunami asked.

"She sends one of her soldiers to the ruins of the Summer Palace pretty much every day," Nautilus said. "Hoping for a message from Queen Coral. That's how we'll reach her."

"Good," Tsunami said.

"Thank you," Sunny added. She turned to Tsunami. "Then we'd better go." *So we can send our messages to the other two sisters. We only have ten days now.*

Tsunami swept her tail through the sand and looked over at Riptide.

"I could . . . come with you," he said hesitantly, as if he wasn't sure he'd be welcome.

"I think," Tsunami said, "it'd be better if you stay and make sure Blister shows up at the stronghold. Then bring some of the Talons of Peace with you — and I'll see you there?"

He nodded, tilting his wings back with a hopeful expression.

"All right," Tsunami said. "See you soon." It sounded like a promise.

"Bye, Ochre," Sunny said, making one last effort to be friendly to the unlikable dragon. The MudWing had gotten his claws stuck in a pineapple as he tried to peel it and was now trying to shake it off. "Have a nice life."

"Yeah, yeah," he muttered. He accidentally whacked himself in the snout with the top of the pineapple and yelped with pain.

Tsunami and Sunny rolled their eyes at each other and lifted off into the sky. They flew over Flame and his mother, still wrapped around each other on the beach. Sunny felt another jab of pity, although she knew the SkyWing dragonet didn't want to be seen that way.

She glanced back as they reached the edge of the beach and saw that the other dragons had turned to leave, but Riptide was still staring after them.

"Are you all right?" Sunny asked Tsunami. "I mean, about Riptide? Have you forgiven him for lying to you about being a Talon?"

Tsunami gave her a rueful look. "It's complicated," she said. "I hate being lied to and the Talons are the worst . . . but when I saw that he was alive, I was just — really, really happy. Is that weird?"

"No," Sunny said. "I know what you mean."

"I'll see how I feel after the war is over," Tsunami said. "When everything's a little more normal. Not that we know anything about normal or what that's supposed to look like, right? But then I think — well, we'll see."

"I hope Blister shows up," Sunny said as they soared up over the cliffs. "I hope this works."

"It will," Tsunami said confidently. "We'll get all three sisters to the stronghold. I'm not worried about that. What happens once we're all there, though. . . . That part worries me quite a lot."

CHAPTER 22

In some ways, Burn and Blaze should have been easier to send a message to. They both had a fixed home base — Burn at the stronghold, Blaze in her fortress in the Ice Kingdom. But Sunny was not about to waltz into either place, and she didn't want to send anyone she knew to face them. She didn't trust Burn or Queen Glacier not to just kill the messenger.

After a lot of arguing, though, Glory had offered a solution for Blaze: send a RainWing disguised as an IceWing to pass the message along.

"Send me," was her actual suggestion. "I could be there and back in a couple of days."

"Absolutely not," Deathbringer had said. "You are the dragon holding this rainforest together. Two tribes depend on you; if anything happens, you're leaving chaos behind. And Blaze will probably recognize you."

"True," Clay had agreed. "But you could send someone else. Maybe Jambu?"

"He's been there before," Sunny pointed out. "He knows where Blaze's fortress is. He's already changed his scales to look like an IceWing, so he should be able to do it again."

Glory snorted. "As long as he doesn't fall asleep or get distracted by something shiny."

"Or I could go," Deathbringer offered. "I know where it is, too."

"Absolutely not," Glory had echoed back at him, only half teasing. "Remember the part where you tried to kill Blaze? You're the last dragon she'd trust. Glacier probably has soldiers prepared to kill you on sight. She's probably told them to kill any NightWing who comes along, just in case it's you."

"Aww," Deathbringer said. "You totally care if I live or die, too."

Sunny could practically see the struggle in Glory's scales as she tried to stamp out any bits of pink that were trying to sneak through. "Well, sure," she said. "A dead messenger wouldn't do us much good at all."

Deathbringer laughed, and Sunny realized that he was deliberately provoking Glory because he liked the way she shot him down. *If that's what he's looking for in a dragon,* she thought, *he's certainly picked the right one.*

"Send Jambu and Mangrove," Sunny suggested. "They both know the way, and they can keep an eye on each other."

Everyone had agreed to this plan, including Jambu and Mangrove, but Sunny still felt anxious as she watched the two RainWings slip into the tunnel that led to the Kingdom of Sand. It was the day she and Tsunami got back from the Talons of Peace; the flight had taken them three days with almost no stops. *Seven to go,* she thought.

"Be safe," Glory said to them. "That's an order from your queen."

"Yes, Your Majesty," Jambu answered, grinning in a way that suggested he just liked saying those words, not that he was actually listening.

"Stay camouflaged as much as you can, the whole way there. And you don't have to go into the fortress, or even all the way to the fortress. If you find an IceWing patrol before you get there, tell them to tell Blaze and then you come home. Right away. Understand?"

"Yup," said Mangrove. "We still understand. Like we did five minutes ago when you last explained it. And five minutes before that. And —"

"All right, go away," Glory said, flicking her tongue out at them.

"Remember to tell them she has to show up!" Sunny called. "Or else she doesn't get to be queen! Make sure that part of the message gets to Glacier!" She was the least sure about Blaze, who seemed perfectly happy to hide in her fortress and let other dragons do all the fighting for her. If she was going to show up, Sunny had a feeling it would be only because Queen Glacier dragged her there.

As soon as their tails had disappeared, Sunny turned to Clay. "Ready?"

"Sure," Clay said. "I mean, I've eaten breakfast. What else do I need to do? Oooh, maybe some more breakfast. That's a good idea."

Sunny laughed, and soon the two of them were aloft, soaring north through the rainforest toward the Mud Kingdom.

"Do you think anyone will listen to us?" Clay asked her after they'd flown for a while. The landscape below was shifting from jungle to swamp, with shorter trees and brownish-green ponds visible here and there. In the distance to their right, they could see a shimmer of water that had to be the big lake. That's where Queen Moorhen's palace was.

They were definitely not going there.

Sunny tilted her wings to the west, heading for the mountains. "I think someone will listen," she said. "We just have to find the right someone. A MudWing patrol, I think, not SkyWings or SandWings. I bet they'll listen to *you* anyway." As far as she was concerned, Clay could talk anyone into anything, because anyone could see that he was sincere and wanted the best for everybody.

Clay rumbled nervously deep in his throat. "Maybe we don't have to do this. Maybe Burn will stay in her stronghold and just be there when we get there."

"She's more likely to go out again, looking for another battle," Sunny said. She thought for a moment, then added, "Or looking for us. No, we have to make sure she'll be there in seven days, or this won't work."

They found a sheltered grove of pines at the foot of the mountains where they could sleep that night. There had been surprisingly few dragons out that day — a few solitary scouts and some two-dragon patrols — but Sunny had decided to avoid them all. She wanted to get farther away from Moorhen's palace, just in case anyone tried to drag her and Clay back there.

She'd expected to see more soldiers out and about, though. It was a little unsettling how quiet the skies were.

Clay was thoughtfully watching the stars as she curled up against him in the dark.

"Sunny," he whispered, "I know I'm bad at remembering stuff, but . . . Pyrrhia only has three moons, right?"

"Of course," she whispered back. "Why?"

"That thing over there," he said, pointing with one of his wings. "It looks kind of like a moon coming this way."

Sunny followed his gaze to a glowing shape in the sky. It was bigger than the other stars, although not quite as big or round as a moon. She couldn't remember ever noticing it before.

"Freaky," she said. "I wonder what it is. Not one of the regular moons — look, you can see all the others, there and there, and over there right on the edge of the mountains." None of them were full, but two of them were more than halfway there and filled the sky with light.

"I might fly up the mountain a ways and take a closer look," Clay said. "Is that all right?"

"Sure," Sunny said, sitting up. "I'll come with you."

They climbed higher and higher, looking for a clear view of the sky, and finally stopped on a ledge not far from the peak. Clay seemed almost entranced by the strange new thing in the sky, and so it was Sunny who looked down, and gasped, and grabbed his arm, and pointed.

"Clay, look!" she whispered.

The valley below them was dotted with fires, almost like a lake reflecting the stars above. But they could clearly see the shapes of dragons gathered around those fires . . . and the glint of weapons being polished and sharpened and readied for battle.

"That's where they all are," Sunny whispered. "The MudWings are gathering for something. This must be almost their whole army."

Clay stared down at them, his tail twitching.

That could have been him down there, she realized. *If there had been no prophecy, he'd have grown up like any ordinary MudWing. He'd have led his brothers and sisters into battle. He'd have fought and died for Queen Moorhen, and by extension, her ally, Burn.*

"They're planning something big," Clay said. "I wonder how soon."

"Let's go find out," Sunny suggested, spreading her wings.

"But you —" he started.

"I'm just a SandWing," she said. "I could be your ally. In the dark, maybe no one will look twice at my tail." She curled it up in an imitation of the scorpion-like way the SandWings often held their tails.

After some arguing, she won the debate, and they flew down to the MudWing camp as cautiously and quietly as they could move. There didn't seem to be any guards on the outskirts, and they slipped in among the campfires on silent feet.

Many of the dragons around them were sleeping, although Sunny saw at least one member awake in each small group. She remembered what they'd learned about MudWings in Clay's home village. Each troop was made up of brothers and sisters, who fought alongside one another through thick and thin, led by whichever one was the biggest — their bigwings.

"Someone here could pass a message to Burn," she whispered to Clay. "But how do we decide who? And what if they're all going off to a battle tomorrow? Do you think we can stop them?"

She had to hurry to keep up with Clay's longer strides. He was pacing purposefully through the camp, studying each group of dragons, and she wasn't sure he was even really listening to her.

Oh! she thought. *I'm an idiot. Of course.* Of course he was looking for his brothers and sisters. He'd only met them once, but they were often on his mind; he'd wondered aloud about them several times in the last few weeks.

Sunny hadn't met them, so she couldn't help him search, but she stayed close on his heels as they walked and walked through the camp, which was even bigger than it had looked from up on the mountain. Here and there she spotted SandWings and SkyWings as well, which made her feel less conspicuous, at least.

Suddenly Clay stopped and blocked her path with his tail. He nodded at a group of five dragons clustered around a fire, drawing formation plans in the dirt.

"Is that them?" Sunny asked softly.

He nodded, then started forward again.

"Reed," he whispered from the shadows. "Shhh. Don't call out. It's Clay."

All five dragons whirled toward him as he stepped into the circle of light.

"Clay!" yelped the smallest one, quietly. He jumped over the fire and bounced around Clay, stepping on his talons a few times by accident.

"Hey, Umber," Clay said affectionately, punching the little dragon gently on the shoulder. "Everyone, this is Sunny. Reed is the bigwings; my sisters are Sora and Pheasant, and my third brother is Marsh."

"Hi," Sunny whispered to all of them, nodding at each of the trusting brown-eyed faces. "It's great to finally meet you." The way they looked at Clay — there was a bit of terrifying hope there, as if they were expecting him to come with extra fireproof scales to protect them all.

"Are you all right?" Reed asked. He was almost, but not quite, as big as Clay, and he held his head up and shoulders back as if he was very aware that he shouldn't have been the bigwings. But he, too, looked at Clay with hope rather than envy or worry. "We've been wondering . . . we've heard rumors. . . ."

"Oh, we're fine," Clay said. "Indestructible. Don't you worry." He grinned at Reed, nudging his side. "What is all this? Why are you here?"

The five MudWings exchanged looks, as if they weren't sure whether to answer that question. Would it be treason to their queen? Or loyalty to their brother?

Reed was the one who nodded: *Yes. Tell them.*

"A huge offensive," Pheasant said, her voice shaded with anxiety and fear and resignation. "Wipe out as many IceWings as we can in one huge sweep, and hope we kill Blaze while we're at it."

"Queen Moorhen is leading us herself," said Reed. "And Queen Ruby is supposed to bring her troops over to attack from the north. The order that came down was we keep fighting as long as any enemies are left alive."

"Take no prisoners," Sora whispered, shuddering. "Kill everyone."

"Burn wants to end the war fast, before you guys mess everything up," Umber added. "That's the word going around the camp anyway."

"And as long as the SeaWings are still in hiding, she can focus all her energy on the Ice Kingdom," Reed explained. "On destroying them."

"Every last IceWing," Marsh finished. "Unless we all die first." He stared into the flames of their campfire.

The three moons were not enough to combat the dark that was pressing in around them, like shadow wings folding over their heads. The fire flickered and spat, illuminating amber underscales and dark brown tails in waves of orange light.

"You can't do that," Sunny said. She could hear her voice shaking. "All of you against the IceWings — you really might wipe them out. The *entire tribe*."

"And so many of you will die trying," Clay said, reaching one wing around Umber. "It's so cold in the Ice Kingdom — we were there, just on the outskirts — and it was freezing. Imagine how much worse it'll be right in the heart of it, or up by Glacier's palace. Hundreds of dragons will freeze to death. *You* might — you mustn't —" He broke off, clearing his throat.

Marsh and Sora shuffled closer to him and he spread his other wing to go awkwardly around them as well.

"He's right," Sunny said. "This is a suicide mission. Suicide or genocide, those are your only two outcomes. Clay, we can't let this happen."

"What else can we do?" Reed demanded. "We're part of an army. These are our orders — orders from our queen."

"You could run away," Clay said. "Come with us. We'll hide you."

"We can, but you know that's not good enough," Sunny said to him. "We have to stop this from happening at all."

"There's five of us against Queen Moorhen, Queen Ruby, and all of Burn's army," Reed pointed out. "Who's going to listen to us?"

"I'm sure you're not the only ones who are worried," Sunny said. She twisted to look at the fires all around them and wondered how many of the sleeping dragons were caught in nightmares about the battles to come.

Nightmares. She touched the pouch around her throat. A possible idea was starting to come to her.

"When are you supposed to attack?" Clay asked.

"We move out tomorrow morning," Pheasant answered. "A few days to cross the mountains and the desert — those who make it — and then we'll be at the Ice Kingdom."

"So we have to do something about it now," Sunny said, standing up and pacing around the fire. "Where is Queen Moorhen? Is she here? Do you know?"

Reed and the others looked alarmed, apart from Umber, who looked excited. "You can't just go talk to the queen,"

Reed said. "She'll never let you get away. There are orders to capture you all if anyone sees you, although everyone's looking for five dragonets together, and most dragons don't know what you look like. But if you walk right into her camp — you might as well put on your own chains."

"We're not going to do that," Sunny promised. "I have a plan. A sort of a plan. A something worth trying anyway. So which way is she?"

Umber flicked his tail toward the center of camp. "Right in the middle of everything," he said. "Like a real bigwings."

"Please don't kill her," Sora said softly. "She's not a bad queen."

"We're not going to," Clay assured her. "We would never. We don't do that."

"We'll be back," Sunny promised them. She plunged into the darkness with Clay close behind her, weaving between the fires again.

"Do you really have a sort of plan?" Clay asked. "Because I have no plan. Except maybe a throwing-up-I'm-so-nervous plan."

"I do," Sunny said, curling her claws around the dream-visitor. "I just have to see the queen and make sure she's sleeping."

"Oh," Clay said. "Aha." He took the lead, adjusting their direction, and soon they saw a brightly burning circle of fires ahead of them. Wide-awake guards were posted between the fires, staring alertly out at the camp and up at the sky.

But beyond the guards they could see a huge dragon, as big as Morrowseer, curled in a slumbering ball. Firelight reflected off her russet scales and caught the glitter of gemstones on her ankles and head. The spines on her back moved slowly up and down as she breathed.

Clustered around her were four other dragons, all smaller than her, all glittering with gems and sleeping as well.

"Her brothers and sisters?" Sunny guessed. They stopped well out of sight of the guards, studying the royal camp.

Clay nodded. "I think so." He grinned. "If Starflight were here, he could tell us all their names and personal histories and what they each eat for breakfast every day."

Sunny grinned back, although inside, her stomach felt as though it was trying to eat itself. "I remember one thing I read," she said. "It said that no MudWing queen has ever been challenged by a sister — only daughters. I didn't understand it then, but I do now. In your tribe, brothers and sisters are always loyal to one another. A sister would never try to take the throne from her bigwings."

Clay nodded. "That feels right to me," he said.

Sunny stared at the queen, trying to memorize her features, or what she could see of them. Would this work? Was she really going to risk it?

The image of hundreds of IceWing corpses flashed through her head. *Of course I am.*

Struck by another idea, she studied all the queen's brothers and sisters, too. She wondered how many times the dreamvisitor could be used in one night.

"All right," she said, pulling Clay away.

They chose the darkest patch of shadow they could find, outside the camp, with the mountains looming over them.

"Maybe you should be the one to do this," she whispered to Clay, trying to pass him the dreamvisitor.

He shook his head and pushed it back to her. "You've used it before. And you'll know what to say. And if it's me — well, she might think it's a normal dream, just another MudWing voicing her inner anxieties or something. But if it's you, she'll know it's real. A real message from the dragonets, because nobody else looks like you."

That's true, Sunny thought. And then, wryly, *So maybe there* is *a good reason to look this weird after all.*

"You can do it, Sunny," Clay said. "I'm completely sure." He twined his tail around hers and she felt a tiny bit less terrified.

Sunny cupped her talons around the dreamvisitor and held it to her head, closing her eyes. She'd only ever used it on her friends.

Please let this work, she prayed.

She thought of the huge brown dragon she'd just seen. *Queen Moorhen. Let me in.*

After a long moment she opened her eyes and found herself standing ankle-deep in mud. Mud stretched around her, an endless warm swamp dotted with mangroves and dozing crocodiles. The sun was high above them in a hazy sky and insects buzzed through the long cattails.

Sunny turned in a circle and spotted Queen Moorhen pacing across a dry island that stuck out of the mud. Several scrolls were scattered around her talons, many of them covered in brown spatters, and a large map of Pyrrhia was scratched into the dirt. The queen lashed her tail and drew long lines with her claws across the mountains, furrowing them through the sketched-out Kingdom of Sand, and then slashing furiously at the corner of the map that represented the Ice Kingdom. She stopped, shook her head, and glanced down at the mud.

With a jolt of horror, Sunny realized that there were dead bodies lying half submerged around the queen's island. She recognized at least one of them as one of the queen's brothers, who'd been sleeping nearby in the royal camp.

This is a real nightmare. She might not be able to hear me.

But Sunny had to try. She waded through the mud, which felt gloppily real against her scales, and clambered up onto the island behind the MudWing queen.

Moorhen whirled around and stared at her.

Sunny spread her talons. "I'm harmless," she said. "I'm here to talk."

"Here? Now?" the queen demanded. "Can't you see I'm in the middle of a campaign? And everyone is dying and it's all my fault and I can't save them?" She slashed her claws across the Kingdom of Sand and turned to look down into the mud again. Her wings trembled and she lowered her snout to the closest corpse. "No. *No, I command* you not to die."

"This is a dream," Sunny said firmly and loudly. "You're only dreaming. I promise you."

The queen drew back from the corpse. "Hmm," she said.

"It's a nightmare," Sunny said. "But they're not dead. Your brothers and sisters are asleep right beside you in the camp. They're safe, at least for now."

"What does that mean?" Queen Moorhen asked. Her voice sounded less strained and her wings were relaxing. "Is that a threat?"

"Not at all," Sunny said hastily. "I want them to be safe, too. I want all your subjects to be safe. That's why I'm here."

The queen looked up at the sky, then around at the swamp, down at the map, and back at Sunny. "This is really a dream? Then how are you here?"

"Old magic," Sunny said. "But that's not important. Do you know who I am?"

"I have a guess," said the queen. "Shouldn't there be five of you?"

"There are five of us," Sunny said. "But I'm the one here talking to you. I'm here to tell you not to attack the Ice Kingdom. Not tomorrow, not ever. Too many dragons will die if you do, on both sides."

"Is that an omen?" Queen Moorhen asked. "Did your NightWing tell you that?"

"You know it doesn't take a NightWing prophecy to see that future," Sunny said, touching one claw lightly to the scratched-up map beside her. "You *know* how many of your dragons you'll lose."

The queen drew a line in the dirt in front of her. "But then the war will be over, and perhaps that'll be worth it. Burn has promised us immunity from attack for the next hundred years if we help her win. If we don't — she'll destroy us. She is a powerful enemy, little SandWing. A lot more powerful than you, and she's an enemy I don't intend to make."

"You don't have to," Sunny said, thinking, *That's how Burn got her MudWing alliance? With intimidation and threats? So Queen Moorhen joined the war to* protect *her dragons. . . . It sounds backward, but I can see it.* "We're going to end the war. We have a message for Burn — meet us at midnight in seven days' time, in the main courtyard of her stronghold. If you can tell her to do that instead of attacking the IceWings, we'll find a way to stop the war. And you can come, too. We want everyone to see that this is the end of the fighting. No more dragons have to die."

Queen Moorhen tilted her head with a skeptical expression. "It sounds like a tale from one of the SeaWing queen's silly romantic scrolls. What are you planning to do?"

"You'll see," Sunny said. "Just be there. Be there instead of watching your dragons die in the Ice Kingdom. Bring the SkyWings, too. Everyone who wants this war to be over."

The queen nodded slowly. "I'll think about it. Are you choosing Burn, then?"

"We're choosing peace," Sunny said. "That's the important thing."

"That sounds like you're avoiding the question," Moorhen pointed out.

"Does it matter?" Sunny asked. "As long as the war is over?"

The queen thought for a long time, and then sighed. "Perhaps not."

"Make sure Burn is there," Sunny said. "It's important."

"It sounds like it," said the MudWing queen. She brushed her tail over the map of Pyrrhia, erasing it and all the agonized clawmarks she'd drawn on it. "I'll see what I can do."

That sounded a little ridiculous to Sunny — if the queen of the MudWings couldn't do as she'd asked, then what chance did anyone have? But she didn't say that. She bowed and stepped back.

"Thank you, Your Majesty," she said instead.

"Good luck," said the queen. "You're very small to be in charge of saving the world."

"And weird-looking," Sunny agreed. "But we can do it if everyone helps."

"Hmmm." Queen Moorhen pulled her wings in close and stared down at the mud-covered bodies of her brothers and sisters all around her. "Maybe."

As Sunny lifted the dreamvisitor away from her head, stepping out of the dream, she thought she heard the queen whisper one last thing.

"I hope so."

~ CHAPTER 23 ~

Sunny was tired after visiting the queen's dream, but she made herself step into the dreams of the royal siblings next. Three brothers and one sister, all of them having similar anxiety dreams, most of them about Queen Moorhen dying in some awful way. One of the brothers was having such a terrible nightmare that Sunny wasn't able to get through to him at all, but the others saw her, and they seemed to listen to what she said. They each answered that it was up to Moorhen to make the decision, but Sunny had a feeling the queen would listen to her siblings more than any other advisors she might have, and if they could persuade her . . . well, it was worth the chance.

After that, as she and Clay were walking back through the camp, past so many sleeping dragons, she stopped, brushing his wing with hers.

"We can do more," she said. "Not all of them, but . . . if even a few dragons talk about having dream messages from us, maybe that'll make a difference."

"Aren't you tired?" Clay asked. "You look like you haven't slept in a week."

There had been a lot of exhausting flying lately, more than she was used to, and all she wanted was to curl up under Clay's wing and sleep for the next month. But that was not an option.

"I can do it," she assured him.

"Let me do some, too," he said, holding out his talons. "You can rest while I do that."

They chose sleeping dragons at random, standing in the shadows nearby and dropping lightly into their dreams. Most of them were nightmares; there were nightmares all through the camp. Sometimes Sunny could break through and show them they were dreaming, and then they would listen. She kept her messages brief: The war is almost over. No more killing. Don't go to the Ice Kingdom. The war will be over soon. You can help. Stop fighting. Spread the word.

They found Reed and the others again as early morning light was beginning to creep across the camp. Umber, Marsh, and Sora were fast asleep in a pile of tails and wings, but Pheasant and Reed were awake, watching for them with matching anxious expressions.

"We did our best," Clay whispered, pressing their talons in his. "Hopefully you'll get new orders soon."

"But we should go before we're seen," Sunny said.

"Do you want to come with us?" Clay asked.

Reed sighed and looked at his sleeping brothers and sister. "No. I mean, I do, but we are loyal to the queen, and we don't want to be fugitives. I wish I could at least give you Umber or Marsh, but they won't leave the rest of us. We stick together. That's our way."

"I'm sorry," Clay said reluctantly. "I wish I could stay. If you do have to fight . . . I wish I could be there with you."

"Me too," Reed admitted in a low voice.

Pheasant shook her head but didn't say anything. She nudged the others awake, and they each hugged Clay good-bye.

"See you soon," Sunny said, trying to sound more hopeful than she felt.

"Be safe," Clay said. "I'm glad you have Reed." He wrapped his wings around his brother again, and then he and Sunny hurried off through the camp, toward the safety of the mountains. They stayed on the ground, afraid that the guards would spot them if they flew this close to the camp.

Most of the campfires were now just dying embers, but a few had been rebuilt and the smell of roasting meat and smoke floated through the pre-dawn air. Birds fluttered and chirped in the trees at halfhearted intervals, as if they weren't sure they should be awake yet. Sunny's eyes ached and her wings had never felt heavier.

They had reached the scrub brush on the hills overlooking the camp when Sunny heard a different sound coming from behind them. Not the rustling and stamping of dragons or the clanking of weapons.

She heard singing.

Oh, the dragonets are coming . . .

"Clay," she whispered. "Do you hear that? Am I imagining it?"

He stopped and lifted his head to listen.

They're coming to save the day . . .

Voices in the camp below — more than one, in different parts of the camp. The MudWings were singing.

They're coming to fight, for they know what's right . . .

It was the eerie version they'd last heard in the Sky Palace, not the usual rousing bar song that Tsunami used to sing around the cave whenever she wanted to annoy the guardians. Sunny had been trapped in her birdcage, alone, on display above the banquet Scarlet was holding for Burn. But everyone there had heard it — the sound of the prisoners singing, echoing over the cliffs in the night. Sunny could remember the shivery, hopeful feeling it had given her, and she also remembered the expressions on some of the soldiers' faces. Hope, dread, longing . . . most of them much more complicated than the pure fury visible on Scarlet and Burn.

She felt it again now, like sand trickling across her scales all the way down her spine. Those dragons singing — those were the dragons who believed in them. They were the reason she and her friends had to do this.

I hope we can do this. I really, really hope we can do this.

She glanced up at Clay, who smiled at her. Just being near him made her feel like anything was possible. Clay was so real and solid and dependable and kind. He would always be there.

Clay had kept all of them from killing each other as they grew up under the mountain, trapped with only one another and their guardians. If he hadn't been there, would they have been more like the "alternates" — the fake dragonets of destiny — who'd hated one another? Could Tsunami, Glory, and Starflight have turned out that way, hostile and aggressive and angry all the time, if they hadn't had Clay to keep them together? Would Sunny have ended up like Fatespeaker, clinging to a belief in a friendship and loyalty that didn't exist?

But that hadn't happened. They'd had Clay, and he stopped them from fighting too much, and he made jokes when anyone was sad, and he made them care about one another, and he believed in all of them. He'd made them a family, even though they were from different tribes.

He really is our bigwings.

"Let's get back to the others," she said, and he nodded, and soon they were winging their way back to the rainforest.

Six more days.

We can do this.

"She's not coming?" Sunny cried. "What do you mean she's not coming?" A shower of raindrops pattered over her wings, sending pink-and-red hibiscus flowers whirling down past her toward the ground far below.

Jambu shook his head, looking very literally blue from horns to tail. "We tried, but every IceWing we talked to basically laughed at us. They said Blaze never leaves her fortress, and she won't until Glacier lets her go, which will be when Burn and Blister are dead."

"They know if she gets near one of her sisters, she's dead," Mangrove said. "She doesn't stand a chance in a challenge duel."

"Then why do the IceWings support her?" Glory said crossly. "Don't they want the SandWings to have a strong queen? No, of course they don't," she answered herself, figuring it out as she spoke. "The one kingdom they share a border with — wouldn't it be great if it happened to be ruled by a vain, silly dragon who was totally in debt to them and did everything their queen ordered. Maddening for us, but sensible for them. Queen Glacier knows what she's doing. Unless she loses — like if Blaze happened to die somehow — in which case she'd have to deal with Burn right on her border, all enraged and looking for vengeance. All right, yes, I can see why she'd keep her safely locked up. Three *moons*."

"That was like watching her brain work on the outside of her head," Fatespeaker said to Starflight.

"Well, we can't let her stay all locked up," Sunny said. "It's not going to work unless all three sisters are there. Right? Don't you agree?"

"Yes," Glory said, and Tsunami and Starflight nodded as well. "If what you want is to forge a peace treaty, all the combatants need to be present to agree to it." Glory scratched her snout, thinking. "Perhaps it would be enough to have Queen Glacier there . . . but I don't think so. Glacier would know that it would look like weakness to come in her place and let Blaze stay in hiding. Safer for neither of them to show up."

"But doesn't Queen Glacier want to end the war, too?" Sunny said. "I'm sure she does. I'm especially sure she would if she knew what Burn and the MudWings were planning a few days ago, even if they've put off their invasion plans for now."

"Are we sure about that?" Starflight asked. "They're really not invading?"

"It doesn't look like it," Glory said. On her shoulder, her sloth woke up, chirruped sleepily, and tucked itself closer to her wing before closing its eyes again. "We've dreamvisited with Clay's brother and also sent out scouts to check. It seems like that MudWing camp is in a holding pattern — no one flying off to kill IceWings, at least for now."

"Queen Moorhen is waiting to see what happens at the stronghold," Sunny said, shaking loose flowers off her wings. "Which means our plan really has to work, or else the invasion might still happen. Maybe if we could tell Queen Glacier that, she'd let Blaze come."

"Maybe," Tsunami said, "but we can't get to the queen if she's in her ice palace, not that it would be safe to go talk to her no matter where she is."

"And none of us have seen her, so we can't even dreamvisit her," Clay pointed out.

"But we *can* dreamvisit Blaze," Sunny said. "I think that's what we have to do. Glory, you should do it. You're really convincing."

Glory looked down at the sapphire as Sunny passed it to her. She thought for a moment, then shook her head. "No, she won't listen to me. She kept saying I shouldn't be part of the prophecy, remember? She wouldn't take me seriously."

"And she's jealous of Glory," Deathbringer interjected. "Blaze doesn't like any dragons prettier than she is. Which Glory is. Not that I've noticed, myself, personally. It's just a fact."

"Enough out of you," Glory said, folding her wings in, but not before Sunny spotted the hints of pink blooming along the edges. "I've already said you can be the NightWing liaison, so flattery won't get you anything else, Mr. Clever Scales."

"It's not flattery to state the obvious," he said.

"It should be Sunny or Tsunami," Glory said, ignoring him and passing the sapphire back into Sunny's talons. "Tsunami actually got wounded trying to help her, so she might be impressed by that. But then, Tsunami is about as diplomatic as a starving rhinoceros, so I'd probably vote for Sunny."

"I BEG YOUR PARDON," Tsunami objected. "I can be VERY DIPLOMATIC when I WANT to be."

"I'm sure," Glory said. "Any other votes?"

As each of them voted for her, Sunny felt as though her own scales might turn pink.

"You are all — you're — you're such a bunch of —" Tsunami sputtered.

"Frog-faced blobs of camel spit?" Sunny suggested.

Tsunami started laughing so hard she nearly fell off the branch. "All right, fine," she said, recovering at last. "I don't see how I can compete with that kind of mastery of language."

"But then you should use the dreamvisitor to talk to your mother," Sunny said. "Or to someone in your kingdom. Some

SeaWings should come to the stronghold, if any of them are willing, to see what happens."

Tsunami nodded, bumping Sunny's shoulder affectionately. "I can do that. I'd like to check on Anemone anyway."

That night, Sunny took the dreamvisitor and flew to the pool by the tunnels. She chose the tunnel that led from the Kingdom of Sand to the rainforest. The one that led to the Night Kingdom smelled of burnt scales and fire, and still radiated heat.

She crouched in the darkest part of the tunnel, where it was pitch-black. There was nothing around her to offer a clue about where she was. Even if the dreamvisitor gave the dreamer a glimpse of her, all she would see was blackness. Hopefully Blaze would think it was a cave in the mountains, if anything.

She closed her eyes and held the blue sapphire to her head again. It hummed in a strange way, like faraway chanting faintly heard through layers of rock.

Blaze. Sunny pictured the beautiful SandWing. They'd only met once, in the Ice Kingdom. Later, she'd overheard Tsunami describing Blaze to Kinkajou: *"She's pretty but silly, one of those overly optimistic dragons. Like Sunny is sometimes, although Blaze is more self-centered."*

This comparison had made Sunny want to shred a tree with her bare claws. She was nothing, *nothing* like Blaze, and if Tsunami thought so, then she really must think Sunny was an idiot with no brains in her head at all.

Don't think about that now. Concentrate on getting into Blaze's dreams, she thought, and then she opened her eyes and realized she was already there. She stood in the desert, claws sinking into warm sand.

Blaze was flying, her polished scales shimmering in the bright hot sunlight. She shone against the clear blue sky, and beautiful jewels sparkled all along her scales. She kept circling in the air and twisting her head to look down, not far from where Sunny was, but she didn't seem to notice Sunny at first. Sunny lifted herself onto her back talons to look around and spotted a clear pool of water not far away. Blaze was admiring herself in the perfectly still reflection.

"Good grief," Sunny muttered. She flared her wings and waved at the SandWing in the sky. It took a lot of flapping before Blaze finally gave a little start and veered around to stare at Sunny.

Sunny beckoned, wanting to have this conversation on solid ground.

Blaze landed in front of her, kicking sand up Sunny's nose without noticing she'd done so. She swished her tail around and sat gracefully.

"Hello. I know you, don't I?" she asked.

"We've met," Sunny said. "I'm one of the dragonets." That was all she had to say. "Dragonets of destiny" didn't sound right to her anymore, not since she'd found out the truth about the prophecy. She wondered briefly what would happen if she just told the SandWing sisters that the prophecy was false.

Then they really wouldn't listen to us, she thought. *We'd have no chance of making this work. We have to let them believe it, at least for now.*

"Oh, of course, the weird-looking SandWing," Blaze said. "Right. Which necklace do you think looks better on me? I've always liked rubies, but these emeralds are smashing, too, right?" She held out two gem-studded necklaces, draped sparklingly across her claws.

"Blaze," Sunny said. "Do you want to go home?"

The SandWing princess looked around, blinking. "Aren't I home?"

"This is a dream," Sunny said patiently. "I mean, really home. Home to the stronghold and the desert, to sand and roasted lizards and warm sunshine every day."

"Oh my," Blaze said with a wistful sigh. "I remember my rooms in the stronghold. They were so big and pretty, with tall windows on three walls. I really do look my best in full natural sunlight, you know." She spread her wings and swished them gracefully around, admiring them.

Sunny managed not to roll her eyes. "So come to us. Don't keep hiding in that cold, dark fortress. If you come to the stronghold, we'll end this war and you can go home."

"What?" Blaze said, tilting her head. "Right now?"

"The third midnight from tonight," Sunny said. "Didn't anyone give you our message?"

"No one's said anything about a message," said Blaze. "From the dragonets of the prophecy! How could they keep something like that from me? Well, I *am* offended." She thought for a moment, then brightened. "Oh! So you *did* pick me!"

"Well, wait," Sunny said. "We haven't picked any of you yet. We —"

"Right, of course, you haven't announced it or anything, but you're going to pick me. The only way I can go home, after all, is if my sisters are dead. Oh, how lovely! I knew you would choose me; I'm very nice. And doesn't everyone want a beautiful queen?"

Not at all, Sunny thought. "We're really looking for a peaceful outcome," she said. "That's our goal. And then whoever becomes queen —"

"I'm going to order a new bracelet to celebrate!" Blaze declared, jumping up and nearly dancing around Sunny. "And a crown! Of course I need a crown! Oh, now I really have to decide, rubies or emeralds? I suppose I could have two crowns! Or lots and lots of crowns! I'm so excited!"

"Blaze, stop," Sunny said desperately. The princess wasn't listening to her at all, and Sunny didn't want to lie to her, or make her show up under false pretenses. "The important thing is that you be there at the stronghold. And then we'll figure out who should be queen. It might not be you. Do you understand?"

"Glacier is going to be pleased, too," said Blaze, talking right over Sunny. "I'll have to convince her to let me go, but I can win arguments when I really want to. I'll tell her there's a new crown in it for her, too. I think *she* looks best in sapphires, naturally."

"So you'll be there?" Sunny said. "Even knowing you might not be queen when it's all over?"

Blaze was already swanning back to the still pool. "You can live in my palace if you like!" she called back to Sunny. "I could give you a really important job, ooo, like helping me get dressed in the morning! Sometimes it takes me simply hours to choose the right anklet."

"Midnight at the stronghold!" Sunny cried after her. "Three midnights from tonight! That means not tonight, not tomorrow night, but the night after that. Will you remember? Will you count right?"

"Queen Blaze!" sang the SandWing princess as she lifted into the air. "Doesn't that sound pretty?"

Oh, dear, Sunny thought. She stepped out of the dream and stared into the blackness all around her.

Will Queen Glacier listen to her?

Will she be there?

What if all of this falls apart and we fail?

She gripped the dreamvisitor tightly in her claws.

That's not an option. If Blaze doesn't show up, I'll fly to the Ice Kingdom and drag her back myself.

In four days' time, either the war will be over . . . or we'll all be dead.

CHAPTER 24

Night had fallen, and the sky was full of dragons.

That was the first thing Sunny noticed when she stepped out of the tunnel onto the desert sands. The air crackled with the sound of wingbeats and the smell of fire. Dragons soared overhead like a million bats, sinuous shapes silhouetted across the moons.

It was time. This was the night. All three SandWing sisters would be in the same place for the first time since the war began.

If they show up, Sunny thought. She glanced at the night sky again. *It certainly seems like every other dragon in Pyrrhia might be here.*

And it was easier to see them than it should have been because of the mystery orb in the sky. It had gotten bigger and brighter every night, and now it was the same size as the other moons — two of which were full. Between the three of them filling the sky, it looked like another brightest night.

A new brightest night when there shouldn't have been one for another ninety-four years, Sunny thought. *If that's not an omen, what is?*

She hadn't said that to her friends, though. She knew

they'd roll their eyes at her and the whole idea of "destiny" or "omens." But still, that third uncanny moon in the sky made her feel somehow a little more hopeful . . . like maybe things would be all right. The way she used to feel when she thought about the prophecy.

Sunny climbed up to the ridge overlooking the stronghold and stood between two cacti, gazing down at it. The long black structure, all shadows in the moonlight, was vast and forbidding even from a distance, and she still had nightmares about the weirdling tower. She couldn't imagine stepping back inside there of her own free will.

But that was exactly what she was about to do.

The sound of shifting sand behind her signaled the arrival of her friends, and Sunny turned to see Clay, then Tsunami, then Starflight and Fatespeaker emerge from the tunnel.

Fatespeaker glanced around at the desert, at the way the sand seemed to run all the way to the edge of the sky. She shuddered. "This place is freaky," she whispered. "Starflight, I don't think it's safe here. Shouldn't you stay behind?"

Starflight shook his head. "No, I have to be here. I'm not missing this — even if I can't see it." He'd been practicing with Tamarin, the blind RainWing, all week. How to fly with someone guiding him; how to sense unexpected obstacles; and most of all, how to ask for help.

Sunny slid down the hill to them and brushed Starflight's wing with hers to let him know she was there. He leaned toward her, touching the bandage on his eyes.

"What *is* that?" Fatespeaker asked, staring up at the sky. "Starflight, why is there a fourth moon?"

Sunny had already described it to him, although his explanation didn't make all that much sense to her.

"I think it's more like a comet than a moon," Starflight said to Fatespeaker. "I remember a scroll that mentioned something like that in the sky hundreds of years ago. Maybe it circles around and only comes back every thousand years or so. Have you noticed the earthquakes? I think they might be caused by the comet."

The ground trembled quietly under them, the way it had several times in the last few days. Sunny dug her claws into the sand, glancing up at the stars.

"But it's not going to, like, land on us or anything, right?" Fatespeaker said. "Because it sure looks like it's gotten bigger. I think maybe it's going to fall on us. OOH, I THINK MAYBE I'M HAVING A VISION."

"Stop that," Starflight said, smacking her gently with his wing. "You know those powers aren't real. Your visions are just your imagination."

Fatespeaker shot him a very indignant look that he luckily couldn't see. "I know that's what Stonemover said, but I think it doesn't apply to me. My visions are TOTALLY real, and when this moon-comet thing CRUSHES US ALL, everyone will be sorry for not listening to me."

"All right," he answered. "We'll see."

"Where's Glory?" Tsunami asked, coming back from scouting the top of the dunes.

"Right behind us," said Clay, and he jumped out of the way as more dragons started coming out of the tunnel.

It was strange to know that all these dragons were RainWings but to see instead SkyWings and NightWings and MudWings. Glory had decided to bring fifteen RainWings along — to be voices for peace, if necessary, and to be dangerous venom-spitting backup if *really* necessary. She'd decided it would be safer for her dragons if they came in disguise, their camouflage scales making them anonymous bystanders. Those three tribes were the easiest disguises — no poisonous tails, webbed talons, or serrated claws among them.

There were five actual NightWings as well, plus Deathbringer, who'd refused to stay behind and let Glory go without him.

"But you could be useful here," Glory had argued back in the rainforest. "You could keep an eye on the NightWings for me."

"I'd rather keep an eye on you," he'd retorted. "And on all the dragons you're about to go chat with who literally want to kill you."

"Hey, that's how you and I met," Glory said. "Maybe I'll charm them out of the idea, too."

"I'm not sure *charm* is quite the word I'd use," he'd mused, and gotten a swat to his nose as a thank-you.

But she'd let him select five NightWings he thought were more trustworthy than the rest, so that the tribe would be represented at this gathering. Sunny thought that was probably a good idea, although she was still having trouble forgiving the black dragons for all their lies. Mangrove and Grandeur had been left in charge of everyone while they were gone.

The five dragonets climbed up to stand on the ridge, surveying the stronghold below and the clouds of dragons who were already descending on it.

"What if they start fighting?" Fatespeaker asked suddenly. "All these dragons from different tribes who've been at war for so long. What if something happens and they start trying to kill each other?"

Sunny curled her tail around her talons. What an awful thought. That hadn't even occurred to her.

"It'd be a huge battle," Deathbringer said. "That might end the war itself."

"With hundreds more dead dragons," Sunny said. "No, that's not all right. We'll stop them if we have to."

"Right," Tsunami said. "By asking nicely? Is that the plan?"

"You'd be surprised how effective asking nicely can be," Sunny said. "Maybe if you ever tried it, you'd know."

"Yowch," Glory said with a grin, and Tsunami glared at both of them.

"Well, let's get down there before anything happens," Clay suggested.

"Before we go," Sunny said, turning to her friends, "I just — I just want you guys to know that I love you. And I don't regret anything that's happened. I'm not mad about the fake prophecy or the Talons stealing us, because without all of that, I wouldn't have grown up with you, and you're more important to me than anything. You're my brothers and sisters. You're my real family. So it was worth it, no matter what."

"Awwww," Clay said, pulling her into his wings for a fierce hug.

"Uh-oh," Glory said. "A mushy speech. We're all going to die, aren't we?"

"She means she loves you, too," Tsunami translated, dragging Sunny away from Clay so she could hug her as well. "And so do I."

"Me too," Starflight said quietly, and they all wrapped their wings around him together. Sunny felt the sinewy curve of his shoulder pressing against her snout and smelled the herbs in the bandage on his eyes. *Poor Starflight. Is that enough of an answer for him? I do love him. But . . . like a brother. I wish I felt more. . . .*

There wasn't time to say anything else. It was almost midnight. They leaped into the sky, soaring down toward the stronghold with the RainWings and NightWings streaming out behind them.

From above, as they approached, Sunny could see that the courtyard looked deserted. The monument to Queen Oasis was a tower of darkness, rejecting the moonlight and casting a long shadow across the sand circle around it. The soldiers' barracks were empty. The flat white stones stretched blankly, glowing as if they were made of the same stuff as the weird moon. Fire flickered from torches that studded the courtyard like claws.

What if they don't come?

The dragons who had flown in to watch were gathered all along the walls, wing to wing. They'd torn out the heads on spikes and dropped the gruesome trophies onto the sands below, making room for the hundreds of spectators instead.

It was hard to tell which tribe was which in the silvery moonlight. All the dragons seemed to have scales of silver and black and gray. But Sunny was pretty sure she spotted SeaWings sitting next to MudWings; IceWings beside SkyWings; SandWings and NightWings and RainWings barely a few claws from one another.

That's what I really want, Sunny thought. *A Pyrrhia where all dragons can see that we're basically the same, no matter what kinds of natural weapons we hatch with, or don't hatch with, for some of us. A Pyrrhia where it doesn't matter what tribe you're from, because you can have friends from any tribe. Like us.*

As her gaze scanned the walls, she spotted familiar SandWing scales and her heart squeezed happily. Thorn was here, along with Six-Claws and Qibli and no doubt more Outclaws. Even if everything went horribly wrong, Sunny had this strange, warm feeling that her mother would care about her and want to know her, whether or not she saved the world.

Sunny was surprised to find herself thinking, *Maybe that's better than a prophecy and a great destiny.*

But I do still have to save the world. Right now, in fact.

She was on one side of Starflight with Fatespeaker on the other; they guided him down to the sand, and Sunny heard

Fatespeaker describing the scene for him in a whisper. Clay thumped down next to her and sneezed as sand went up his nose.

Tsunami and Glory arrived without Deathbringer, who had been sent to the walls along with the dragons they'd brought with them. Sunny was a little surprised that Deathbringer had agreed to be that far away from Glory, but she glanced at the determined look on Glory's face and figured she wouldn't have argued with that either.

Glory herself was disguised as a SkyWing, red and gold scales rippling along her wings. "Ironic, right?" she'd said, lashing her crimson tail. "Now at least I look like I belong in the prophecy."

And judging by the murmurs coming from above them, the audience was thinking the same thing.

The five dragonets, Sunny thought. *As Morrowseer foretold. Here we are, prophecy or no prophecy.*

Now where are the queens who blister and blaze and burn?

A rumbling growl came from the dark entrance to the old palace.

And Burn stepped out into the moonlight.

CHAPTER 25

Three moons, Sunny thought, *she's even bigger than I remembered.*

Burn was a massive, heavy dragon with jagged scars all over her pale yellow scales, including a particularly vicious one all along her side under her left wing. A more recent wound was slashed across her snout, oozing olive-green pus and dark blood. Her black eyes glittered and her stained claws gleamed with what looked like fresh blood as she slithered across the stones toward them.

"So you came," she hissed. "I thought the rumors couldn't possibly be true." She cast a seething look up at the hundreds of watching dragons. "I hope you have a good reason for disrupting my battle plans."

"This war is over," Sunny said, as loud as she could. There was a ripple of whispers along the walls as her words were passed along.

"Really," said Burn. "Because you say so, is that it?"

"Because we all say so," Tsunami retorted. She flared her wings to include all the dragons above and around them.

"Interesting," said Burn. "But I see a problem. In fact, I see two problems, flying this way right now."

Sunny whirled and saw a mass of dragons arriving from the east. *Blister and her forces,* she thought hopefully. She looked north and spotted flashing silver scales. *Please let that be Blaze with the IceWings.*

"It's possible I won't kill you," Burn said. "After all, you've brought me my sisters to kill, which is more help than any other dragons have been. Then again, you're very annoying."

"This is not about killing," Sunny said. The sounds of wingbeats were getting closer, so she turned to watch Blister land next to the Queen Oasis monument. Blister sank her talons into the sand for a moment, shooting a deadly look up at the obelisk.

Blaze and Queen Glacier landed a moment later, off to Sunny's left. Blaze eyed her sisters nervously, staying close to the IceWing's side.

Blister slithered out of the sand and paced slowly between Sunny and Clay, her snakelike gaze pinned on Burn as she circled her older sister.

"You're still alive," Blister remarked in a cold, calm voice. "That's a pity." She paused and narrowed her eyes at the dragonets. "I was hoping you'd have my sisters dead before I got here."

"What?" Burn snarled. "They've chosen *me* as queen, not you."

"No way!" Blaze cried, then hurriedly backed into Glacier as her sisters whipped their heads toward her. "They picked me! They told me to come here!"

"We haven't chosen any of you," Sunny said firmly. "And we're definitely not killing any of you."

"Unless we have to," Glory observed. "Feel free to provoke us."

"Shh," Clay said, nudging her.

"We're here to find a peaceful solution," Sunny announced. "Either you three decide among you, *peacefully,* who's going to be queen, or everyone else here will decide for you. No more armies. No more dead dragons."

Burn barked a harsh, disbelieving laugh. "I have a better idea," she snarled. "First I kill my sisters, and then I kill all of you, and then I stuff you and spend the next hundred years telling your dead face about peaceful solutions."

Out of the corner of her eye, Sunny saw a flurry of movement from the part of the wall where Thorn was perched. "No one is going to let you do that," she said to Burn, trying to sound much braver than she felt.

"In fact," Blister interjected suddenly, "I've already made a gesture of peace. Didn't you get my present, Burn?"

An eerie silence fell for a moment as Burn stared down at her.

"I was thinking," Blister hissed into the stillness, "that this war has gone on too long. I thought if I sent you a gift . . . something I know you've always wanted . . . that perhaps we could . . . mend fences and reunite the family." She bared her teeth at the palace entrance and Sunny spotted Smolder just inside the doorway, where she'd first seen him.

"Aha," Burn snarled. "That was from you. Smolder, bring me the box."

"Now?" he said.

"Don't argue with me," she growled, and he vanished into the palace.

A gift? A gesture of peace — reuniting the family? That doesn't sound like Blister. Sunny flicked her tail anxiously. *Or is she really willing to stand down and let Burn be queen?*

Smolder returned a few moments later, carrying the box that Sunny had seen on the top floor of the weirdling tower, when she'd been chained up there. As he set it down in front of Burn, it let out a malevolent hiss.

"Burn, be careful," Sunny said. She had a horrible sinking feeling in her chest, and she really didn't like the look on Blister's face. "I — I think this might be a trick."

"Of course it is," Burn said. "Especially if it's from my clever little sister. Sending me a present, thinking I'll open it without any suspicion. As if I don't recognize the hiss of the dragonbite viper when I hear it."

"It's not a trick," Blister said coolly. "I know you've always wanted one for your collection."

"Dragonbite viper?" Fatespeaker whispered to Starflight.

"Rare and deadly," he whispered back. "The only snake in Pyrrhia that can kill a dragon with one bite." He shifted nervously on his talons. "If that's really what's in there. . . . I hope that's not really what's in there."

"Well, the trick's on you," Burn said. She sank her claws into the top of the box and ripped it off with a vicious tearing sound. Fast as lightning, her talons shot into the box and lifted out a writhing, hissing rope of scaly fury.

The snake's head was pinned between Burn's claws so it couldn't bite her. Its whole body wriggled and lashed like the eels attacking in the SeaWing prison.

"I know your sick, twisted mind. You thought this would kill me," Burn snarled at Blister. "So it'll be very poetic when it kills you instead." She took a step toward her sister and then stopped suddenly, looking down.

"Oh," Blister said, "I got you two. Did I leave out that part?"

A second dragonbite viper lunged out of the box and sank its teeth into Burn's ankle. Its venomous fangs slid like shards of ice right between her scales.

The screaming seemed to come from everywhere at once. Blaze was probably screaming the loudest, shrieking and flapping her wings as if she were the one who'd been bitten. All along the walls, dragons were pushing and yelling and leaning in to get a better look or taking off into the sky to get as far away from the snakes as possible.

Burn stamped one foot down on the second snake, crushing it, but it was too late. Black veins were shooting up her leg and spreading through her scales.

"What's happening?" Starflight asked, reaching out for Sunny.

Sunny touched his wing with her own. "There was a second snake in the box — and it bit Burn." This *was Blister's plan — the one I overheard her talking about in the mirror. Send Burn something she really wants and figure out a way for it to kill her. Clever and evil and sinister.* She looked over at

Blister, who was watching her sister's death throes with an enthralled, smug smile on her face.

We can't let her be queen. All of Pyrrhia would be in danger if Blister were queen.

But what else can we do? She's not going to accept Blaze on the throne instead . . . and it looks like this is the end for Burn.

Burn let out a furious roar and collapsed to the ground with a crash that shook the earth. Her wings twitched and convulsed as if they were possessed. She clawed at the air, reaching for Blister.

"I'll kill you," she snarled. "I'll claw that — I'll — it hurts — stop it, stop the —" She roared again, howling her agony at the sky.

Her ankle was entirely black now, the claws curling in and shriveling. The venom marched up toward her heart, fast and unstoppable.

"Is there anything we can do?" Sunny asked. "Clay? Starflight?"

Starflight shook his head mutely.

Burn rolled onto her back, wheezing as the black tendrils looped together in the center of her chest. Her arm flopped to the ground, her talons opened, and the first snake slithered loose onto the stones of the courtyard.

"The viper!" Blaze shrieked. "It's going to kill us!"

Pandemonium erupted along the walls.

"Fly!" screamed several dragons.

"Kill it!" roared others. "Or it will kill us all!"

Blister was in the air already, hovering over them and

watching gleefully as the snake shot toward the dragonets. It moved like lightning, zigzagging across the stones faster than flight.

"Up! Up! Up!" Tsunami shouted, shoving at her friends.

"Starflight!" Fatespeaker screamed.

Sunny whirled and saw Starflight stumble forward, his wings unfolding but slowly, too slowly. His talons reached out, trying to orient himself. The snake was nearly at his feet already.

Sunny and Fatespeaker reached him at the same time, grabbing his forearms and trying to lift him bodily into the sky. But they were both small, and Starflight was heavy and confused and unwieldy. His tail thwacked the ground and his wings nearly overbalanced them all as they tried to struggle into the air.

The viper hissed and it sounded as if it was coming from inside Sunny's skull.

It's going to get one of us, Sunny realized with a jolt of horror. *Let it be me. Please don't let Starflight die.*

And then something hit her, like a boulder slamming into all of them. Sunny, Fatespeaker, and Starflight tumbled backward, a tangle of wings and tails catapulted across the courtyard. Sunny was flung loose from the others and skidded across the sand, crashing finally into the Queen Oasis obelisk.

She shoved herself back up, dizzy and disoriented. What had happened? Had someone pushed them? Did the snake bite anyone? Was Starflight all right?

Her head took a moment to clear, and then she realized there was a dragon lying on the stones where she'd been standing a moment before. The dragon who'd slammed into them; the dragon who'd saved their lives.

It was Clay.

CHAPTER 26

"No!" Sunny screamed.

"Sunny! Stay back! The viper's still alive!" Deathbringer yelled from overhead. She realized that he was holding Glory in the air, and the RainWing queen was fighting to get away.

But no one was holding her back, and she didn't care about the snake. She didn't care if she did get bitten; she wasn't going to leave Clay lying there, dying.

She scrambled across the courtyard and threw her wings over him, shaking him with her talons. "Clay!" she yelled. "Clay!"

He looked dazed but his eyes were open. Maybe the snake had missed him. She couldn't see it anywhere. Maybe —

"Ow," Clay said, trying to sit up. "Ow, I — my leg — wow, that *really hurts* —" He pressed his claws to his head and looked as if he might pass out.

And then Sunny saw the wound — the fang marks in the flesh of Clay's right thigh. A black starburst had already appeared around the two holes, pulsing bigger and bigger across his warm brown scales.

"Clay." Sunny started to cry. "Please don't die."

"I'm — I'm, uh — open to suggestions," he said with a small, breathless laugh. He reached toward his leg then flinched back, gritting his teeth in pain.

Tsunami thumped down on his other side and let out a gasp at the sight of the snake bite. She twisted to look at the courtyard around them. "Where's the snake?" she said. "Where did it go?"

"I don't know," Sunny said. She could barely see through her tears. She leaned against Clay, trying to send all the warmth from her scales into him.

"Hey, it's all right," Clay said, although his claws were clenched and his wings were starting to shudder. "It's not such a bad destiny, Sunny. I'd die to save you and Starflight over and over if I had to." His voice caught on the last few words and he stopped, breathing hard.

"I order you not to die," Tsunami said, grabbing his shoulder. "Clay, stop, STOP IT. Stop dying RIGHT NOW." Her normally bossy voice was full of panic.

"Ow!" Deathbringer roared from up in the sky, and a moment later, Glory crash-landed into Sunny.

"No, no, no," Glory said, looking at the growing burst of black. Her scales had turned lily-green and white — the colors of fear and panic and pain. "No, we have to be able to stop this. There must be something we can do. Starflight!" she bellowed. "Think! How do you stop a dragonbite viper's poison? The scrolls must have said something," she muttered, touching Clay's scales. He winced as her claws brushed the blackened area. "Why can't I remember anything? Why is it spreading so fast?"

Sunny looked around for the first time and realized that the dragons along the walls had fallen completely silent, staring at them. Blister and Blaze were watching, too, one with cold interest and the other with horror.

Over by the wall, Starflight was trying to find them, stumbling forward with his claws held out, although Fatespeaker was trying to drag him back.

And . . . there was something hurtling out of the sky toward them. Something that blazed fiery orange and trailed smoke. A dragon with burning scales.

"Out of the way!" Peril yelled. "Sunny! Get everyone out of the way!"

Tsunami reacted first, leaping over Clay to shove Sunny and Glory back. The heat from Peril's scales swept over them as the SkyWing hit the ground and nearly slid into Clay.

"You can't die!" Peril yelled at him. "I won't let you!"

"Don't —" Tsunami started forward. "What are you —?"

"I'm burning out the poison," Peril said, and she stabbed her smoldering claws straight into the center of the black starburst on Clay's leg.

With a roar of crazed agony, Clay surged up as though he was trying to fly away. Tsunami, Glory, and Sunny flung themselves at him and pinned him down, but he was bigger and stronger and fighting hard.

"Deathbringer, get down here!" Glory yelled, and a moment later the NightWing was there, adding his weight to theirs.

Sunny grabbed Clay's front talons in hers and held on for dear life. "Clay, it's all right! She's helping you!"

But Clay was in too much pain to hear her. He jerked and thrashed, his howls digging into Sunny's heart like IceWing claws. She closed her eyes and leaned into him. The awful smell of melting scales and burning flesh assailed her, as if she were burying her snout in the NightWing volcano.

She felt more dragons join them, holding down Clay's wings and keeping his claws away from Peril. When she opened her eyes again, it was who she expected: Riptide and Starflight — and also who she didn't: Thorn, clasping Sunny and Clay's talons between her own.

"Mother," she whispered with relief, resting her head against the warm SandWing scales.

"This should have been me," Thorn said, "but I couldn't get to you in time."

Sunny shook her head and chanced a look at Clay's leg. Peril still had her talons buried in his scales, carving out everything that had been touched by the black venom. There was a scorched, gaping, bleeding hole in Clay's thigh and Sunny had to look away quickly before she threw up.

"I'm not sure he can survive this," Thorn whispered gently to Sunny. "That big of a burn . . ."

"He can," Sunny said fiercely. "Maybe no one else could, but *he* can."

"Fireproof scales," Starflight said, across from them.

"Oh. I hope . . ." Thorn said, and then she spread her wing around Sunny's back and pulled her close, falling silent.

A few moments later, Peril said, "That's all of it," in an exhausted voice, and stepped back. "I think. It better be. I don't see any more venom, do you?" she asked Sunny. "Clay? Clay? Are you all right?"

Clay had passed out. His wings were limp and his head lolled to the side when Riptide let go of it.

"Is he all right?" Peril said, her voice rising. "Tell me it worked!"

"It worked," Glory said. She rested her talons on Clay's chest, which was rising and falling evenly.

The black venom had stopped spreading; Peril had burned it all out of him. Sunny could see his fireproof scales trying to fix themselves, warm brown smoothing over the scorched spots. But the hole Peril had had to gouge out of his leg was too big for the scales to knit over. Clay was going to be scarred and probably limping for life.

But he was alive. He'd survived the snakebite. That was all that mattered.

"Thank you," Sunny said to Peril. She automatically reached to hug Peril, but the SkyWing jumped back before they could touch.

"Seriously," Tsunami said, rubbing her face with her talons and sitting back. "You — that — I don't know what to say."

Glory had her tail curled around her talons and was holding her wings in close as wave after wave of odd colors spread through her scales. Deathbringer put one wing around her, gently, and she let him.

"Maybe," Clay mumbled, and they all leaned closer to hear him. "Maybe Peril is the wings of fire." He lapsed back into unconsciousness.

Sunny saw the nervously delighted expression on Peril's face and felt as if her heart might explode.

The NightWings just made that up — "wings of fire" was nothing but a pretty phrase to them. But it is something, and it's more than Peril's burning scales. Peril helped us because Clay is wonderful. He was kind to her when no one else ever was, and he believed in her, no matter what she'd done. His heart is the real wings of fire.

She glanced around at her friends. *Clay's heart, Tsunami's courage, Glory's determination, Starflight's loyalty . . . I think the wings of fire are inside all of us, inside every dragon. Maybe you just have to reach inside and find it.*

A sinister hiss interrupted her thoughts, and she whirled around as a jolt of fear ran through her.

The dragonbite viper was slithering up between two of the stones, eyeing the group of dragonets with a dark, cold, lidless glare.

Peril leaped forward and smashed her talons down on it. The snake flailed horribly for a moment, and then crumpled into a shriveled, burnt-out husk.

"Ah, well," said Blister's voice, behind them. "That would have been convenient, killing all my enemies with one snake, so to speak."

Blister flicked her tail up and studied them for a long moment as they turned to face her. Tsunami squared her shoulders and glared back at her, talons clenched as if she was ready to fight.

"But I think I'll deal with you later," Blister said. Her eyes shifted toward the hordes of gathered dragons and Sunny realized that Blister wasn't sure what they would do. If Blister tried to kill the prophecy dragonets, right here in front of everybody . . . would they stop her? How would they all react?

"For now," Blister said, "I'm finally just one step away from the throne that is rightfully mine. And that step, of course —" She turned to her sister, Blaze, who cowered back against the IceWing queen.

"Is killing you."

CHAPTER 27

"You don't have to kill her," Sunny protested as Blister advanced on Blaze.

"Perhaps," Blister said over her shoulder. "But I certainly want to."

"Can't you fight for me?" Blaze pleaded, turning to Queen Glacier. "I don't want to die like this."

Queen Glacier looked torn. She had to know there was no chance Blaze would survive this duel, which meant she'd get none of the promised territory for the IceWings — and she'd be left with a bordering kingdom ruled by a queen who'd been her enemy for eighteen years.

But Sunny could see that Glacier wanted to be just and fair. She couldn't fight a SandWing's battle for her, not one-on-one for the throne like this.

The IceWing shook her head. "I'm sorry, Blaze. This is your fight." She touched Blaze's wing with her own, briefly, then turned and flew up to join her fellow ice dragons on the wall.

Blaze faced her sister, wide-eyed with fear.

"You can forfeit," Sunny cried. "You don't have to fight! Let her be queen and live."

"It's too late for that," Blister snarled. "She wanted to be queen badly enough to fight for it all these years. She can't back down now that it's just the two of us." With a swift, sudden movement, Blister darted at Blaze, bit down viciously on the edge of one of her wings, and darted away again.

"Ow!" Blaze shrieked. She staggered back, staring at her wing. "Three moons, it's bleeding! I'm bleeding!"

"Oh, brother," Glory said, but there was pity in her expression.

"Shouldn't we stop them?" Sunny asked her friends.

"It's royal SandWing business now," Starflight said, touching the bandage around his eyes and ducking his head. "They'll fight, and Blister will win, but the important thing is that it means the war is over. There will be a queen on the SandWing throne, and no one else has to die."

"Except Blaze," Glory observed.

The two SandWings circled each other, hissing and jabbing with their tails like two scorpions.

"Poor Blaze," Sunny said. "It doesn't seem fair." She curled into Clay's side, leaning against his scales.

"I wish someone else could be queen," Fatespeaker said. "Blister is so creepy."

"And smart," Starflight agreed. "Who knows what she'll do once the throne is really hers." He scratched his claws across the stone. "With a united SandWing army at her clawtips and the treasure, if she's the one who stole it . . . she could easily be the most dangerous dragon in Pyrrhia."

"Isn't there anyone else?" Sunny asked. She turned and saw Smolder still standing in the shadows of the doorway.

He met her eyes and started toward her, carefully avoiding his sisters.

"I don't think so," Starflight said. "None of the three sisters have exactly taken the time to have dragonets."

"Hello," Smolder said, sliding up to them. Flower was perched on his shoulder, staring around at all the dragons with her big, brown, dragonlike eyes. "Aren't you all dramatic troublemakers. Do you think Blister is going to let me live? I'm guessing no. This would probably be a good time for me to run away." He cast a speculative glance at the sky. "But to where? Could you use another Outclaw, perhaps?" he asked Thorn.

"You have some nerve," Thorn snapped. "I should kill you myself for that trick you played, locking us in the library."

"As if I had a choice," Smolder said reproachfully. "And it didn't even work. Burn was this close to killing me until she got your message about meeting her here tonight."

I should be mad at him, too, Sunny thought, but she couldn't be. He wasn't evil — he wasn't even mean. He was a dragon in a terrible family, in a hard situation, in danger of being put to death like his brothers at any moment. He could have killed her the moment he got his talons on her. He could have left her in the tower. Maybe she shouldn't like him, but she did anyway.

Smolder pointed to his sister's dead body with a rueful expression. "I must admit, I never expected to outlive *her.*"

"It probably won't be by much, if that's any consolation," Thorn said bluntly.

"Smolder," Sunny broke in, "are there any other dragons in line for the SandWing throne? Did Queen Oasis have any sisters or other daughters? Or did any of these three have dragonets?"

Smolder shook his head. "Mother was very strict and very careful. She had just the three daughters, so someone could inherit one day, but she didn't want a lot of challengers. So she had no more eggs, and the rest of us were not allowed to have dragonets either." He fell silent for a moment. "I was in love once. She was so angry when she found out. . . . I don't even know what she did, but I never saw Palm again."

"You should have better choices," Sunny said, stamping her foot. "All three of your sisters are terrible." Blaze let out another yowl of pain as Blister slashed her claws across her nose. Sunny had a feeling this fight could have been over already, but Blister was playing with Blaze, showing off for the audience.

"Why can't someone else be queen?" Fatespeaker asked. "If Glory can be queen of the NightWings . . . who says it has to be a member of the royal family?"

"Good question," said Glory.

"Who else would have the authority?" Starflight asked. "Why would the other SandWings listen to anyone else? If any dragon could take the throne, it'd be anarchy. There'd be challengers trying to grab it every other day."

"I know," Sunny said, "but still . . . if all the royal options are awful . . . it seems like there should be a way to give the SandWings someone else, a better queen." Her wings drooped. After everything they'd been through, all the worry about the prophecy and all the danger they'd been in and all the dragons who'd tried to kill them . . . was this how it ended? They stopped the war, but gave the SandWings an evil queen? Was she supposed to say, "Oh, well, good enough?"

Flower wriggled off Smolder's back and came over to pat Sunny's talons in her odd comforting way. The little scavenger looked up at Sunny and squeaked, waving her paws.

"Scavengers are so crazy," Tsunami said. She ducked her head to sniff at Flower. "Look at her, just standing here in the middle of all these dragons. Where's her survival instinct? This is the one who stole the treasure, right? Hey, squish-face, this is all your fault, you know."

Flower wrapped her arms around one of Sunny's ankles and tugged as if she was trying to drag Sunny somewhere, squeaking loudly.

"What?" Sunny asked. She looked at Smolder. "What's she trying to say?"

He shrugged. "I never know."

Flower jumped up and down, flapping her paws. Sunny tilted her head, confused. The scavenger ran over to the pit of sand, flapped again, ran back to Sunny, tugged on her ankle, and ran back to the sand. To Sunny's astonishment, Flower threw herself down and started to dig with her paws.

"What in the three moons . . ." Smolder said. "I'll never understand scavengers."

"She's trying to tell us something," Sunny said. She followed Flower to the sandpit, glancing up at the obelisk. Did

Flower know that the dragon she'd killed — or helped to kill — was buried here? "This is a little morbid, Flower."

Flower whacked Sunny's front talons, pointed at the sand, shouted something like "YIBBLE FROBBLE!" and went back to digging.

"All right," Sunny said, and she started to dig, too. *What could she be trying to tell us?*

"What *are* you doing?" Glory demanded.

"Digging," Sunny said. She glanced up at Blaze and Blister. Blaze had three more bleeding wounds, and Blister was pacing smugly around her. Surely the fight couldn't last much longer.

"Why?" Tsunami asked, coming to stand next to her.

"Because Flower wants me to," Sunny said. "I don't know, but it feels like maybe it's important."

Tsunami and Glory exchanged glances. Sunny could guess what those looks meant: *"Another crazy Sunny idea. Look at her, following a scavenger's instructions, as if that makes any sense."*

"Scoot over," Tsunami said. She flexed her claws and drove them into the sand.

"You too," Glory said to the scavenger, joining them.

Tsunami and Glory began to dig, wing to wing with Sunny. A moment later, she looked up and found Thorn digging busily beside her as well.

She tried to hide her smile, but she couldn't.

Their talons swept the sand away quickly, and soon Sunny could see the gleam of white bones below them.

That's Queen Oasis. Why does Flower want us to dig her up?

Before long, they had the front half of the dragon's body uncovered. She was huge, too, even bigger than Burn. She must have been terrifying when she was alive.

Flower scrambled into the hole they'd dug and carefully climbed around the bones until she was standing beside the dragon's skull. She tapped on the skull's jaws and looked up at Sunny.

A sudden shiver went down Sunny's spine, as if she knew what was about to happen, although she couldn't have put it into words.

She reached down and pried open the queen's mouth.

Inside were two sacks, falling apart and full of holes, but otherwise just like the one the scavengers had given her in the forest.

Behind her, she heard Glory gasp. She understood what this meant.

Twenty years ago, the night Oasis died — Flower must have hidden some of the treasure in the dead dragon's mouth, before she ran off to hide in the dunes. Maybe she thought she'd have a chance to go back and get it, or maybe she didn't want to be caught with it.

Sunny carefully lifted the sacks onto the sand. Emeralds and gold coins and tiger's-eye bracelets spilled out through the holes. She sliced open the sacks with one of her claws.

And there it was at last: the Eye of Onyx.

CHAPTER 28

"By all the moons," Thorn whispered.

Sunny slid her talons around the black sphere and lifted it up. As she did, she realized that it was set on a chain of hammered gold links so it could be worn as a necklace.

And then she took a closer look at the setting.

In molded, beaten gold, on either side of the onyx stone, were two dragon wings. They caught the firelight of the torches and glowed red-gold-orange as she held the necklace up.

Wings of fire.

Had somebody known, somewhere along the line, and told the NightWings? Was it just a coincidence?

In a way the prophecy turned out to be real after all.

Even if somebody thought they made it up, it's real to me and to all the dragons who need the war to be over.

But the prophecy didn't make this happen; no all-powerful fate or guiding force in the universe made this happen.

We made this happen. Me and my friends and all these dragons here and even Flower.

She could feel power thrumming through the sphere,

like the Obsidian Mirror or the dreamvisitor, but stronger and lighter, somehow. She wondered if animus-touched objects had different auras based on which dragon had enchanted them.

"No wonder no one has been able to take the SandWing throne all these years," Tsunami said.

"It's like Queen Oasis was still hanging on to it," Glory agreed, nudging the bones with her tail. Flower was watching them nervously from on top of the skull. Sunny held up the Eye of Onyx and made a little bow toward the scavenger.

"Thank you," she said. "This is what we needed."

"Sunny," Tsunami said, "with this, *you* could be queen. You'd be a great queen."

"It's true," Glory said. "Nobody wants Blister. They'd follow you, if you want the throne."

They were right. Sunny could sense that the magic in the sphere was not confined to royalty. Any SandWing who held the Eye of Onyx could command the kingdom. Even Sunny, with her harmless tail, could be queen.

Another earthquake shook the ground under her talons.

"And I promise not to be jealous," Tsunami said, "even though this is all *highly unfair* because why aren't thrones just falling into *my* lap, is what I'd like to know."

Sunny imagined it: a palace, an army, treasure, and power. She'd command the largest kingdom in Pyrrhia. She could make the Kingdom of Sand a safe, peaceful place to live. She could change the laws and stop dragons from fighting each other all the time.

She looked up at the wings and claws and teeth lining the walls. Or could she? Would she be strong enough to punish anyone who opposed her? Would she know how to defend her subjects if another tribe attacked them? Would she have to become a different kind of dragon?

I don't want to be queen, Sunny realized. *I don't want to fight for my throne or worry about the size of my territory and how much is in my treasury.*

I want to be with my friends. I want to teach dragonets how to make peace and how to find other solutions instead of war.

I just want to be me, Sunny.

But it still didn't have to be Blister. There was another choice.

She could feel the eyes of every dragon on her; even Blister and Blaze had stopped fighting, alerted by the silence that something significant was happening. Blister stepped toward them with a hiss.

Sunny looked right at her, then turned and gave the Eye of Onyx to Thorn.

Something crackled between them as their claws touched — a tiny jolt of purple lightning sparking along the curve of the black stone.

"This is the new SandWing queen," Sunny said, hearing her voice echo across the courtyard. "She is our choice. She is the right choice."

Murmurs and gasps rippled through the watching dragons.

"Fourth moons and fireballs," Thorn said, awestruck. "Me? Are you sure?"

"I'm extremely definitely sure," Sunny said.

"Awesome," Glory whispered, and when Sunny looked over at her, the RainWing queen winked. Beside her, Tsunami was nodding, too.

"Absolutely not," said Blister, advancing on them. "That is mine. I *deserve* it. *I* took the rest of the SandWing treasure. I tricked Mother into flying to her death alone." She gave the old queen's bones a scornful look. "I used my *brain* to get out of facing Burn in a challenge duel, by turning our fight into a war." She hissed at the dragonets, her usual stillness broken into trembling anger. "*I* am the smartest dragon in Pyrrhia. *I* am the rightful SandWing queen."

She flicked her tail at Burn's body, then at Blaze, who was crouched on the stones, bleeding from several small wounds. "Besides, it's in the prophecy," she growled. "Of three queens who blister and blaze and burn, two shall die . . ."

"And one shall learn," Sunny quoted back at her, "if she bows to a fate that is stronger and higher, she'll have the power of wings of fire." *Morrowseer was talking about the NightWings, hinting that the winning queen would have to submit to the NightWing tribe. But this is much better.* "This is your fate — to accept your new queen." She nodded at Thorn.

Blister coiled her venomous tail up, giving Sunny and Thorn a cold glare that was unsettlingly like the dragonbite viper's. "You don't seriously think that's going to happen, do you?"

"So fight me," Thorn said. "I'm not afraid of you. I can win this throne in battle, if that's how you want to do it."

She tossed her head toward Blaze. "Or are you only willing to fight weak and cowering dragons?"

Blister's expression was hard to read. *Is she afraid to fight Thorn?* Sunny wondered. *Or is she calculating her next move — coming up with another evil trick?*

"I don't have to fight you," Blister said, pacing closer and closer. Her obsidian eyes glittered in the moonlight. "You have no right to this throne. The Eye of Onyx is *mine*." Suddenly she lunged forward and snatched the smooth black sphere out of Thorn's talons.

Orange sparks flew off the Eye where Blister's claws touched it. There was a hissing, crackling, spitting sound that seemed to fill the whole courtyard and expand outward, shock waves spilling over the walls and the desert beyond.

Blister's talons started shaking. It looked as if she was trying to drop the Eye but she couldn't. Lightning flickered across the black stone and then out, darting along Blister's arms and up into her wings. She jerked back, nearly lifting into the air, and fell, still clutching the sphere.

But she didn't scream. She never made a sound, even as her tail smashed into the ground and her head thrashed from side to side.

The lightning cracked again, faster, ripping through the SandWing's body.

And then Blister, the dragon of their nightmares, the sister whose evil schemes had started the whole war, exploded into a pile of black dust.

Nobody moved.

Nobody spoke for a long, long moment.

And then Blaze said wonderingly, "It's me? *I'm* the sister who survives?"

Thorn stepped forward and gingerly picked up the Eye of Onyx again. It made a little humming sound and flickered with dark purple lines, just once, then went quiet.

"What happened?" Starflight asked. Beside him, Fatespeaker shook her head, for once too shocked to speak.

"I think we'd better do some research about the exact enchantment on that thing," Glory said, giving the Eye of Onyx a wary look.

"I can see why Oasis kept it in her treasury instead of wearing it," Thorn said. "I'm a little traumatized right now." But she lifted the necklace over her head and let the chain settle around her neck, with the onyx stone and the dragon wings resting in the center of her chest. They bumped against the moonstone that was already there, and Sunny thought of her father.

We proved him wrong. We really did it. We ended the war.

She looked up at all the dragons who were watching — from the walls, from the sky, and now spilling into the courtyard — SandWings coming forward to greet their new queen. Blaze was the first one to reach her, crouching and bowing low to Queen Thorn. Behind her, others followed suit.

"This is really strange," Thorn whispered to Sunny. "I hope you're planning to help me figure this all out."

"I will," Sunny said. "But you'll be brilliant." She caught a glimpse of Smolder, Six-Claws, and Qibli among the bowing dragons, and she saw Queen Glacier, Queen Coral, and Queen Moorhen watching from the walls, looking relieved. "And I think there will be lots of other dragons willing to help you figure it out, too."

She realized that Clay was sitting up beside Starflight, rubbing his head, and she hurried over to him with Tsunami and Glory right behind her. His bewildered, worried, wonderful face — alive, alive and all right — made her whole body feel as though it was full of light.

"Wow, everything hurts," Clay said. He blinked at them and at the sky where the sun was rising and at the courtyard full of dragons. "Uh . . . did I miss anything?"

It was a perfect day for flying.

Trails of white clouds splashed across the bright blue sky as if they'd been painted on in long, thin brushstrokes. The wind whisked around them, fast and breathless and playful, and the mountains below looked like sharp green gemstones in the warm sunlight.

"Can't you imagine it?" Sunny said to her friends. "Wouldn't it be perfect?"

They stood on one of the peaks of Jade Mountain, with all of Pyrrhia spread out below them. From here, on a day like today, Sunny could see the white sands of the desert far off to the west and the dark green of the rainforest to the east. She could see the ocean glittering blue in the south and the jagged teeth of the mountains stretching in a long line north toward the Sky Kingdom.

She opened her wings and felt the wind whoosh around her, nearly lifting her off her talons.

"I can see it," Tsunami said. "We could use the caves as classrooms but have everyone outside as much as possible."

"Lots of sunshine," Glory agreed. "Mandatory sunshine."

"And field trips," Clay suggested, limping over the rocks to them. "So every dragonet can feel mud and sand and the ocean and snow and also eat mangoes." He grinned at Glory. "Mandatory mangoes."

"And scrolls, right?" Starflight said. "Lots and lots of scrolls. All the scrolls in Pyrrhia. We could have the biggest library in the world here." He paused, and even with the bandage over his eyes, they could see his face fall. Sunny twined her tail around his, knowing he felt more comfortable when he was touching another dragon.

"Don't worry, Starflight," Fatespeaker said from his other side, nudging him gently. "We'll figure out a way to make scrolls that blind dragons can read, too. And until then, I'll read you every single scroll we find, I promise. I'm not going anywhere."

He smiled shyly in her direction, and Sunny felt another stab of guilt.

They'd talked about it, finally, once they were all safely back in the rainforest. Sunny had found him by himself for once, lying in the sun on one of the leaf platforms, and she'd curled up beside him until he woke up.

"I'm sorry, Starflight," she'd said, and he'd known right away what she was talking about.

"I know," he'd answered, turning his head away from her.

"I just — I love you. But —"

"Like a brother."

She'd hesitated, then said instead, "Not like Fatespeaker loves you."

He'd folded his wings over his face and coughed, embarrassed.

"It's all right if you love her, too," Sunny said. "You should. She's . . . she cares about you. And she's hilarious."

He hadn't said anything for a long time. Finally Sunny had said, "I brought you something." His head lifted at the sound of the rustling scroll. "Remember *Tales of the NightWings*? Want me to read it to you?"

"Ha," he'd said, actually smiling. "It'll sound a little different now that we know none of it is true. Sure, please do."

Here, now, on the mountaintop, Sunny thought . . . well, she hoped . . . that everything would be all right between them. He'd be a great teacher; he didn't need his sight to do that. And his flying was getting more confident every day.

If she ever found someone she cared about that way . . . well, then things might be awkward again for a while. But he had Fatespeaker. They'd all be all right.

"Do you think anyone will actually come?" Tsunami asked, pacing back from the northern ridge. "I mean, a school for dragonets from all the tribes — no one's ever done anything like that before. The queens might not *want* their subjects to 'understand each other better.' What if we build a school and no one comes?"

"They'll come," Sunny said confidently. "We're not the only dragons who want to avoid any more wars. This is the best way. Dragonets who grow up together will see how alike they really are, no matter what tribe they're from. Then they won't judge each other, and they'll be much less likely to kill each other."

"Like us," Clay said, grinning at her.

"Unless they're all like Tsunami," Glory joked. "And then getting to know each other will make them *more* likely to want to kill each other."

Tsunami smacked her over the head with her tail.

"Hey!" Deathbringer shouted from overhead, where he was swooping about surveying the mountains. "No hitting the queen!"

"Yeah," Glory said saucily to Tsunami. "No hitting the queen."

"You're only *a* queen," Tsunami said. "You might have the RainWings and NightWings wrapped around your tail, but you're still not the boss of me. And neither are you, Mr. Moony-Eyes," she said to Deathbringer as he landed beside Glory. "I bet I could knock you off this mountain if I wanted to."

"I think you're proving my point," Glory mused, and then ducked as Tsunami tried to swat her again.

"My brothers and sisters will come," Clay said. "I think. If they know I'm here. Umber was telling me he hardly knows any history, and his reading's not so great. He'd love to learn more."

"We should ask Webs to be one of the teachers," Sunny said. "Now that he's all recovered — I mean, whatever else you guys think of him, you have to admit he was a good history teacher. And he can't go home to the Kingdom of the Sea. Coral's never going to forgive him, even if she lets all the other Talons come back one day."

"I vote yes. I'd be happy to finally get him out of my

rainforest," Glory said. "Much as he would clearly prefer to stay in bed eating fruit forever." She flicked her tail, turning orange around her ears. "Kinkajou and Tamarin will want to come, for sure. They need real teachers, not the scraps of time I have for them. I'll send some others, as long as you promise they'll still get their afternoon sun time."

"Don't forget Mightyclaws," Deathbringer suggested. "And that little NightWing whose mother hid her egg in the rainforest."

"Moonwatcher," Glory said, nodding. "Poor little nervous dragonet."

"And my sisters!" Tsunami said. "I bet I could get Mother to send Anemone and Auklet — although then we might have to let Queen Coral visit, like, pretty much every day."

"Wow," Sunny said. "They all survived. All these dragons we care about. Isn't that amazing? I mean, except Dune and Kestrel." She looked down at her talons.

"And Viper," Fatespeaker added.

"And my father," Tsunami said quietly. Sunny reached over and twined her tail around Tsunami's.

"The other great thing about this school idea," Sunny said after a moment, "is that this way we can all stay together. I mean . . . if you want to. If you want to go back to your families, you can, but we'll always have a place where we can be together."

"I'd rather be with you all than in the Mud Kingdom," Clay said readily, "especially if I can get Umber and the others here."

"Same," Tsunami said. "I'm afraid if I go home, Mother will somehow get a harness on me, or at least want to watch me every moment of the day. And it'll be easier to learn Aquatic here than in the Deep Palace, where there would be a million eyes on me all the time and hardly any chances to come up to the surface to talk." She shuddered. "Worse, no one could understand *me*. How would I boss *anyone* around?"

Sunny giggled and Tsunami shot her a grin.

"I have to stay in the rainforest," Glory said. "But it's not far. I could visit all the time."

Starflight didn't say anything, but they all knew he had no attachment to the NightWing village that was being built in the rainforest. His father, Mastermind, was in prison — or the closest thing the RainWings could come up with anyway — until Glory could figure out how to try him for his crimes. And Fierceteeth was still in the Scorpion Den. Sunny reminded herself that she had to talk to Thorn about her and Strongwings . . . once they figured out what they wanted to do with them.

"Oh, I know! Peril!" Clay said suddenly. "Peril could be one of the students. She's got nowhere else to go, and we'd know how to take care of her."

Sunny caught the look that went between Glory and Tsunami. They all knew they owed Peril Clay's life, but it was still hard to feel entirely safe around her.

"She really doesn't know where Scarlet is?" Tsunami asked. "Isn't that a little weird, that she rescued Scarlet, and then Scarlet just vanished on her?"

"Peril's out looking for her now," Clay said. "She said Scarlet was appearing in her dreams all the time before the rescue, but she hasn't come back since."

"Maybe we could use our dreamvisitor to look for her?" Sunny suggested. "Except then she'll see us, too, which makes me so nervous. I wish we'd found the Obsidian Mirror." She'd gone back to the outskirts of the Scorpion Den to look for it, but as she'd feared, every sand dune looked the same, and a day of digging had turned up nothing. Either someone else had found it — which was also a worrying thought — or the desert had swallowed it up.

"It is disturbing," Deathbringer said, frowning up at the sky. "She's going to come for you sometime, especially you," he said to Glory.

Glory shrugged. "I'll let you worry about that," she said.

"Oh, thanks," he said. "You know I will."

"Fine by me," she said, and despite their sarcastic words, the look they gave each other made Tsunami roll her eyes at Sunny.

I wonder if they'll have dragonets together one day. Will anyone complain that the queen of the RainWings should be with another RainWing instead? A half-RainWing, half-NightWing dragonet — what would that look like? Everything in one dragon, or something different, like me? Then I wouldn't be the only half-tribe dragon in the world.

Below them, in the caves, Sunny knew her mother was having an awkward reunion with Stonemover. They'd both changed so much over the last seven years; there wasn't much in common between the new queen of the SandWings and the partly stone enchanter hermit of Jade Mountain.

Sunny had been with them for the first few moments, but it had been way too strange, so she'd fled out here to her friends instead.

"Oh," she said, remembering something. "One of the things we have to teach everyone is that the NightWings don't have any of those powers that they've been claiming to have. We can't let everyone still be afraid of them. Right?"

"Except me," Fatespeaker protested. "I totally so do have powers."

"Fatespeaker," Glory said sternly. "We talked about this."

"All right, all right, Your Majesty," Fatespeaker said, subsiding grumpily. "But I swear my visions really do *feel* real."

"But that comet went away again without falling on us," Starflight pointed out. "Didn't that convince you?"

Fatespeaker had the grace to look a little embarrassed. "Well," she said. "IT COULD STILL COME BACK."

Sunny started giggling, and after a moment Fatespeaker's dramatic face cracked and she joined in.

"What about our prophecy?" Clay said. "Won't it confuse everyone if we tell them it wasn't real after all?"

Sunny thought about that for a moment. "Maybe we could say the NightWings lost their powers along with their home. So that was it — the last prophecy."

"The last prophecy," Starflight echoed.

"Three moons, yes," Tsunami said. "That is what I vote for. No more prophecies, ever again."

"I guess we just make it up from here," Sunny said, watching the wind tug at her wings and tail. Far below them, hawks soared over the ridges and valleys.

"Bad news, Sunny. I'm *pretty* sure we've been making it up this whole time," Glory said.

Sunny laughed. "That's true. And things turned out all right anyway."

"Well, I know what I want my destiny to be," Clay said. "I want it to be sleeping and being friends with you guys forever. Oh, wait, also feasting! Lots of feasting."

"That sounds great," Starflight said. "Best destiny ever."

"We can make that happen," Sunny said, smiling, and all of them spread their wings and leaped into the wide open sky.

WINGS OF FIRE

will continue . . .

The war is over. The false prophecy has been fulfilled.

But the dragonets still have enemies.

A dark evil, buried for centuries, is stirring.

And a young NightWing may have had the first true prophecy in generations . . .

Something is coming to shake the earth.
Something is coming to scorch the ground.
Jade Mountain will fall beneath thunder and ice,
unless the lost city of night can be found.